WHAT SHE DESIRED

Kitty kept her eyes strictly on his hands though she could almost feel his gaze warming her cheek, her neck.

He repeated the musical phrase.

"Faster," she said.

He played it again. And again. "Now I think I am getting the idea."

She turned toward him with a smile. Too late she realized her mistake as she met his clear blue eyes directly. In an instant, his finger lifted her chin and he pressed his lips to hers.

This was exactly what she feared.

This was exactly what she desired.

LEAST
LIKELY
LOVERS

VICTORIA
HINSHAW

ZEBRA BOOKS
KENSINGTON PUBLISHING CORP.
www.kensingtonbooks.com

ZEBRA BOOKS are published by

Kensington Publishing Corp.
850 Third Avenue
New York, NY 10022

All Kensington titles, imprints, and distributed lines are available at special quantity discounts for bulk purchases for sales promotion, premiums, fund-raising, educational, or institutional use.

Special book excerpts or customized printings can also be created to fit specific needs. For details, write or phone the office of the Kensington Special Sales Manager: Attn. Special Sales Department. Kensington Publishing Corp., 850 Third Avenue, New York, NY 10022. Phone: 1-800-221-2647.

Zebra and the Z logo Reg. U.S. Pat. & TM Off.

ISBN 0-8217-7841-2

First Printing: August 2005
10 9 8 7 6 5 4 3 2 1

Printed in the United States of America

ONE

The argument raged for three days.

"You *must* come with me to live at Charsley, my dearest Kitty." The insistence in Lady Dunmark's voice edged into pleading with her daughter. "There is no alternative. Our house is let, and you cannot set yourself up somewhere alone."

"Why not?" Miss Kitty Stone already knew the answer.

Her mother groaned. "You have no money and neither do I. We spent everything in London, and we owe every cent we will reap from the lease. I know your feelings about living in the duke's house, seeing him every day. But Beatrice needs us."

"Beatrice needs you, Mama, not me. Most definitely not me."

"But there is no other place for you, Kitty. An unmarried girl of two and twenty! You know you must stay with your mother."

Both knew the other's position by heart, could play either role in the familiar dialogue.

The two ladies were equally adamant. The younger—tall, slender, and exceptionally pretty—had been clever enough to endure several months of Society's closest scrutiny, during which her every word and gesture had been discussed, reiterated, and evaluated by every tabby in London. The elder—her lovely face touched by few indications of her age of three and forty—had suffered the same examination. Her status as a widow capable of doing the best for her daughters had been challenged and her implied lack of parental abilities had been blamed for the inexorable foundation of the scandal.

After their trial by tonnish fire, neither daughter nor mother would give way to the other. The dispute raged on over their breakfast coffee and continued while they strolled the lanes to the village, while they watched the repairmen trod the roof, and while they packed their belongings for storage. It even continued at the dinner table and during preparations for retiring.

The disagreement repeated itself on the day the Duke of Charsley's fine chaise, adorned with liveried postilions, waited outside their door, and Nell handed their bandboxes to the footmen from Charsley Hall.

Lady Dunmark summoned all the authority she could muster. "You must come, Kitty."

Miss Stone spoke through tightly clenched teeth. "Why?"

"There is no other place for you."

Kitty watched their maid, Nell, climb into the coach while carrying their luggage. The new tenants for their house were to arrive by five that afternoon. Short of making her bed in the hayloft, where was she to go? Suddenly limp with frustration, Kitty took the footman's hand and stepped into the chaise.

Once the horses moved off, with mother and daughter side by side on the plush cushions, silence reigned.

Kitty had lost.

She was on her way to reside in the home of the man who had courted her for six months, then eloped with her little sister.

* * *

Kitty stared out the window at the springtime green as the well-sprung coach carried her farther and farther from her childhood home. Though she had not deigned to admit it to herself, she had known for the last week that she would have to accompany her mother to Charsley. Without money, without a convenient aunt or cousin, without a well-established married friend who would welcome her prolonged presence, she had no choice. She would have to make the best of it for a few months, at least until Beatrice was safely through her confinement in November. Six months ought to be bearable.

Her mother might well choose to remain at Charsley indefinitely. That Kitty could not do.

The only alternative was to find a position as a governess or a companion; any other employment necessitated paying for a place to live. In those long months after Bea eloped with the duke and the scandal reverberated through London drawing rooms, Kitty often wished she could disappear into one of the little villages near town, take a new name, and make a new life for herself far from the gossipmongers of Mayfair. In fact, she went so far as to make inquiries, inquiries that vividly showed the cost of maintaining independence. Even if she sold her fine wardrobe and pawned every bauble she owned, she could not afford to keep herself for more than a few months. The salary of a shop girl would never suffice to make ends meet.

Could Kitty see herself as a governess, teaching trifles to little girls? Or trying to tame the wild pursuits of little boys? Or would she rather be a companion, to fetch and carry for some valetudinarian? In either case, she would be a servant, but she would have a place to live and duties to perform.

The important thing was to have a life for herself and of her own choosing, however narrow the range.

After Christmas, Kitty promised herself. After Christmas, she would go to Bath or London and seek a position. Between now and then, she would save every penny that came her way. Was that not better than living in the house of her former suitor, tending to the frailties of his wife who just happened to be her very gooseish sister? But if her mother gained an inkling of her plan, Lady Dunmark would do all she could to put a stop to it.

"I wonder what sort of society one will find in the neighborhood of Charsley?" Lady Dunmark had wiped away the last tear she had shed upon leaving the estate she would no longer occupy, the estate to which her husband had brought her almost a quarter century ago as a fresh young bride.

Kitty sympathized, not happy herself to be torn from her childhood home. "Being so near London, I would think that most of northern Kent is well populated with agreeable families."

"With some eligible sons, I hope."

Kitty took a deep breath before replying. "If you are referring to possible matches for me, Mama, I will say again that I have no intention of marrying anytime soon."

Ever, she added to herself.

"But you have said you never loved the duke."

"You know I never fell in love with him, though I was quite prepared to marry him, to provide for myself, for you, and for Beatrice. He is a wealthy man from a distinguished family. When he ran off with Bea, I gained a reprieve. I do not now intend to burden myself with some other man."

Especially one as dim as the duke with his never-ending verses. Pretentious, ponderous, and preposterous poems, too clumsy to be taken seriously.

"You do not want to be a spinster, Catherine."

"I have had enough of making myself perfectly amiable for a man who ultimately jilted me."

"Kitty!" Lady Dunmark pressed one hand to her heart and clutched at her throat with the other. "Do not say that awful word!"

"Jilt? That is exactly the word used by all our supposed friends, as you well know."

"But, really—"

"Look, Mama, you and Bea will be well taken care of forever. I have the luxury now to do whatever I wish."

Lady Dunmark fluttered her beringed hands in the air. "Oh you will be soon rid of such nonsensical notions, dear. The first few days living so near Char may be awkward, but I feel sure he is devoted to Beatrice. After all, a baby already on the way . . . perhaps an heir if she is fortunate enough to have a male child."

"Yes, Mama. I am certain their marriage will be brilliant." Kitty settled back against the squabs. Last winter, while she had ruminated on her apparent future with a dull husband she did not love, Beatrice and Char spent long afternoons together. Char spent hours struggling with a few inelegant lines, lines he enjoyed reciting, reworking and reciting again. And again.

Apparently Bea had found them more amusing than Kitty had. Sometimes Char taught Bea card games. They both giggled over their hands like schoolchildren, causing shudders in Kitty. If she had given more consideration to those tête-à-têtes, she might have been less astounded when, in early February, they hared off together and married without the knowledge of either family.

When her initial shock had passed, Kitty felt relief that the welfare of Mama and Bea was no longer her concern. How very wrong she had been.

The dark eyes of the Dowager Duchess of Charsley glittered with disapproval. "I may as well tell you, Lady Dunmark, I did not approve of having you come here. I have had far too many upheavals in my life and I do not wish to have any more."

Kitty and her mother shivered on hard stone floors in the cold entrance of Charsley Hall, a mansion of vast size and ancient provenance. Geometric displays of spears, arrows, and muskets covered the walls—enough arms to supply an entire militia. Though large enough to roast a whole ox, the mammoth fireplace held not one glowing coal to break the April chill.

The dowager spoke from a distance in a harsh tone. "Your daughters are silly chits and I blame them entirely for the ridiculous bumblebroth into which we have landed. Charsley had his head turned by one, then the other. Now there will be a child! Unseemly to come so soon!"

She gave a showy shudder, then continued her harangue. "I maintain strict rules for this house. The first one is that the servants answer to me and to me only. Your maid is included in those rules. I will now withdraw to my apartments; I do not wish to be disturbed. Dinner is at five."

Dressed in mourning and looking like a gaunt black crow, she turned quickly and disappeared through a door under the wide marble staircase.

Kitty snapped her mouth shut.

Her mother gaped for another moment, then brought her lips together in a moue of disapproval. "Well, I never!"

"Char always said she was a dragon. An understatement, I believe."

"A most unpleasant woman. One would think she would be thrilled to have a grandchild on the way. And why is she telling the servants what to do? That is now Beatrice's responsibility."

Kitty was not surprised. At barely eighteen years of age, her sister was just out of the schoolroom. How could Bea wrest control of the household from a personage like the dowager duchess? Char had not the spine to stand up to his mother, and his new young duchess was unlikely to insist.

The very starchy butler reappeared with the housekeeper. "Here is Mrs. Wells. She will show you to your apartments." Before leaving, he made a shallow bow.

Mrs. Wells's curtsy was equally half-hearted. Her mouth was drawn up in a tight line, echoing the dowager's disapproval. "Your chambers are this way." She stomped up the stairs, leaving Lady Dunmark and Kitty to follow.

At the end of a long corridor, Mrs. Wells threw open a door. "If you need anything, a footman will be nearby."

"Thank you." Lady Dunmark put her reticule on a table as the door closed behind them.

Kitty looked around at the dim sitting room, modestly but comfortably furnished. "I would have thought they might have dressed up this room a bit, at least with a vase of flowers."

Lady Dunmark moved a chair closer to the grate. "At the moment all I care about is the fire. This house is icier than the coach was."

Kitty investigated the two adjoining rooms. "There are fires lit in the bedchambers too. And the cans of water are still warm to the touch."

"Bea wrote that we would be given the apartments usually reserved at Christmas for the dowager's brother and his wife, otherwise they would have to open a whole wing. I thought it was to keep us nearby in this huge pile, not because of some nip-cheese cost-cutting."

"Most likely to put us in our place, if the dowager duchess had anything to do with it." Char's wealth was immense. A centuries-old dukedom and its huge estates certainly had sufficient resources to provide comfortable accommodations for two guests. But these dark rooms seemed downright inhospitable, almost as unwelcoming as the dowager's uninviting attitude.

Poor Beatrice, what would she have to endure?

Kitty walked to the window and threw back the draperies. The verdant green park spread to a faraway line of trees. A herd of deer with strange antlers grazed in the distance. As beautiful a scene as it was, she felt grateful it was Bea's prospect, not hers.

"Mama! Kitty!" Beatrice, Duchess of Charsley, rushed into their room on a cloud of perfume. With countless little squeals, she hugged them. "I am so glad to see you. I thought you would never get here. Then I fell asleep and no one wak-

ened me." Dressed in a frilly pink gown with her hair frizzed
into ringlets, Bea threw herself into her mother's arms and
burst into joyous tears.

Kitty watched with amusement as Lady Dunmark also
succumbed to emotion, joining in her daughter's happy sobs.
The two of them were much alike both in looks and sensibil-
ity: quick to laugh and cry, quick to judgment, and short of
patience. Kitty thought herself to be a different sort of person, one less emotive and perhaps more critical by nature.

When the sobs faded, Kitty hugged Bea. "Are you very
happy, my pet?"

"Yes. No. I do not know." Her tears flowed again, and
once more, Lady Dunmark embraced her younger daughter.

Eventually they all sat, Mama and Bea wiping their eyes.

"What we need," Lady Dunmark said, "is a pot of tea.
Can I call someone, Bea?"

"Oh no, the dowager has told them all to follow her strictures, not to listen to me. That footman outside the door does
nothing I ask of him."

For a moment, Kitty thought her mother would rise up in
anger, but after an initial swelling of her breast, Lady Dunmark
sat back. "Never mind now, my dear. I take it you and His
Grace are getting along well?"

Bea smiled and nodded. "Very well, Mama."

"He is pleased about the baby?"

"Yes, of course he is. We are both happy about the child.
It is just . . . if the dowager was not so very maddening."

Kitty held her breath. It would not do for her or her
mother to criticize Char to his wife, though he had obviously
shirked his duty to establish a proper household routine and
move his mother to the dower house. "The park outside is
lovely, Bea."

Bea's face grew more animated as she spoke. "Other than
the awful presence of the dowager, Charsley is the most
wonderful place you can imagine, though even I have yet to
see all of it. There are hundreds of acres, Char said. Or did
he say thousands? I cannot remember. But it is very large.

There are many farms leased to tenants. The home farm is the biggest and Char sees his steward there sometimes. Of course the dowager tries to run everything, but at least the steward is polite enough to talk to Char. Though do not breathe a word of it. Anything that goes on has to be kept secret, even from the servants. They all tattle to Mrs. Wells and she goes straight to the dowager with every little complaint."

"An abominable situation indeed." Lady Dunmark clenched her hands and pressed them into her lap. "It makes my blood boil."

Kitty patted her mother's knee. "Do not fret, Mama. We will be able to help Bea a little at a time. If we challenge the dowager on every front, she will keep the upper hand. Slowly and steadily is the way to go."

"Yes, my dear Kitty, I know you are correct. But it is wrong and I do not like it. Nevertheless, we must be careful or things will be worse than ever."

Bea flung her hands into the air. "I do not know how things could be much worse. Char's mother makes him miserable every night at dinner. And her minions are everywhere, prying into my things."

Lady Dunmark glanced at Kitty, then gave a shrug. "Tell us about your wedding trip and your journey back here to Charsley, my dear."

Bea broke into a grin and waved a hand about. "You saw how we traveled, Mama, with a great chaise and two coaches full of servants . . ."

Kitty sighed with relief that her mother had changed the subject of conversation. They would have to tread lightly if they were to make things better here for Beatrice. Thank heavens Mama swiftly caught the drift of things.

Bea prattled on as if she had not a care in the world. "So we climbed all over the ruins of the castle and Char picked a bouquet of wild roses that grew in the bailey. Very romantic, he was. Now I want to have more roses planted in the gardens, but the dowager says. . . . Oh, Mama, she is simply beastly."

Kitty took her sister's hand. "Perhaps she is still surprised by your marriage."

"But it was months ago, Kitty. You and Mama were accustomed to the idea almost right away."

Kitty bit back a sharp retort. Bea had not the slightest idea of what her scandalously sudden wedding had meant to her mother and Kitty, what they had gone through to hold up their heads in London Society. Bea was hardly more than a child, nothing but a schoolgirl, and she was quite unaccustomed to giving the slightest consideration to others.

Kitty squeezed her sister's hand. "Perhaps the dowager just needs more time. You have the baby to think about."

"But she says she will take care of all that too, arranging a nursery and hiring nurses. And she hardly ever speaks to me. She tells Char what he should have me do, and there I am, sitting right in front of her."

"Oh my dear!" Lady Dunmark's voice was almost a moan.

Kitty jumped in quickly. "Where are Char's sisters?"

"Both of them, Char says, had the good sense to marry at young ages and move far away. They rarely come here, and I do not blame them, for the dowager talks of them in the most unflattering terms, as though they were vulgarly married to rogues. And we know they are both nice and have perfectly respectable husbands. Char only sees them in London, you know."

"I did not realize that." Kitty remembered them from early in the year, but neither sister had stayed long in town.

Bea wore a plaintive pout. "And then there is Char's cousin Jack, Jack Whitaker. First the dowager complained that he was away with the army, Char said. Then he was wounded and returned here. She nursed him with all the kind consideration she ought to show toward her own son. I think she almost suffocated him with her ministrations. Then last month he went away to London and now all she does is worry about him."

"But Char so admired his cousin in the military!" Kitty spoke too quickly, and tried to cover her gaffe. "You say he lives in London now?"

Bea made a dismissive gesture. "He owns the neighboring estate, called Nether Acker, but his house has been closed up for years so he stayed here. I do not know when he will return from London. I wish the dowager showed just a tiny bit of concern for Char instead of fretting about Jack, who is not even here."

Kitty gave her sister a sympathetic hug. "I do not know just how, Bea, but Mama and I will help smooth things over with the dowager. It may take a while, but her moods must not spoil your happiness."

Lady Dunmark joined in. "Indeed we shall help you, my darling. You must save your strength and think only of yourself and of the baby."

"Mama, you and Kitty will stay, will you not? I could not even think of having the dowager in the room when I am. . . . Well, I do not know what to think about the birth. I—" Again the tears began to fill Bea's eyes.

"Do not think about that, Beatrice. You have many months before you need to think about the birth. Now, darling, I want you to know we brought some of your things from the manor for you. Your dear little desk and the rest of your clothes, your fans, and your doll, the lovely one Papa brought you from Paris."

Bea smiled through her tears. "I want her so very much, to save for my own darling daughters. For even though Char wants a son and heir this time, I do hope to have some little girls eventually."

"Of course you do," Lady Dunmark said.

Kitty watched Bea's face cloud up again.

"But wait," Bea wailed, "that means you have closed the manor, does it not? Oh, is everything gone, all our happy days?"

Lady Dunmark's lips began to tremble. "No, nothing is gone, my dear." She gave a big sniff and touched her lacy handkerchief to her mouth.

Kitty patted her mother's shoulder. "Bea, everything is just in storage. The house is let to a nice family. All the servants are still there to take care of them. Someday we will be able to go back if we wish." Kitty knew her words were foolishly optimistic, but for the moment, what did it matter?

Bea's voice was melancholy. "How I miss dear Dunmark Manor. I wish Char and I could go and live there, get away from his mother . . . have our baby to ourselves . . . with you and Kitty, of course."

Kitty stood and nodded to her mother. "Which reminds me, I need to go and supervise the placement of my harp."

Bea brightened immediately. "Oh Kitty, I am so happy you brought your harp. We can practice our duets and play together again."

Kitty almost winced at the thought. Beatrice was less than accomplished at the pianoforte, no matter how hard she tried. It often seemed their attempts at playing together ended with Bea in tears, which was not a good way to win the dowager's admiration, or even tolerance for her son's wife.

TWO

Major Jack Whitaker, formerly of the 22nd Foot, accepted a glass of claret from his old friend Colonel Townsend. "Thanks, Ken. I hope my visit will not keep you from any pressing responsibilities." They sat in Townsend's regimental headquarters with two bottles and a pair of goblets before them on the oaken table.

"Ha! I detect a note of irony in your voice, Jack. As you well know, we have far fewer duties than is healthy, even for a regiment billeted in the heart of Town. It's more than an annoyance when I have to drag my men out of gaming hells, completely foxed and often poxed as well."

Jack chuckled. "You do not have to convince me, but I will not include your rhyme in my next report to Sir Arthur Wellesley, if you do not mind." He shifted in his chair to change the pressure on his hip and thigh, stifling a grimace at the pain the move also caused in his shoulder. "It is deuced hard to see what I have accomplished in months of calls at Horse Guards. I got a letter from Sir Arthur yesterday, full of complaints. About his men. About the lack of supplies. About the impossible Portuguese officials. But mostly about the lack of support from our government."

"It is pathetic." Townsend fingered his wine goblet.

"Everyone expects news of victories from the Peninsula, without sending more men or more money."

Jack nodded and stared into his wine. If he were entirely healthy, he would have been at Wellesley's side, an aide to the commander of the British expeditionary forces in Portugal. He would be preparing for battle instead of here in London trying to influence the influential.

Before he embarked for Portugal a second time, Wellesley had written to Jack, giving him unique orders. "See the members of Commons and the Lords. Talk to the political leaders, both Whigs and Tories. And cultivate your contacts at headquarters, Whitaker. I will write you with my specific requirements. The dunces need to be constantly reminded of my army's needs."

Those had been Sir Arthur's instructions. However much Jack would rather be back in action, he had to admit he understood Wellesley's thinking. As the grandson of a duke, Jack had access to both the nobles and the gentry. As an injured officer still drawn and pale from his wounds, Major Whitaker carried some weight with the desk lieutenants and in the regimental dining rooms. And, not to be too modest, as a handsome officer with a decided limp, he was often a center of attention in the salons of Mayfair.

But had he really accomplished anything?

Jack shook off his dejection. "With summer almost upon us, most people are getting ready to move to the country. I think I might as well head to my cousin's place in Kent. I trust you will keep me informed about the situation here."

"Certainly," Colonel Townsend replied, "and I expect you to return the favor when you hear from Sir Arthur."

"Without delay."

"I envy your service in Portugal, Jack. I have not seen action for almost two years. But I suspect you still have some healing to do."

"I despise the remnants of my wounds, not because of the pain but because they keep me here in England. I was barely off the ship when we went into battle, and I was wounded the evening of the first day. Damnable bad luck!"

"At Vimeiro, was it not?"

"We had the French running away, without time to regroup. They had only one cannon left, and it did not last long after it killed three men and left my horse dead beneath me." Fragments of the explosion had peppered Jack's left side, embedding sharp steel fragments in his arm and leg.

"You showed them what the British Army was made of that day. But how did you manage to save that leg? The surgeons usually have a mangled limb sawed off in no time at all."

"Of that I was well aware! I waited until the day after the battle to find one who would extract the pieces of metal. I knew if I went to the field hospital immediately, I would have lost the leg and probably the arm too."

"And you did not bleed to death?"

"Too stubborn by half, Ken."

"Nevertheless, although I don't begrudge you the wounds, I would trade your experience for mine. Mountains of paperwork cross my desk every week, the men complain and carouse, and my wife insists on dancing every night until dawn. Now she wants to move to Brighton. For the sea air, she says; for the entertainment and the gossip, I say."

"We both want to be in the field. I almost begged Sir Arthur to take me along to Portugal last winter; he scoffed at my request."

Jack remembered Wellesley's precise words. *Bravery you have in spades, Major, but I do not need a partial man. And you can be of use to me in London.* Jack did not repeat them, not even to his friend.

Colonel Townsend tossed down the last of his wine. "I too groveled. I wanted my regiment in the fray, but Sir Arthur claimed his hands were tied by the empty uniforms that run headquarters."

"Bumblers and nitpickers. Some of them are not competent to lead mules away from a salt lick."

The colonel chuckled. "All too true. When next you write to him, tell Wellesley we are still waiting for our orders."

"I shall." Jack stood slowly. He was determined to exit the room without hobbling. "I will write to you. If you take lodgings in Brighton, let me know your direction."

Colonel Townsend gave a hearty laugh and waved him away.

Once back in his carriage, Jack allowed himself an ironic chuckle at the colonel's dilemma. Wives could be the very devil!

Not quite ready to call it a night, Jack stopped at his club and joined a group of men sharing a last drink after an evening of faro. Captain Foster of the Life Guards moved beside him.

"Jack!" He raised his glass in a salute. "To your health."

Jack returned the gesture. "To yours, Foster."

"How are you getting on?"

"Improving. Too slowly, but improving."

"At least you saw some action, Whitaker."

Foster, Jack thought, was another son of a younger son, holder of a minor position in a great family. Like Jack, Foster possessed a substantial income, enough to provide the finest tailoring, the best made boots, and the finest Irish bloodstock mounts. In Foster's case, however, that money also had to support his habitual gambling losses, whether at Ascot or Newmarket, at White's or Watier's, at the cockpits or mills. Foster tended little to his supervisory duties of his regiment's ceremonial functions.

But he had somehow managed to wheedle a place in Wellesley's entourage for the attack on Copenhagen.

"I suspect your experience in Denmark only whetted your appetite for battle, Foster."

"For months afterwards I could not imagine why I was so demoralized and unable to concentrate. When you returned, Jack, I caught on to the source of my afflictions. I missed that thrill, though I got only a short dose, but enough to make me eager for more."

"I understand, but do not be too anxious to find more of it. A prolonged battle is very different, you know."

"Ah yes, now that you are the celebrated hero to the foolish young striplings, you can warn them off. But they won't listen, and neither will I."

"Be careful of those romantic yearnings for the sword, Foster. Having your horse killed beneath you and waiting a day and a half for a surgeon takes all the allure right out of the show." He saved his descriptions of the piles of dead, the horses with their guts spilling out, the muck and filth, the flies and maggots, carrion crows—and even more disobliging than nature, the human scum stripping the dead and dying where they lay.

"Some of the men are pushing for our regiment to be sent off. I want it myself."

Jack made a dismissive gesture. "If you want to decimate your ranks, see your men and cattle sacrificed, see the—" He paused. "I know, Foster, that I am wasting my breath. The fact is, I wish I were back there myself. I would go in a minute if Sir Arthur would have me, which he will not."

"Why not?"

"I am not fit."

"Ah! But you soon will be."

Jack was not so sure. Getting back to full strength was proving to be difficult. The hunks of flesh cut out along with the metal were slow to heal fully. His thigh and calf and even his knee, almost a year later, were weak and seemed to be missing significant chunks of muscle. And he needed more surgery, not a thought that gave him comfort.

He soon made his good-byes, feeling weary of talking about the war and being able to do so little. What Wellesley wanted from him seemed far beyond his capability.

As he traveled the short distance to his rooms, Jack was certain the streets were less crowded than usual. The capital emptied out as the summer heat approached. The great families scattered to their country estates and slid into the long evenings of bucolic twilight pastimes so different from the social whirl of the London.

He needed some relaxation himself. He fought off the frequent attacks of the chills and the headaches that plagued him, but he knew he needed rest. His daily exercise to improve the operation of both leg and arm could continue at Charsley, his cousin's estate. If he needed to escape the exaggerated nursing attentions of the dowager duchess, perhaps he would start opening up his own house at Nether Acker. He had not entered its doors for at least five years. Probably would have to have parts of it pulled down for it was sure to be infested with numerous pests.

At Charsley Hall, if he could stomach the silly lines of poetry the duke wrote to his feather-witted young bride, he would eat well and try to put some meat on his bones. He was quite sick of rich food that soured his stomach. Not to mention overlarge amounts of wine which dulled his pain but clouded his mind.

At Charsley Hall, he would not have to bother himself much with the rest of the family. Since Nether Acker lay just a half-mile from his cousin's family seat, he could spend most of his time there. He could tolerate a few evenings dozing through Char's recitations after dinner. And his presence might even moderate the dowager's sharp remarks to her son and that mite of a gel he had married so suddenly, and obviously without his mother's knowledge, much less her approval.

At Charsley Hall, perhaps things had improved now that, according to the brief note Char had sent, his young wife was increasing. Surely the dowager would soon come around to approval of the match if the chit managed to spawn an heir for the line.

Luckily, their tribulations were no real concern of his. Jack sank back onto the cushions, relieving the strain on his leg, and started to plan a mental list of things for his man to pack.

The day after she arrived at Charsley Hall, Kitty wandered through five connected salons after breakfast seeking her harp. The beautiful rooms had been elegantly designed by Robert Adam or one of his followers. The windows were half shuttered everywhere, making the light dim against the morning glare, but the splendor of the furnishings was still evident. Tables of ormolu and marble, sofas and chairs upholstered in rich satins, tall candelabra, and ornate clocks ticking softly. Pianofortes stood in two of the salons, but her harp was nowhere to be seen, not even shoved into an obscure corner. After retracing her steps and checking each room again, Kitty searched for the housekeeper or the butler, and eventually found Mrs. Wells in the corridor to the kitchen.

"May I ask where my harp was placed?"

Mrs. Wells turned a hostile gaze on Kitty. "Her Grace does not wish to have music in the house except immediately following dinner."

"But, my sister—"

"Her Grace, the dowager duchess, I mean."

Kitty tried to give the housekeeper a withering look to express her disapproval. "But that does not explain where my harp is."

Mrs. Wells arranged her lips in what could only be called a smirk. "It has been stored, miss. Safely put away."

"Where?"

"Oh, that I could not say, miss. The footmen took it, but I do not know where."

Kitty stifled her growing fury and thanked the housekeeper far more politely than the woman's impudent manner merited. That was the dowager's fault. What kind of mistress allowed a servant to address guests in such a manner?

Though Kitty had been dreading her first meeting with Char, now she sought it. But she would not give the disagreeable Mrs. Wells the satisfaction of asking where he could be found. Instead, she marched off to search the outbuildings. Once, early in their acquaintance, Char told her he had a private retreat of his own, where he could write and think without being disturbed by the estate workers. Now she understood why he needed such a place, though it seemed to be his mother he needed most to avoid. However lovely, the mansion had a dreary atmosphere, not conducive to poetry. Or to any kind of comfortable life for the young duchess or for her mother.

Once outside, Kitty looked toward the folly at the top of a distant hill, a columned temple in the classical style. It would be a long hike, and she did not recall that Char had a great taste for walking. His sanctuary would be closer.

She hurried through the gardens, almost oblivious of their abundant beauty, to the kitchen garden and through the neat rows of lettuce and carrots to the adjoining stable block. There, in the cobbled yard, she saw Char talking to a pair of grooms as they studied a rangy chestnut mare.

Of medium height, Char had a pleasant face and wavy hair in an ordinary shade of light brown. He wore a yellow waistcoat under his bottle green coat with tan breeches and knee-high boots. Looking at him from a distance, Kitty could hardly believe she had once considered becoming his wife. Besides the fact he was her sister's husband, she felt quite indifferent to him. No stab of excitement had ever pierced her heart when she saw him. No feeling of warmth or affection had ever washed over her. No quickening of her heartbeat had ever met his arrival. Instead she felt more than a little irritated at him, and profoundly grateful it was Bea who had wed him. If it had been Kitty and not Bea who had to deal with the dowager, she knew she would have harangued Char like a fishwife to remedy the situation at Charsley Hall.

Kitty had never found Char a man of strong convictions, and now she understood why. His mother had probably expressed all the opinions that were allowed in this house since the old duke died a dozen years ago.

She waited near the gate until Char dismissed his grooms and came over to make his bow to her.

"As always, I am your servant, Miss Stone." He looked distinctly ill at ease.

She dipped a shallow curtsy. "Good morning, Your Grace." Though this was the first time they had spoken outside the presence of Bea or her mother, Kitty felt no embarrassment, but Char nervously shifted his hat from one hand to the other and back.

"Call me Char, please. As you have done for so long." He gave a self-conscious little laugh. "Trust you and Lady Dunmark had a reasonably comfortable journey here."

"Yes, and we thank you for the fine equipage. Even over the worst of the roads, we were comfortable."

He rocked from one foot to the other. "Glad you have come. Beatrice is very lonely, I fear."

"The situation is unusual, Char, is it not? But for Bea's sake, we will have to endure it."

"Sincerely sorry if you feel awkward, Kitty."

Awkward was not the way Kitty felt, but she could not exactly find a word to define her feelings, so she merely shrugged.

Char glanced down at the hat in his hands and fingered the brim nervously. "I will endeavor to make everything go as smoothly as possible. Stabled your mare just inside."

Kitty could not help smiling, to think of her little mare in the fine stable full of racing bloodstock. "Thank you, Char. I shall look in on her in a few moments."

"Want to make you and Lady Dunmark welcome."

Then pack your infernal mother off to the dower house, she wanted to say, but she knew it would be too direct. Even insulting.

Char went on. "If there is anything I can do—"

"Yes, there is. That is why I have sought you out. As you

know, we have let Dunmark Manor for the next several years. I did not wish to leave my harp there, and so we brought it along. But apparently the dowager duchess does not wish to have it in the music room. I wonder if you might suggest some alternative arrangements."

"Ah, dear me." He frowned and wagged his head from side to side. "As you often heard me say, Mama can be difficult . . . er . . . is always difficult, as a matter of fact. Claims to be sensitive to noise. Cannot bear even to have a pianoforte played during the day. Does love music after dinner, though. Likes to hear us sing."

"Would it bother her if I played my harp in our apartments? It seems the house is quite large enough to prevent the sound from disturbing the dowager in another wing."

He turned his hat round and round. "You are probably correct that she could not hear it. The servants would tell her, though. We'd all be in the suds."

She felt a twinge of exasperation. "Well, perhaps I could play out here in the stables. I am sure the horses would not mind."

He gave a bark of anxious laughter. "No, and the grooms do not ordinarily run into the house and tattle to Mama either. Let me think about the situation for a while. Talk to my bailiff. Know we can find a place for you to practice that will satisfy both you and Mama."

"In the meantime, Char, I do not know where the instrument has been stored. I am concerned that it not be in a damp cellar or near an attic window where it would be in direct sunlight. Not that it is terribly fragile, but the strings are sensitive to changes in temperature and moisture in the air."

"Can't imagine what they did with it. I will look into it, Kitty. Now come and see your mare."

She followed him into the stable, so clean and neat it could have been a well-kept kitchen. "Diamond?" she called softly.

At the sound of her voice, the gray mare came to the stall

door just down the row. Char opened the upper half of the door and Kitty patted the mare's neck.

"She looks wonderful, none the worse for the journey."

After a few more minutes, Kitty gestured to Char to close the stall. "Now I must get back to Bea. She and Mama are enjoying a good coze, but I promised her I would help her get started on embroidering a cap for the baby. And by the way, Char, congratulations on your impending fatherhood. I am happy for you."

He looked befuddled. "Well, ah, yes, indeed. Very pleased. Hope Beatrice keeps her health . . ." His voice trailed away.

"Bea is a robust young lady, Char. Neither of you should be concerned. We will keep her fit and happy for the next six months." *And we will think of a way to get your abominable mama out of that house,* she added silently. *Then I shall go off and find myself a position, far away from all of you. Start a new life!*

"Thank you, Kitty. Always been the most amiable and gracious of ladies."

As she walked back to the house, she mused about his phrase for her. Already, she sounded like a companion to some elderly old countess. An amiable and gracious lady, indeed.

When she reached the boudoir, Kitty paused in the doorway as her mother posed a question to Bea.

"Is there no dower house, my dear?"

Bea lay upon a velvet chaise. "Yes, a perfectly fine one, just the other side of the church. It is occupied by Char's cousin Fanny and her mother, Lady Euphemia, sister of his grandfather. He could not possibly displace them."

Aha! Perhaps that explained part of the dilemma.

Lady Dunmark stood looking out the window, fingering the draperies. "But does he not have other properties?"

"I think he does," Bea said. "But I know nothing of them."

Kitty stepped into the room and took a seat beside the chaise. "The duke will find my harp, and he will find a place for us to play together, Bea."

"I am so happy to hear it. I have hardly begun to investigate all the buildings near the house, but Char will know of a good room somewhere."

"Is the dowager duchess always uncivil to you, Bea?"

Bea drew a fluffy white shawl around her shoulders. "She is even ruder to Char. I do not understand it. She is infinitely kinder to his cousin Jack than she is to Char."

Kitty patted her hand. "I do not understand her attitude toward Char either."

Lady Dunmark cocked her head to one side. "Who is this cousin Jack? You spoke of him earlier, but I did not get the connection."

"Char's cousin," Bea said, "was wounded in some battle and came here to recuperate. The duchess nursed him herself and took the best care of him. Never said a word of reproach, even though he sometimes cried out at night and woke her from a sound sleep."

"Why did he come here, my dear? Does he not have a home and a family of his own?"

Bea shrugged. "I never figured it all out. Jack owns the neighboring estate, but the house there has been closed ever since his father died a long time ago. Jack and Char grew up together as boys. Both Char and his mother wanted him brought here to mend. I think Jack will be back here soon, for he is only in London on some business for the army."

Kitty and her mother exchanged glances. How could the arrival of a cousin so favored by the dowager do anything but make the situation here worse?

THREE

Lord Pearson's study in his Grosvenor Square townhouse was furnished in the style of the reading room of Boodles, Jack thought. All it lacked were several more elderly men nodding off over their broadsheets.

Lord Pearson usually held his hands tightly together to disguise their palsy, but at the moment he raised both of his trembling arms in a gesture of entreaty. "I tell you, Jack, we risk losing everything. All the government support for Wellesley in the field. I cannot believe how good men, some of the finest in the land, have become obsessed with other problems to the extent of ignoring those troops. I find it appalling. And dangerous."

Jack agreed. "We cannot fail in the Peninsula. If we were to give up that campaign, what would the other powers do? Not that anyone else is mounting an effective resistance to Napoleon."

"Castlereagh and Canning argue incessantly, and Portland does nothing. The government is hobbled by squabbling."

The two men sat for a moment in gloomy silence. Jack stared at the tooled leather wallcoverings of Lord Pearson's study and saw in his head only the bodies hefted away from the front lines at Vimeiro. Many were dead already; others had been gravely wounded. Not one deserved to be forgotten by the King's ministers.

Lord Pearson lifted the wine bottle and shakily refilled their glasses. "I know what you have been doing, going everywhere and talking to people on behalf of the cause, Major. At the risk of your recovery, I must surmise, for you do not appear to be fully restored to good health as of yet."

Jack kept his gaze on the wall. He feared the pain he felt was too easily evident in his eyes. For every shard of metal they had dug out of his arms, his hip, his back, there were a dozen more festering deep within his flesh. Or slowly working their way to the surface, like the sliver of iron he'd picked out of his knee just yesterday. When he got back to Charsley Hall, he needed to have the surgeon come by again and extract more.

"Are you tired, Jack, or just thinking about your injuries?"

Jack tried to wipe the frown from his forehead. "Thinking about the troops, Lord Pearson. And worrying about the duke and the new commander in chief."

"Ah! Enough to make any man blanch. The Duke of York had myriad faults, but on the whole, I believe he was a positive force for the army. Few were able to say no to him, until he had to resign."

"Yes. I know how you fought for years to make him see the error of his ways and then tried to defend him."

"Futile gestures, which have compromised my voice, I fear. He never appreciated my interference. And General Dundas is not a great supporter of mine, not any more. Not even Castlereagh has time for me."

"That is a great pity, though your voice is sure to find a receptive audience again before long."

"Nevertheless, Jack, we need some new blood, some younger voices who can make sure the needs of the war, of the army, are given full consideration. And I do not mean just the design of new uniforms. The ministers are mired in one quarrel after another. The new commander of the army, old Dundas, is too old for the position. We must have some new men to invigorate the government."

Jack gave a half chuckle. "I am sure you are correct. But where are these new voices to be found?"

"That is one of the reasons I summoned you."

"Me? I have certain access to some in power, but I can only advise, not speak on the floor of the House."

"It is the Lords I am thinking of, Jack. Your cousin, the Duke of Charsley. He rarely attends and has spoken only once. But with your guidance, I hope we can count on him."

Jack's mood took a desolate swerve downward. Char, with his poetry, his new wife, his overbearing mother—how could anyone expect him to stand up in the House of Lords and deliver a speech worthy of attention? He was far more likely to recite a paean to romantic love than express an opinion on supplies for Wellesley's army.

Lord Pearson drained his glass and poured more. "Well? You do not look very optimistic. This is not an idea which meets your approval?"

Jack chose his words carefully. "My cousin will eventually grow into his duties, but for the moment, he is, ah, devoting himself to his estate, and takes little interest in other matters."

Jack knew Lord Pearson must have heard about Char's quick marriage. Or elopement, as some gossips termed it. Just another of those little scandals that had occupied the tabbies of the *ton* for a few weeks, greatly overshadowed by the much more perilous and spiteful mess created by York's affair with Mrs. Clarke.

Though he had heard few details of his cousin's notorious exploit, Jack gathered that it was little more than a quick change of mind that resulted in the near-jilting of the young bride's sister, hardly a matter for ruffling the feathers of government leaders. On the other hand, Mary Anne Clarke's solicitation of bribes in exchange for army promotions, all secured between the sheets, was a disgraceful national outrage.

Be that as it may, would Char be amenable to attending to government business next winter when the Lords sat again? It seemed unlikely to Jack. Char would be simpering over a squalling infant by that time.

"Lord Pearson, I regret to say that I doubt my cousin will take much notice of Parliament in the next year or two. I am afraid he is more than occupied at Charsley Hall, and tells me he had enough of London in the last two seasons to last him a lifetime, though I assume his duchess will be anxious to take her place someday in the future." For the next few years, he added to himself, he assumed she would be busy breeding a passel of little Charsleys, one after another.

Lord Pearson stood and walked to his desk, turned and faced Jack again. "Then you shall have to convince him, Jack. Make him promise to join our coalition to support Sir Arthur."

Jack started to protest, but Lord Pearson continued without a pause. "It is your duty to the King and to England, Major Whitaker. I speak not only for myself, but for several others who are sincerely concerned. In fact, I will hold you personally accountable for your cousin's participation."

Jack wanted to slump back in the chair and refuse the charge, but deep in his heart, he knew Lord Pearson was correct. He continued to sit tall and ignore the pains that never left him. Char might not be the most promising of young voices in the realm, but he represented an old and distinguished family. Someone just needed to show him the way to go on. And it appeared Jack had received the assignment.

Lord Pearson was not finished. "One more thing, Jack. Char controls two seats in Commons, as you know. That old fellow from Bluestone ought to retire. And you must stand for it. Give us an eloquent spokesman in the lower house."

Jack felt his jaw drop in surprise. And in anguish. He devoutly wished he had refused to see Lord Pearson. All Jack wanted was to return to Wellesley in Portugal and take up his commission with his regiment. But he was getting farther and farther away from assembling his kit for the Peninsula.

When Jack arrived at his rooms, Baldwin, his batman and valet, was almost wringing his hands outside the door.

"Major, I hope I have not overstepped my instructions."

"What are you doing here on the doorstep, Win?"

"It is those three men, sir, the three you said could go to Kent with you. I did not know what to do when they arrived. They just came in and helped themselves. But I know you had asked about them, and I—" He stopped abruptly as a blast of raucous laughter sounded from inside.

"The devil! I was hoping they had forgotten." Shaking his head, Jack went inside. Three men, none too clean, were dressed in flashy if soiled satin coats that seemed to date from forty years ago. Each held a brimming glass of wine; one empty bottle already lay on its side on the desk, and one of the men was trying to remove the cork from another with his teeth.

When they recognized Jack's presence, all three struggled to their feet, one of them staggering over to embrace him.

"Major Whitaker, we're waitin' fer you."

"So I see, Bart. How very much you warm my heart with your solicitude. Be seated."

Jack took the bottle from Tommy's hands and handed it to Win. "You may as well open this. I have a feeling they will be sleeping here on the floor, with or without it."

Win extracted the cork and poured Jack a glass before handing it to Bart.

Bart started to raise it his lips, then shook his head and waved the bottle in the air. "Thank'ee, Major. I've always said you was the fines' of the fine." He filled his goblet and splashed more wine into those of his friends.

"You said nothing of the sort when I sent you to the brig! Which is what I ought to do with all three of you right now."

"Aw, no, sir. You promised us—what did he promise, lads?" Bart asked.

Jack shook his head at his own imprudence. Some foolish impulse while he was on the ship bound for England had caused him to offer a home to the three of his wounded men. Now it appeared he would have to honor his promise.

* * *

Leaving her mother to fuss over a few last curls, Kitty took the opportunity of the last half hour before they were to gather for dinner to take a closer look at the rooms she had passed through earlier while looking for her harp. The previous night, after their arrival at Charsley, they had been served dinner in their rooms. But tonight, the dowager had sent word they would dine together in the Red Salon.

Kitty admired the first floor apartments with their justly famous Adam decoration, beginning with a colorful anteroom decorated with lifesize marbles of ancient gods and goddesses, athletes and warriors. She paused in the small ivory salon, a jewel of a room with insets of colored marble grapes flanking the grinning face of Bacchus centered on the fireplace surround. Around the walls were gilded sconces twined in shining golden vines with sparkling grapes of crystal and amethyst. The delicately colored carpets reflected the colors of the sylvan scenes and woodland nymphs painted on the ceiling. How very bizarre, she thought, that in this home where the sour grimace of the dowager duchess seemed to set the tone for behavior, someone had once celebrated the fruits of the vineyard and the bucolic pleasures of a classical arcadia.

Kitty drifted into the adjoining Green Salon and heard childish laughter from the next room. What children could be about? Or perhaps it was just a youthful maid with a particularly babyish laugh in response to some footman. That might show that the dowager was not as much in control as she thought.

Kitty moved slowly and soundlessly across the carpet toward the Rose Salon. When she gazed into the next room, she was surprised to see a young girl seated beside the dowager on a sofa. Who in the world was this child? As she stepped closer, Kitty saw a tall woman in gray, obviously a governess, standing behind one of the chairs.

In order not to startle them, Kitty gave a little cough before speaking. "Good evening, Duchess."

The dowager's head snapped up and quickly changed from an expression of surprise to one of disapproval.

"You are very early, Miss Stone."

"Yes, I am. I could not resist the opportunity to have a closer look at the furnishings of these beautiful rooms."

The dowager's eyes narrowed as she glanced at the child, who wore a look of curiosity. "Miss Stone, may I present Mary Reynolds, my ward?"

"Miss Reynolds, I am happy to make your acquaintance."

The dowager gave the child a little push. Mary stood and dipped a curtsy, mumbling her greetings.

"Speak up, Mary." The dowager's voice was harsher than it should have been when speaking to such a young child, Kitty thought.

"I am happy to meet you." The child spoke clearly but kept her eyes on the carpet.

She had long curls of a light brown shade, and wore a simple white dress with a yellow sash.

"You may take Mary upstairs now, Miss Munstead," the duchess said.

Kitty watched them leave, their sudden departure before her mother or the duke or duchess came in adding to her curiosity about Mary.

The dowager cast a frown at Kitty. "I try not to think of Mary as a burden, but it is difficult to raise a child in such surroundings without others of like age. She has an unfortunate tendency to be headstrong."

To Kitty, the child had seemed just the opposite, a quiet and shy girl completely deferential to the dowager. "Does she ride? I would be happy to have her accompany me in the morning since His Grace has been kind enough to stable my mare."

"Mary has a pony, but must stay near the stable. She is not experienced enough to venture farther."

"I see." Kitty paused, waiting for the dowager to say more, but she sat in silence. "Perhaps if we took along two grooms?"

"I would prefer that you not interfere with Mary's program of instruction, Miss Stone. She and Miss Munstead should not be disturbed. If you have any desire to visit the schoolroom, please put it out of your mind. I shall not allow it, and I hope I will not have to instruct the butler to make use of the locks to that wing."

Kitty said no more, astonished at the venom in the dowager's voice. How could she be so unkind?

Instead of speaking her mind, she forced herself to remain silent, staring at the painting on the room's longest wall. Of very large size, it showed a sweeping plain on which two armies faced one another. Puffs of smoke and a few fallen soldiers occupied the center where the advancing ranks fired on each other. Though the action of the picture was clearly its focal point, the figures involved in the murderous scene were dwarfed by the sweep of the surrounding hills and the stormy sky. Yet the subject matter was all too suitable, Kitty thought, for this very house.

The dinner seemed interminable, a meal made unpleasant by the dowager's continual critical remarks about the affairs of the estate. No one was able to establish a topic of conversation that suited her. Not even Lady Dunmark's admiration of the gardens brought an agreeable expression to the dowager's face.

Char declined to stay behind when his mother rose, calling for Randall, the butler, to bring a bottle of port to the music room. His mother grimaced at that, but for once held her tongue.

Once seated again in the Rose Salon, the dowager announced her desire for a short musicale, instructing Char to save his poetry recitations for another evening. "You may play the pianoforte, Miss Stone. Your sister has a feeble talent at the keyboard, to be sure. I trust you can improve upon her accomplishments."

Kitty longed to make a sharp retort, but tried to keep her anger under wraps. "My sister performs creditably, in my experience, Your Grace. But I have always thought of her as a better soprano. Will you join me at the instrument, Bea?"

Though Bea's cheeks were as intense a shade as the deep pink silk-clad walls, she came to the pianoforte and sat beside Kitty at the keyboard.

Kitty kept her voice to a whisper. "We will do a few simple songs. Do you remember the one about the birds of June?"

Bea nodded.

When their voices blended together, Kitty thought both of them sounded better than performing solo, and they followed the first song with another and a third. At the end of each, the duke and Lady Dunmark applauded enthusiastically. Kitty did not bother to look at the dowager, but was quite sure she heard only two pairs of hands clapping.

They both arose from the bench and curtsied to their audience of three.

The dowager's face was actually free of scorn as she called for the tea tray.

A half hour later, Lady Dunmark softly closed the door of their apartment behind her, but the look on her face was anything but composed. Kitty knew what was coming. When her mother got into a pelter, there was nothing to do but let it run its course.

Lady Dunmark drew herself up and, eyes flashing, trembled with fury. "That woman's treatment of Beatrice is inexcusable." Her words flowed out in a torrent. The dowager duchess was trying to make Bea even more helpless, Lady Dunmark proclaimed; the dowager disapproved of anything Bea said; the dowager's compliments to the cook were effusive while she did not deign to comment on the lovely songs Bea and Kitty sang. The dowager was all criticism and no positive remarks. The dowager complained that Char was not living up to his responsibilities; the estate managers needed closer supervision. The acidity of the dowager's voice reflected her meaning, even when her words were milder.

The dowager had no right to disapprove of Bea's wardrobe, nor Bea's choice of new draperies for the ducal chambers.

Lady Dunmark was almost breathless with anger. "She is one of those women who rule through constant criticism, who do not allow any evaluation of themselves." The dowager was rude, arrogant and a model of incivility. She fancied herself the greatest of ladies, but she acted like a vindictive witch. She made it clear that no authority but herself would be allowed, then reviled her son and Bea for taking on no responsibilities at all. The contradictory nature of her views, even when Lady Dunmark had attempted to point them out, remained beyond the dowager's comprehension.

At last Kitty broke into her mother's litany of anger. "Perhaps it is not an inability to see what she is doing, but a purposeful strategy to enhance her own authority."

"Indeed, I assume you are correct, Kitty." Lady Dunmark launched into another list of evils and exclamations of disgust. Kitty listened with only half her attention. She was beginning to work on an idea about bolstering Bea's spirits.

Lady Dunmark dabbed at her eyes with a lacy handkerchief. "Beatrice is a gentle gel, sweet and accommodating. And why the duke does not see he must assert himself I will never understand."

Kitty knew precisely why Char was so deferential to his mama. It was the result of many years of being manipulated by her, years after his father had died and he had only his mother. He had grown used to it—and dependent upon her maneuvering. After all, if he spent many hours running the estate every day, he would have less time to write his poetry.

Kitty tried to think of words to comfort her mother. "In time, Mama, we will find a way to help Bea."

The next morning after her ride, Kitty sat at the dressing table, watching in the mirror while Nell arranged her dark hair in a knot atop her head.

"What have they asked you to do, Nell?"

"Mrs. Wells wants me to tell her what you are doing. I say sewing baby clothes. I am to report where you go, but since I am supposed to be at Mrs. Wells's disposal, I say I don't know because I am waiting for her in the servant's hall."

"I hope you know how much Mama and I appreciate the hardships you are going through and also your loyalty to us. Together we all must sort out this muddle and do something about the stranglehold the dowager has on the household."

"I know you do not approve of servants' gossip, miss, but I have been keeping my ears open to learn who is in charge."

"I would like to hear your views, Nell. The situation here is extraordinary and the servants are part of it, answering as they do to the dowager instead of the new duchess."

Nell put down the brush. "That nasty housekeeper, Mrs. Wells, is devoted to the dowager, but some of the servants, like the cook, Mrs. James, have a frown whenever the duke is overruled by his mama. The maids and footmen respect Mrs. Wells, though they sometimes talk about how Miss Beatrice, or Her Grace, as I should say, ought to take over the household, because everyone is very excited about the baby. They dare not say so to Mrs. Wells."

"What do you know about the governess, Miss Munstead?"

"She keeps strictly to herself. They say she only takes her meals with the little girl or alone. I've not heard the nursery-maid say a word."

Kitty nodded, setting the curls to jiggling and the ribbons woven into her braid to swaying. "Thank you, Nell. You know how Mama and I appreciate your service to us, even though now Mrs. Wells can tell you what to do."

"Don't worry about me, miss."

"You are a dear, Nell. I also wonder what the dowager does all day in her apartments. She is never at breakfast or luncheon."

"I asked about that. One of the maids serves her during the day. She meets with the estate steward and Mrs. Wells, but there are long hours in which no one is allowed in."

"The duke says she has a large collection of miniatures,

which are famous in some circles, among people who know of that sort of thing."

Lady Dunmark walked into the room, the dark cloud of a frown marring her forehead. "Good morning, Nell."

Nell dipped a curtsy. "Good morning, milady."

Lady Dunmark patted her shoulder. "Kitty, did you see the diamonds the dowager was wearing last night? I expect that most of those jewels ought to be on Beatrice instead of her."

"I cannot quite see the duke asking his mother to give them to Bea, Mama."

"If she were to follow the usual protocol, she would present all the Charsley family jewels to the new duchess. Knowing Bea, she would probably give most of them back to the dowager to wear anyway. How foolish it is of the dowager not to be generous! Surely munificence evokes its own reward." Lady Dunmark turned to Nell. "What do the servants say?"

"Milady, they are curious about Miss Beatrice—the duchess, I mean. They find her sweet, but they know the dowager is in charge, through Mrs. Wells. They will not defy her and risk being discharged without a character. They are also curious about you, Lady Dunmark, and Miss Stone."

"Thank you, Nell. Now I suppose it is best for you to go along and follow Mrs. Wells's instructions. We certainly do not wish to have you get into any trouble. And we thank you for your service."

When Nell had left the room, Lady Dunmark put her head into her hands. "I do not know what to do, Kitty. Or where to start."

Kitty put her arm around her mother's shoulders. "I have been thinking about it too. What I propose is that we begin with a few simple things, to test the waters."

"Like what, Kitty?"

"Bea says Char cannot absolutely count on the butler and the footmen to do his bidding because they also answer to the dowager. But he has more success with the grooms in the stable. I think we will have some luck with the gardeners, who have little to do with the servants in the house."

Lady Dunmark broke into a smile. "You are always so clever, Kitty. You see things I never do."

"I also want to try to use the stillroom, and I will go directly to the dowager and ask. We will see what she does."

"Well, you are also braver than I am. I cannot imagine approaching that woman on her own ground."

"If that does not work, I propose to get to know the cook, Mrs. James. She may have a great deal of independence from the housekeeper."

Kitty only hoped her efforts were half as fruitful as her ability to bring a cheerful twinkle to Lady Dunmark's eye.

FOUR

Kitty reined up her mare beside Char's mount at the top of a long slope. Below them stretched the park with its lake and clumps of trees, the very epitome of a Capability Brown landscape. In the distance stood the mansion, its porticoed façade presenting a dignified, even austere, contrast to the emerald green of the grass and cloudless azure of the sky. Kitty appreciated the beauty of the scene, though she silently held an ironic view of the very human complications beneath the idyllic surface. A domineering dowager duchess who tyrannized her son and bullied his wife. Servants who answered to the dowager and ignored the needs and desires of the young couple.

Char sat in his saddle and stared silently at his holdings. Whether he would ever assume full control of those estates remained an open question to Kitty. If she were to help her sister, she had to think of a way to raise the issue with him, yet she feared a direct approach would only spook him like a colt shying at a wind-blown scarecrow. No, an indirect and gradual approach would work best with Char as well as with Bea.

Kitty's mare backed up a few steps and pawed at the

ground as if wondering why they had come to a halt. "You must be very proud of Charsley Hall, Your Grace."

The duke looked startled, as if he had forgotten she was there. "Oh, er, yes. Ancient, you know. In the family for centuries."

Kitty grinned to herself. "I suspect you were composing some lines of verse to celebrate this view."

He cleared his throat and spoke in stentorian tones. "*Amid the verdant lawns of deepest green, The stately columns from a distance seen*—That is as far as I have got."

Kitty refrained from voicing the next line that jumped into her head. *And many crested peacocks strut and preen.* Char was unlikely to appreciate any unsolicited contributions. Based on her previous exposure to his poetry, he was more than capable of coming up with another hundred lines of meandering blather.

For shame, she thought. After Char had so kindly offered to show her around the neighborhood this morning, such insolent thoughts were disrespectful and entirely ungrateful, especially right here in his presence. Yet a little bubble of laughter remained to tickle her throat.

"A very lyrical beginning, Char."

"Thank you, Kitty. I rather pride myself on my lyricism these days, a new direction for my work indeed. But now, I am neglecting my promise to show you around, am I not?"

"If you need to return to your desk to suit your muse, please feel free to do so. We can continue our tour another day."

His voice took on a less pompous tone. "No, indeed. As long as we have begun, I think we should continue."

"Whatever suits Your Grace."

"Below us you see the house and park. Beyond the larger grove of trees to the north lies the Acker River. My cousin Jack's property spreads out from there. The village of Acker Ford and two smaller hamlets are to the east, where we will ride later. To the south, as far as we can see today, is my land.

The home farm is just past the stables. Several more villages sit along a stream near Bluestone Mill, but that we will save for another day."

"It is very impressive, Char. Think of how many families depend upon your land." As she spoke the kernel of an idea began to form. If she let it develop in her head before she spoke, she might just have the answer to her initial problems.

Char urged his horse forward. "We shall head for the closest village to continue your introductory tour."

For the next hour, they rode among Charsley's farms and settlements, skirting the land belonging to Nether Acker, and seeing dozens of people in the fields and at work in the villages. All bowed or bent their heads at the duke's approach, and he greeted them warmly, though he appeared to know few of their names. Kitty wondered why he did not recognize more, since she remembered how her father and mother knew every detail of the lives of their tenants. She was willing to wager that the dowager knew most of their names.

As they rounded a bend in the lane to return their horses to the stable, Kitty noticed a cottage almost hidden behind overgrown bushes and a screen of trees. She decided to walk back to it after finishing their ride.

They were met in the stableyard by half a dozen grooms, who whisked the horses away to be cooled down, curried, and fed. Char, once she reminded him of his two lines of verse, hurried off to his writing sanctuary. Kitty was too interested in the cottage to accompany him, for she was sure that if she accompanied him, he would favor her with numerous poetical compositions before she was again free. Luckily he was preoccupied with his verse and neglected to offer to escort her back to the house.

She headed back down the lane to the cottage, hoping it would look as promising on second view. She had the sense it might be perfect for her musical studies, within easy distance of the house, but out of hearing and screened from view, hardly visible, she suspected, even from the upper story windows of the mansion. The cottage sat far back from the road in a thicket of brambles behind a low stone wall. The long neglected pathway to the front door was overgrown and the gate rusted shut. It took her several tugs to open it. The thatched roof hung low, but there was definitely an upper floor.

Up close, the cottage had a cheerful charm, covered in clouds of pink and scarlet rosebuds about to burst into bloom. A jumble of fragrant flowers and weeds crowded the front garden. Even with the full skirt of her habit draped over her arm, she could not get near enough to peek in the windows.

Finding the door locked, Kitty walked around to the back and looked at the clutter behind the house, comprised of two sheds, a chicken coop, and a well house, all in tumbledown condition. The remnant of a kitchen garden was dense with plants and vines going wild. From the positions of the chimneys, fireplaces occupied both ends of the house.

She looked into the back windows and could barely make out a heap of furniture covered with cloth. It appeared there were two rooms on each floor divided by a corridor and staircase. The back door was also locked, and she did not try to force her way in. That could wait for another day.

Feeling a tinge of optimism for the future, Kitty sat on the stone step, unmindful of the dirt. She was certain she had found the perfect retreat for herself, just a simple room in which she could play her harp. It did not look like it would take a great deal of effort to make it usable.

As for her other idea about getting Char and Bea started on assuming the real responsibilities of a duke and duchess, she thought a festive summer party for the neighborhood might serve a number of useful purposes. First, she needed to maneuver Char into thinking he had hatched the idea himself. The dowager would probably withhold her approval, thus letting Kitty and Bea and their Mama plan most of the activities, along with Char and his bailiff.

They could plan the festival for some traditional summer holiday and combine it with a special service in the church.

All the people of the neighborhood would no doubt welcome a celebration and feast.

The very best part would be watching the reaction of the dowager duchess.

Jack scratched his head and stared at the floor. Any method he concocted for getting his three reprobates to Nether Acker had more traps waiting 'round the bend than the French-occupied ravines of Western Portugal.

Baldwin refused to ride with them, citing their noise, their stench, and their complete lack of companionable conduct. Even though Jack secretly laughed at how Win—his companion through the battles of Copenhagen and Vimeiro—had become so starchy, he understood Win's reluctance. Bart, Tommy, and Yates would be in high spirits once the effects of last evening's wine wore off. Who knew what kind of pranks they might get up to?

So Win would have to ride in the curricle with him after Jack engaged some sort of equipage to ferry the others to Kent. Fortunately, it was not a long journey, and he'd caution the hired driver to stay with him, not to stop unless Jack did. After the raunchy mutterings he'd heard last night, not a female was safe if the three of those scoundrels were on the loose.

Yates, though full of quick laughter, had grown up in the stews of London, and had no trade but scrounging an existence out of dark alleys and filthy gutters. Tommy, a hearty soul from North Yorkshire, full-girthed and red of face, had briefly been apprenticed to a shoemaker. Bart's mama fell in love with an Irishman, he claimed, the source of his coppery hair. If Bart had ever mentioned another detail about his life before the army, Jack never heard about it.

They got off to a late start because Yates disappeared. Only when they had all grown sweaty and irritable, tired of searching, did Yates saunter up.

Jack tried to control his temper. "Another five minutes and we would have been gone, you silly nodcock."

"Had t'say my farewells to the chuffs at Hal's, Major. Growed up on the coins I filched from them sots. Wouldna' been right not to wish them luck."

Jack waved toward the hired coach. "How much did you take them for?"

Yates began to climb aboard, then turned around and gave Jack a wink. "Jest enuf to keep the boys and me in spirits for a few days." With that, he swung aboard and slammed the coach door.

With a groan, Jack hoisted himself into the curricle, and ignoring Win's snicker, nodded to the boy to release his horses.

As they negotiated the crowded streets out of London, he tried to set aside the pains that skittered up his side and down his leg, and fought off a sudden wave of nausea as they turned a quick corner. Almost as bad as his aches were his doubts about his three charges. For the moment he ought to avoid thinking of what he was going to do with the Three, as he had come to think of them. Instead, he concentrated on his driving and watched the horses carefully. He'd borrowed the pair of bays from his cousin Char, and he wanted to be certain he was returning them in prime condition. When they reached the outskirts of town and the traffic thinned, he could no longer avoid the nagging question of how he would keep the Three from setting the entire neighborhood of Nether Acker and Charsley Hall on its proverbial ear.

If they had not hauled him out from under his horse after the explosion and dragged him to shelter away from the battle, and wrapped his wounds tightly, he might have bled to death. If Yates, the least wounded, had not filched most of the officers' dinner, carrying off the pot of meat and vegetables, and going back for a pile of blankets, they might have succumbed to hunger and cold. They all had decided to wait until the next day to see the sawbones, because none of them wanted to lose an arm or a leg. So Jack owed them not only his life but the fortunate fact he had all four of his limbs. When he went to visit the Three in the hospital in London and they confessed they had no place to go, he offered them work on his estate.

But neither gratitude nor charity provided all the answers. First there was the problem of where to put them. There was a little inn at the village of Acker Ford which might accommodate them, but that was only a temporary solution. Even more at issue was useful employment. Not one of the three seemed to have a practical skill. Tommy had been learning to make shoes, he said, but for less than a year before signing up with the King's representative. It was doubtful he could resume his craft, though he might be able to patch leather goods and keep the harnesses mended. Yates was essentially a street tough and a pickpocket. Bart's only accomplishment, Jack suspected, was his amazing capacity for ale. The fellow had never met a man he couldn't outdrink.

Worse yet was the thought of how they would mix with the local folk, who seemed set in their ways and not particularly welcoming to strangers in their midst.

Jack gave a silent snicker at his momentary oversight. The women of the neighborhood might find the new arrivals to their liking, all right. Three new men with whom to flirt would gladden the heart of many a village maiden. Stir up some jealousies, too. Why, oh why had he not considered all these complications before he promised them a home?

Carrying a basket that held the cap she was embroidering for the baby, Kitty joined her mother in Bea's boudoir. Folded lengths of white fabric and assorted spools of lace and ribbon were spread on the chaise while Bea and Lady Dunmark turned the pages of pattern books, looking at drawings of baby clothes.

Bea beckoned Kitty to look at a page. "This gown is

lovely, but I am not sure I can follow these instructions. Do you understand this part about the sleeves?"

Kitty took the book and read the instructions for making the sleeves. "Yes, I think I can help you, my dear duchess. If you sew the long side seams and the shoulders, I will show you how to gather up the sleeves."

Lady Dunmark looked up from the pattern she studied and smiled at her daughters. "You see, Beatrice, I told you Kitty would understand."

Kitty smiled indulgently. Neither her mother nor her sister were eager needlewomen, and it seemed likely they would have to employ a few women from the neighborhood to stitch clothing for the child. But that could wait a little longer until Bea visited more of the tenants and got to know them, a program that was sure to annoy the dowager. First Kitty wanted to plant the idea of a festival.

After they spent a quarter hour admiring various patterns for infant garments but doing no sewing, Kitty broached the subject. "This morning, when the duke showed me around the estate, he mentioned its very ancient history."

"Oh, yes," Bea said. "The family has lived here for ages and ages."

"I suppose there must be all sorts of traditional celebrations and seasonal festivals throughout the year."

Lady Dunmark looked up from a page she was studying. "Does he wish to plan something soon?"

Bea broke into a broad smile. "I would like a festival above all things."

Kitty nodded. "I think he may have had something in mind. Perhaps you could ask him when we have luncheon, Bea."

"Oh, yes, I shall indeed. A festival is just what we need at Charsley Hall."

An hour later when they sat down to a cold collation, Char was eager to recite his poem, grown now, he reported, to twenty-two lines.

But Bea shook her head. "You can read it to us a little later, Char. I am much more enthusiastic about your idea for a festival."

Char looked bewildered, and Kitty held her breath.

Bea was not deterred. "This morning when you and Kitty were riding, you said something about a festival."

"I did?"

Kitty buttered a roll, purposely keeping her eyes from meeting his. "You were speaking of the many years of traditions, of celebrations, of the habits and likes of the workers and their families and of the tenants."

She could still hear the surprise in his voice. "Yes, I did say something about that. Festivals, eh? I remember many from my childhood. When my father was alive, but since he died, I do not remember—"

Bea's fervor bubbled over. "You are exactly right, Char. This is what we should do, let the people know the old ways will return. Will a festival not make them very happy? It will be a return to the days when your father was alive."

Kitty risked one more sentence, to set the hook. "I think your idea is just perfect, Char. Very inspired."

"Yes, er, thank you. I will definitely give it some more thought."

Lady Dunmark looked thoughtful. "I would expect your steward, Mr. Edgerton, would have a record of all the details."

"Yes." Char chewed a moment, a small frown on his forehead. "I remember a few things, like the year we had the fire-eater."

"What?" Bea's voice was a squeak. "I cannot imagine such a thing."

Char patted her hand and spoke with an indulgent tone. "It was a trick, of course. A troupe of traveling performers came that year. Probably a host of charlatans and gypsies, but to a small boy they were amazing."

"But how did a man eat fire?"

"When he held the flame up to his mouth and blew on it,

it flared out in a huge blue conflagration. Then he stuck it in his mouth and appeared to swallow it. I assume it just went out when he closed his mouth."

Bea was still wide-eyed. "But was he not badly burned?"

Char chuckled. "No, and he repeated the feat several times a day."

"Ooooh, I do not think I want to have one of those. What if the trick did not work and he hurt himself?"

Just like the tender-hearted Bea, Kitty thought, to be more concerned for the state of the fire-eater's tongue than for the coins he had no doubt extracted from the audience. "But Bea, there are many more things you will like. Did you not say, Char, there were services at the church for various saint's days?"

Before Char could think of an answer, Bea chimed in again. "How lovely. How very wonderful that would be."

Char nodded. "Yes, I remember some, like taking a basket of chicks one year when they blessed the baby animals. Mama was speechless." He paused, suddenly growing red in the face. "Mama! What will she think of this idea? I greatly fear—"

Kitty interrupted. "I suggest you say nothing until you have the details worked out, Char. Then I am sure you can convince her that reestablishing an old custom will be a good thing."

Bea grabbed Char's hand. "Just think of how she is always saying you should be more involved with the estate business, Char. She wants you to do more."

He was shaking his head and his frown was back. And deeper.

Now, Kitty could only hope that he would follow through. And that the dowager's inevitable opposition could be surmounted.

"Your Grace." Kitty made a low curtsy, carefully holding the vase of flowers to prevent spilling water on the carpet.

The dowager acknowledged her with a quick curt nod of the head. "Miss Stone."

"The duchess and I cut a few roses this morning and brought these for you." Kitty set the vase on a table near the dowager's chair.

The dowager's frown deepened. "I am not fond of roses. Their odor is cloying, overpoweringly sweet."

Kitty bit back a grin. Too sweet indeed for an acidic personage such as the dowager! Kitty carried the vase across the room and set it in front of a tall pier glass. "Perhaps you can enjoy their beauty from a distance and the fragrance will be less noticeable."

Kitty stole a glance around the room. A chaise longue with a novel opened on it, a writing desk with several quills. The pictures on the wall were mostly landscapes. It was a most pleasant room, nothing like the sober mien the dowager presented to the world. A real person lived here. There were several of the glass-topped tables which must have held the dowager's collection of miniatures. Char claimed she had one of the realm's finest collections, including examples from the Elizabethan era. But supposedly she allowed them only to be seen by experts from London.

The dowager polished the miniature in her hand and put it back in the case. "I am surprised the gardener allowed you to cut flowers. Usually he supervises all the—"

"Why, certainly he could not have denied the duchess her pleasure. Indeed he was most accommodating and even helped us choose which blossoms were best for clipping."

"I shall have to speak to him."

Kitty purposely misconstrued her statement. "Oh, yes, that would be most kind. Bea, Mama, and I would so appreciate your indulgence, Your Grace. We need the cooperation of the gardener and just a teeny corner of the stillroom. You see, at Dunmark Manor, we always collected and dried a number of fragrant petals to make a potpourri. It would give Mama great comfort if we could do this here at Charsley

Hall. I assure you we will take care not to trouble the staff or interfere with their duties. And it will be good for Bea to be outside in the beautiful gardens you developed, Your Grace. I commend you on your excellent taste in design. Mr. Henry said you were responsible."

Kitty closely watched the dowager for any sign of reaction and at her last words she was sure she saw a little motion of the woman's shoulders, perhaps just a hint of preening. Perhaps just a hint of appreciation for Kitty's appreciative comments.

Kitty went on, almost without pause. "He said you re-designed the parterre on the south side of the house and in-corporated all sorts of new plants from abroad."

"That was a very long time ago, Miss Stone. As for the stillroom, that is the province of Mrs. Wells, and she has many uses for the room. I do not wish to have her inconvenienced. Perhaps if Lady Dunmark wishes to preserve flowers, she should go back to her home and proceed with her customs. It is not a matter which concerns me."

This was the answer Kitty had expected. The dowager duchess was rigid, unbending.

The dowager went on. "Now, as you can see, I am busy with my collections, and I would appreciate no further disturbances."

Kitty maintained a perfectly courteous expression and curtsied as though the dowager had been watching her instead of polishing another miniature. She had wanted to be certain that no effort went unmade to invite the dowager's cooperation before she began to probe the inevitable fissures in her iron-fisted control. There was, Kitty thought as she left the dowager's apartments, more than one way to pull the petals from a blossom.

"I had no idea my steward had hired a lady gardener."

A deep baritone cut into Kitty's humming as she clipped at the rosebush that covered the cottage window. She held the thorny branch in her heavily gloved hand and turned slowly to face the source of the voice. "Are you addressing me?"

"I am addressing the person who is cutting flowers on my property, yes."

Kitty lifted one eyebrow and contemplated the lean form of the man sitting in a curricle outside the cottage gate. As he climbed down and motioned to his man to walk the horses, a sudden spasm of pain shadowed his face, gone as soon as it appeared. He was attired in a perfectly tailored dark blue coat, buff breeches, and well-polished leather boots. His face was pale but his eyes seemed to sparkle, whether with anger or amusement she was not certain.

"I have the permission of the Duke of Charsley to—"

"Ah! I had forgotten that it is usual, in fact, typical of His Grace to assume the entire neighborhood belongs to him. But why are you trimming those roses? This cottage has been abandoned for many years."

Before she answered his question, she had one of her own. "Is this your concern, sir?"

He leaned against the stone pillar beside the gate. "When I come upon a young lady chopping away at my foliage, I consider it my legitimate concern."

"*Your* foliage?"

"This little structure, despite what my cousin might think, lies on my property."

"Your cousin? Then you must be Jack Whitaker. I should have realized more quickly. And if this cottage is yours, I beg your pardon on my behalf and on behalf of the duke as well." She thrust the branch of pale pink rosebuds toward him.

He grabbed it and immediately winced. "Ouch." He dropped it and pushed it away with the toe of his boot. "That is full of thorns!"

"Pardon me, Major." She could barely keep from laughing out loud. "I did not wish to confiscate your belongings."

He snorted derisively, then looked at her quizzically. "I fear you have the advantage of me, ma'am."

"I am Miss Stone, sister of the duchess."

"Ah! I see." From the tone of his voice, she assumed he knew the entire story of the duke's abandonment of her and his marriage to her sister.

She took off her gloves and set them on the wall beside the scissors. "Since you claim this is your property, I shall not continue my activities here, sir."

"And just what were you attempting to do, Miss Stone?" He gave her an engaging smile, all evidence of coolness fading. "Do you have designs upon this place?"

"Yes, rather. But I do not wish to trespass and I hope you will not consider the trimming of the roses to be serious enough damage to approach the duke for compensation."

He laughed, a sharp bark that seemed laced with real amusement. "This place belongs to me, on the edge of my land, but if you have a use for it, Miss Stone, I am willing to consider a request. You can easily see that I have never needed it. What is your purpose?"

"I plan to make it a music room, in which I may practice out of range of the dowager duchess's hearing."

He renewed his laughter. "Ah, yes. The duchess and her infamous crotchets."

"I am not so characterizing the situation." Had Bea not said Jack was the dowager's pet? The last thing she wanted was to spread her opinion of the dowager beyond Bea and her mama.

"You need not be so careful with me. Feel free to allow yourself to criticize her, Miss Stone. Everyone else does so, you know."

Kitty plucked a rose blossom. "But I am not qualified to say she has crotchets."

"You are being excessively courteous, are you not?"

She gave a little shrug, dropping her reluctance to speak. "To tell the truth, crotchets sound rather too benign in my opinion. I find her imperious and rude."

"How very correct you are, Miss Stone. Obviously I under-estimated you."

"No, you did not expect me to match her rudeness, and perhaps I should not have done so. But I am a little befuddled as to why it should be necessary for me to remove myself from the house when I am quite convinced she could not possibly be disturbed by my practicing. Charsley Hall is a very large mansion. How could sound carry from the music room to her suite in another wing?"

"I should say that the sound has little to do with it. It is rather a matter of control. She wants nothing to go on in that house, indeed on the entire estate, that she does not rule, though she is usually prickly only about the house. So she sent you out here?"

She lifted a rosebud and breathed its sweet fragrance. "The duke suggested I might find another place, and I saw this little cottage overrun with vines. He said I might do with it as I wished. The gardener and a few housemaids and some footman were coming tomorrow to prepare it. But since it is your property, I will cancel those plans."

"What are you planning to do here, practice your high Cs?"

"No, I have no high Cs. At best, I am an indifferent alto. And there is no pianoforte here. I had thought to bring my harp, but I shall find another place." She gathered up the thick gloves and the scissors, in readiness to return to the house.

"Miss Stone, I am prepared to allow you the use of this cottage. For a small price."

"What?" She hoped her face and her voice did not betray the stab of shock his words caused her.

"Would you allow me to come occasionally and hear you play?"

She stared at him. After his rather cynical remarks and her equally cynical answers, she wondered that he would be remotely interested in the meager skills of an amateur musician. "I have no particular aptitude beyond a few familiar melodies, Major. I am quite sure my paltry efforts will bore you excessively. But if you are interested in listening, I am willing to play for you."

"Good. But do have Char cancel those workers. I have

some men who need a project, though they are not experienced at such tasks. What, besides cutting the shrubbery and washing the windows, will be required? I have not been inside for many a year."

"I peeked through the windows, and the furniture appears to be pushed into the middle of the rooms. Who lived here?"

"I have been away at school and with the army for more than the past dozen years. I do not know when it was last inhabited. I assume that Char knows where to find a key?"

"He mentioned no former inhabitants, and yes, I also assume he can get a key."

"There you are, then. I'll bring my men over tomorrow."

Kitty looked him straight in the eye. "I thought you were in London. I believe the duke said you had frequent business there."

"London is growing thin of company. I thought a few weeks in the country might be enjoyable."

And perhaps help to cure the cause of those grimaces of pain, she thought. "Will you be staying at Charsley Hall?"

"Yes. I was just on my way there after leaving those three men at the Cross and Bell. Three fellows from my old regiment, who seemed to be at loose ends in London, and need something to do with themselves."

Kitty opened her mouth to ask for more information, but changed her mind before uttering a sound. What Jack Whitaker did was no concern of hers. She certainly did not want to pester him with pointless questions.

He motioned to his man to bring back his rig. "I expect I shall see you at dinner, Miss Stone."

"Yes, so I assume, major."

He kept his head turned away from her as he gingerly climbed back into the curricle. When he faced her again to say good-bye, his face was free of the brief flash of anguish she had seen before.

"Adieu, Miss Stone."

She lifted a hand and waved. "Until dinner," she murmured.

FIVE

The door of Charsley Hall opened even before Jack's curricle had rolled to a stop on the smoothly raked gravel drive. Two footmen hurried down the steps behind the butler.

Jack winced as he stepped down, bringing a look of concern to the butler's wrinkled face. "Here now, Major, let these men help you."

Jack waved them away. "Not necessary, Randall, I'm just a little stiff from sitting too long. Thank you just the same, but I don't want to spoil myself."

"Nonsense, Major. You drive yourself too hard. The duchess . . . er, the dowager duchess . . . gave us strict instructions to assist you at all times."

"Be assured I shall call upon you whenever I need you. But for now, I can make it upstairs on my own."

Jack turned back to the curricle. One of the footmen had removed the box with the few clothes he brought along from London, and Win had taken the reins to continue on to the stable. "I shall see you in a half hour."

Win touched his hat and clucked to Char's pair of bays, which looked none the worse for their sojourn in London and the trip back to Kent.

Jack forced himself to walk steadily up the staircase behind Randall and ahead of the footman, but when the door of his bedchamber closed behind them, he dropped wearily into a chair. His left hip was afire, the pain stretching down past his knee and even into the small of his back. More metal fragments embedded deep into his flesh were slowly being pushed toward the surface of his skin. He would have to have the surgeon again, much as he hated it, to dig out the pieces before the pain became unbearable. He should have done it days ago in town, but here in the country, Jack knew Mr. Lanark and what to expect from him. Though he was elderly and had treated the old duke, even attended the deaths of Jack's father and many other members of the family, Lanark did a neat job of cutting and sewing, kept his leeches to just a few, and did not insist on keeping Jack flat on his back for weeks on end.

Jack reached for the brandy Randall had thoughtfully placed on the table and filled a glass, squinting at it against the sunlight of the west-facing window. He took a sip and let the mellow liquid soothe his throat and warm his innards. Did the pain begin to fade a bit, or was it just his imagination?

He leaned his head back and drew a deep breath. Much as he hated to admit it, the drive from London had been excruciating, the arrangements to put the Three up at the inn more complicated than he expected. The stop to speak with Miss Stone ate up the last of his spare time. Instead of having the opportunity for a much needed rest, he would have to get out of his dirt as soon as Win arrived, then visit Mary and pay his respects to his aunt before dinner was served.

He untied his neckcloth and let his mind wander while he waited for Win. He hoped the dowager was beginning to cease her fussing at Char. Perhaps the arrival of Miss Stone would bring a change in the atmosphere.

But what was Miss Stone doing here? After Char had dropped her to marry her sister, why would she come to live at Charsley Hall? Jack found it hard to believe that any man would prefer Bea, a mindless chit, over Miss Stone, a young lady of considerable good looks and agreeable countenance, a person who cared enough about her music to arrange a special practice venue, but most of all, a female who showed spirit and wit.

Jack swallowed more brandy. He wondered what Char thought of the gossip his marriage engendered. Of course, Char was rather a special case, a duke since he was barely more than a lad and the object of an odd upbringing. It might be said he already showed signs of developing into a genuine eccentric.

Miss Stone seemed a capable person, without unconventional tastes or peculiar habits. In fact, once he started thinking about it, Jack wondered that Miss Stone had been attracted to Char at all. Even in town, while otherwise trying to live up to the *ton*'s expectations of an ancient dukedom's titleholder, Char was likely to have recited his verses to her.

However, Jack mused, Char was a duke and wealthy. Even young ladies of impeccable taste, spotless virtue, and upright piety could have their heads turned by a noble title and overflowing purse. Jack knew nothing about the words gentlemen spoke into the eager ears of maidens angling for a husband. Perhaps every suitor was expected to spout passionate soliloquies in rhyme. Jack had consistently avoided any activity that hinted at the marriage mart since he came of age.

Only in the last few months had he tasted the sharp ambiguities of the London social scene, and those only from the sidelines. But he had been at several gatherings where his cousin's elopement was the first topic on everyone's lips. Jack had not met Miss Stone in London, though she had been pointed out to him more than once. How had she managed to survive the gossip? The cruelty of Society was just one more reason he avoided the *ton* until recently. Indeed, he recalled hearing many a transparent declaration of compassion for the young lady the duke abandoned for her sister. The pretense of sympathy had amused him at the time.

Such spurious pity would not have been a matter of hilarity for Miss Stone, of that he was certain. To be the object of pervasive gossip could not please any lady. Indeed, he wondered how she had endured it. For a moment, he felt a twinge of remorse that he had not sought her out, tried to ease her discomfiture. But perhaps she had put the tattlers of the London ballrooms behind her, escaped to the Sussex seaside or the windswept moors of Devon before she came here.

Jack's mind continued to roam over the riddle of Char's taste in females as Win brought up a can of hot water and shaved him, then helped him into his dinner attire.

"Win, I am going to visit Mary. I will not need you before retiring, so take the whole evening off. You deserve it after putting up with my three scalawags. And no doubt your lady friend has learned of your return to the neighborhood and will be expecting to hear from you."

Embarrassed, Win colored and stammered in answer. "Th-thank you, major. I w-would not want you to overdo, sir, so I will b-be here at eleven."

"Deuce take it, Win, I will not need you until tomorrow, and if I see you around here later, I shall send you to that inn to keep tabs on Yates and company. Permanently."

"Yessir, I can make myself scarce, sir!" Win swept a brush across Jack's shoulders and turned to busy himself with wiping down Jack's Hessians.

"Enjoy yourself, and that is an order."

"Yes, Major. I will do my best."

Grinning to himself, Jack headed for the nursery and schoolroom on the upper floor.

Mary greeted him with a hug and a warm smile.

"Have you been studying hard, Mary, and practicing your sums?"

"Oh yes, and I can recite all the kings and queens from Henry the Eighth and all his queens to His Majesty King George the Third and Queen Charlotte."

"You don't say! All of Henry's wives? I hardly remember how many he had."

Her eyes were bright as she stood and clasped her hands before her. "Six wives. Three Catherines, two Annes, and Jane."

"Why, that is remarkable, Mary." Jack turned to Miss Munstead. "Very fine, indeed."

Miss Munstead curtsied and nodded to Mary. "Go on."

"Then his children, not in order. Poor little Edward. Mary. Then Elizabeth. I like her the very best of all."

Jack raised his eyebrows and nodded. "So do I, Mary. She was a great queen."

They were interrupted by the arrival of the nursery dinner carried in by two footmen.

Mary looked decidedly disappointed.

Jack patted her shoulder. "Well, my dear, you must eat now. Tomorrow, may I come and watch you ride? Before long, as soon as I can spend more than a quarter hour in the saddle, I shall take you riding across the bridge to Nether Acker."

"Oh, yes, Major. I so want to go with you."

Jack placed a kiss on her forehead and waved good-bye.

There was just time for him to pay a quick visit to his aunt and escort her to dinner. She liked to share a glass of sherry with him before they went down, and he tried hard to converse with her without criticizing her conduct towards Char or her control of the estate. He had to choose his moments of influence carefully, for if he defied her directly, he had no doubt he would be relegated to the same status of everyone else in the house, that of an adversary. It often puzzled him to consider what drove his aunt, why she was so rigid and went out of her way to be unpleasant to everyone. With the exception of him. And of Mary. He had his conjectures, but until he sorted them, he tried his best to stay on her good side, for the benefit of Char as much as himself.

The dowager duchess waited for him, dressed in her finest, a diamond circlet glittering in her hair. "My dearest Jack. You look surprisingly fit."

He bowed low and lifted her hand to his lips. "Aunt Adelina, my best regards. I trust I find you well."

She sighed, giving a little shake to her shoulders. "As well as can be expected under the circumstances. I should warn you that the mother and sister of Charsley's wife are in residence. Despite the frail state of my health, Char insisted."

Good for Char, Jack thought. That was more gumption than he had guessed his cousin had. Even so, the dowager looked in the full bloom of health, and when she smiled, she was as comely as a young girl. It was her perpetual frown and her tightly pursed lips that usually spoiled her looks.

The duchess continued, oblivious to Jack's private thoughts. "I suffer, but no one seems to care."

"You spent too much of your energy on caring for me over the past few months—"

"It was all that kept my fragile hold on life itself, knowing that I was assisting your return to good health. I owed it to the late duke, and to your father. They would expect me to do my utmost for you, darling boy."

"But not at the cost of your own comfort, Aunt Adelina."

"Pooh, that is nothing. But you are certainly the only one who cares a fig for my delicacy. Char is oblivious of everything but the happiness of that ridiculous little gel he married. She has not an ounce of sense. Nor has she the decency to know her place in this household. Further, she is often ill, from nothing that I can ascertain." She leaned closer and lowered her voice as though the duchess's condition were a secret. "She is increasing, and carries it poorly, giving in to the faintest of discomforts, revealing her true state of unworthiness for her exalted position."

Jack swallowed his distaste. "And with no regard for your feelings, I am sure."

"Ah, Jack, how satisfying it is to have a kindred spirit on hand. But what of you, my boy? I fear you still have a pallor beneath that sun tone. You do not look quite yourself."

"I will not pretend I am free of all pain. I will send for Mr. Lanark soon to extract a few more fragments of metal from my leg. But that is a minor inconvenience, Aunt."

"Jack, you are not putting one over on me! But I will

bend to your bluff. Far be it from me to deny you your pride."

"Your Grace, you are kindness itself. Now may I offer you an arm, however unsteady, to take you downstairs?"

"I should like nothing more."

When they entered the drawing room, the dowager carried herself like royalty, acknowledging with a slight nod of her head that the others stood until she was seated.

As soon as Jack had made his bows to the young duchess, Char nodded to a chestnut-haired lady on the sofa beside his wife. "Lady Dunmark, I wish to present my cousin, Major Whitaker. Jack, Lady Dunmark is Beatrice's mother."

Jack bowed to her and welcomed her to Kent.

Char gestured to Miss Stone. "And this is Kitty, Miss Stone, Bea's sister."

Jack bowed again. "I am pleased to make your acquaintance."

Before Kitty could answer, the dowager called to him. "Come, Jack, and sit beside me. You know," she said to Lady Dunmark, "Jack is a great war hero, badly wounded in the Battle of Vimeiro in Portugal last year. He still suffers terribly but bears it with commendable fortitude, I must say."

Jack lowered himself into the chair beside the dowager. "It is a great pleasure to be in the company of four elegant ladies, every one of whom quite dazzles my eye."

"Dazzle!" Char scrambled to find a scrap of paper in his coat. "Dazzle. Exactly the word I need. I need to write that down. Yes, it will fit perfectly in my last line of my ode."

Jack drew a flat leather case from a pocket in his waistcoat and handed it to Char. "There is paper and a small pencil inside."

"Oh, I say, this is a clever thing. I must have one."

While Char opened the case and exclaimed over the contents, showing them to the ladies, Jack let his gaze linger upon Miss Stone. Her gown of rose silk showed off her slender figure to advantage, but had a modest neckline, causing him a touch of disappointment. She watched Char with an expression of amused tolerance, almost as if she were watching a child. Or a friendly puppy.

The dowager's voice broke into Char's enthusiasm. "Really, Charsley, why such goings-on over a commonplace thing?"

Char handed the case to Jack. "Thank you," he murmured.

"Any time." Jack replaced it in his waistcoat.

The dowager returned to her praise. "Jack, the major, that is, has been in London conferring with the government. Is that not correct, Jack?"

"Yes, that is so," Jack said.

"And he has risen fast in the army—"

Jack wished he had a ready quip at hand to stop the dowager's effusive acclaim. It embarrassed him and, by implication, belittled Char. Jack could not see why his aunt was so disapproving of anything her son did or said. Though he had often tried to talk to her about her treatment of Char, she had nothing but criticism of him, making one unfortunate comparison after another to her late husband, the seventh duke, or to Jack's father. Or to Jack himself. She refused to acknowledge that her own sharp words only made things worse, that her disapproval made Char uncomfortable and nervous, bringing on even more bumbling. It was little wonder that he hid himself away all day and lost himself in composing lines of verse.

Char claimed to disregard her words. He had told Jack, at least a dozen times, not to interfere with his mother's criticism of him. In fact, just before he had left for London some weeks ago, Char had forbidden Jack to mention his concerns to the dowager, and Jack had to respect Char's view.

When dinner was announced, the dowager was still singing Jack's praises and disparaging her son's. The other three ladies looked pained, but hardly spoke a word, boding ill for a pleasant time at table.

He escorted the dowager to the head of the table and, at her indication, took his place beside her, all proper idea of precedence completely askew.

Jack had no idea how to stop his aunt's rambling rants.

Unless he went back to London. Or removed himself from
Charsley Hall. He could make the old house at Nether
Acker livable again. If that small cottage could be opened
up and used, why not the big house on his land, shut up for
a decade, ever since his father's death? Certainly the steward would have inspected it from time to time for dry rot or
pests. If he was not here, he would not have to listen. Though
his departure would not improve things for the rest of them,
would it?

He shut out the dowager's shrill account of how Charsley
had disliked going away to school and had not excelled as
Jack had. As Jack remembered it, his aunt had been the one
to bring Char back to the Hall instead of spending more time
at Harrow. He might have developed a bit of independence if
he had lived away from her. She had always been eager to
stamp out any hint of initiative on Char's part.

At least, he thought, if he removed himself, Aunt Adelina
might not use his accomplishments to disparage Char. Yes,
the only answer was to set himself up at Nether Acker and
make the best of it for the next few months. As for his wish
to talk Char into devoting some time to supporting the army
in the House of Lords, that discussion was best postponed
until the poor man could get away from his mother's acid
tongue.

Kitty could hardly swallow a single bite of food. What
sort of mother would pour scorn on her son for hours on end
in the presence of virtual strangers? She felt she ought to
stand and confront the dowager for her unseemly words and
rude conduct. But matching disrespect with disrespect hardly
seemed to provide a solution.

She stole a glance at Major Whitaker and tried to remember exactly how he had characterized the dowager that afternoon. Crotchets, he had called her actions? That did not
seem to approach the strength of what her tart comments deserved. His expression looked strained, but she did not know

whether that meant he disapproved of the dowager's lecture or he was in considerable pain. In any case, her little ideas for a summer festival and making her way—and Bea's—into the stillroom seemed wholly inadequate to the situation.

If she could only think of a way to move the dowager to some distant location, preferably abroad—or the Scottish highlands—she would put the plan into instant motion.

As it was, only a slow and gradual approach would bring improvement for Bea and Char. They would have to move one step at a time to assert their rights and privileges, if indeed they even knew what those were. Mama had already outlined to Bea the duties of the chatelaine of a great estate, at which the young duchess had dissolved in tears and declared herself overwhelmed.

Lady Dunmark had spoken sternly to Bea, the first time Kitty recalled such an incident. "These are the responsibilities you must take on, Beatrice. You are the Duchess of Charsley, and you are accountable for the lives and prosperity of hundreds of people. No matter how difficult the dowager is and how many obstructions she throws in your way, you have a duty to your child and your future children."

Kitty had almost cheered, but by now, the effect of such talk seemed diluted by the interfering maliciousness of Char's impossible mother. It would not be easy to pry the reins of the household from her grasping fingers.

For the moment, Kitty wished this charade of a dinner would end. A few weeks ago, she had despised attending dinners where she was on display as an object of considerable gossip. Every eye seemed fastened on her, waiting for the slightest sign of disappointment or a broken heart. Those wretched dinners had been a delight compared to the two evenings spent in the company of the Dowager Duchess of Charsley. She could not think of a word to say, not even about the weather. For if she observed that the day had been fine, she imagined the dowager would find a reason to say it had been foul.

Kitty's attention returned to the dowager as she again

asked Jack to tell them what he had been doing in town. Whether it was the look of pleading Kitty sent to Jack— which he met with a crooked smile—or Bea's eager encouragement, at last he acceded to their wishes.

"I fear you will find it dull stuff indeed, for I rarely have direct success." Jack looked directly at Char. "As you know, Duke, Sir Arthur Wellesley was entirely absolved of blame for the Convention of Cintra which was forced upon him by generals who took over command from him at the conclusion of the battle. Lady Dunmark and Miss Stone, forgive me for repeating what you may already know, but it might make more sense if you had a little background."

"Yes, go on," Lady Dunmark said softly.

"Wellesley—and the rest of us, I might add—had been eager to pursue the French and drive them away for good. But the new generals refused to press our advantage immediately, and the enemy had more than enough time to regroup while they dithered."

Char nodded. "Foolish old men, that's what they were."

"But you were already grievously wounded," the dowager said.

Jack spoke again before the dowager had a chance for further comment. "I knew what was going on, however. Eventually, our navy carried the French army back to their home soil, from which point they marched right back to fulfill that Corsican madman's fanatical ambition to rule the entire continent. Once the inquiry into the matter was completed and Wellesley cleared, he began to plan his return to Portugal. You will remember when he came here for a brief visit."

Char nodded again. "Damn fine man, Wellesley. Excuse me, ladies."

Jack plunged back into his account quickly. "He told me he wanted me to stay in England instead of returning with him. He asked that I meet with members of the government and other men of influence to build support for his operation. And with the resignation of the Duke of York as the commander in chief, not to mention the competition among the various ministers, there is plenty of talking to be done. Wellesley believes that a successful army is well supplied with equipment and well fed. But once the expeditionary forces have crossed beyond the horizon, many in the government, even at Horse Guards, find it convenient to forget their existence. So I, along with a number of others, have to keep reminding them of what the army needs."

The dowager put down her spoon and pointed a finger at Jack. "As I said, Jack, you are a true hero, doing all this before your wounds are entirely healed."

He shook his head. "The job is far from heroic. What the men do in battle can be heroic, but I merely talk. Only, however, until I am fit to return to Portugal. I am determined to go as soon as I can manage a day on horseback."

"Oh, no," Lady Dunmark cried. "You cannot think to endanger yourself again."

Kitty stared at Jack. How could he think about fighting more?

The dowager, looking pleased, nodded her head in approval.

Jack held up a hand as if to ward off their thoughts and words. "I fear I have talked too much at this table, ladies. I am sorry to have gone on so long, for you must be more than ready to depart."

Char stood. "If you don't mind, Jack, we'll go right along with the ladies. It is my usual custom to accompany them to the drawing room instead of sitting here alone, and I find I quite prefer it."

"As you say." Jack carefully pushed himself to his feet.

Kitty followed the others to the Ivory Salon, wondering about Jack's wish. How little she understood the thoughts of such a man. What would drive him to face the enemy's guns far from home?

After a few moments in the Ivory Salon, the dowager called for a short musicale. "Jack has an excellent voice and will make the rest of you sound much better."

Kitty wanted to pick up the china shepherdess from the

table beside her and toss it at Jack, then follow it with the matching shepherd aimed at the dowager, but she meekly went to the pianoforte and sat down, seething inside. Jack strolled over and spoke in a near whisper. "The good thing about this part of the evening is that Aunt Adelina prefers a very short musicale."

"So I understand."

Bea came more slowly to sit beside Kitty, her face sulky. "Let us do the same songs we sang last night and see if she notices. She will only be listening to Jack anyway."

"Exactly." Kitty struck a chord. "We all know 'Sir, Bring a Rose,' do we not?"

Char, the last to reach the pianoforte, chimed in and they made it through all three verses of the song without incident. Kitty was forced to acknowledge that Jack indeed had a good voice though he did not use it to outshine the rest of them.

Lady Dunmark applauded when they finished the last chorus, but the dowager did not look any more pleased than usual, despite her favorite's participation.

"Here," Jack said, pulling a sheet of music from a stack on the side table. "And we all know this one, about the river, right?"

Bea nodded. "Since I was about five years of age."

Jack leaned down and whispered in the ears of the two sisters. "Some day when I have drunk a glass of wine over my usual limit, I will tell you the words we soldiers sing to this tune, but I am afraid the dowager would box my ears if I tried them tonight."

Bea giggled, and Kitty had to admit she rather liked Jack even though he was the dowager's pet. After the dowager's constant praise of Jack over the last two hours, Kitty wanted to spurn him, but he had an engaging way about him. Somehow she had to enroll him in her plan to rearrange the situation in this household.

When they finished the second song, Bea asked to be excused. "I am rather fatigued tonight and I beg to be allowed to retire."

Kitty and her mother both rose immediately to accompany her upstairs and managed to leave the room before the dowager could break into Char's and Jack's wishes of a good night.

When they reached her boudoir, Bea flopped onto a chair and started to pull the ribbons from her hair. "Jack, Jack, Jack. You have no idea how I wish he were not back here to make that woman compare him to Char at Char's expense. And yet I like Jack. He is kind to Char and to me."

"He has a tolerance for the dowager," Lady Dunmark said. "But I am certain he sees what she is doing. He had quite a frown when she spoke of Char so disparagingly."

"He was here when you and Char came to live at Charsley Hall?" Kitty asked.

"Yes, the dowager was caring for him. I think he had been here since last fall."

"How was he injured?"

Bea went to the mirror and made a face at herself. "I do not understand it myself, Kitty, but he says he was in an explosion, and pieces of metal pierced his body all over. I think he is still in some pain, but he went to London shortly after we arrived."

"Why does the dowager favor him over her own son?"

"Char told me Jack's mother died when he was quite young. His father, Lord John Whitaker, never had much use for his son. Char says Jack was always good at everything, at games, on horseback, even swimming."

Lady Dunmark went to Bea's side and shook her head. "Do not make faces, Beatrice. What happened to Lord John?"

"Both he and the seventh duke died at relatively young ages." Bea broke into a little grin. "Char says one died of too much wife and the other of too little."

"A rather macabre joke," Lady Dunmark said. "Beatrice, I said to stop twisting your face."

"Mama, I know you used to ask what I'd do if my face froze this way, but that will never happen."

"But you will create more wrinkles, my dear. Here, let me help you rub in some Denmark lotion."

Kitty ignored her mother's beauty advice to her sister. She let her thoughts stay on Jack. He seemed fond of Char, and showed no evidence he disliked Bea. But he had said little to counteract the dowager's remarks about her son. Kitty had another matter to add to her list of chores to be accomplished: convincing Jack to join in her efforts to change everything at Charsley Hall.

SIX

Jack woke in a sweat at the sound of his own moaning. A thousand knives stabbed his side and his leg, twisting deep as he thrashed at the pain. His breath came in short pants and he could hear his pulse pounding in his ears. A pinpoint of light pierced the darkness, and he bit his tongue trying not to cry out at the shattering explosions and anguished shouts.

He had to get back to the action. Save his men. Where were they, lost in the darkness and shrieking for him? But he was pinned beneath his horse. Drowning in blood.

"Here, major. Drink this."

Jack tightly grasped a handful of sheet to keep from jerking upright and opened his eyes.

Win held a glass toward his lips.

"No. Only water, not that." His voice rasped in his ears.

"Major, just a few drops—"

"No laudanum. Bring me water. Or better yet, brandy."

It was only a dream, those catastrophic outbursts. A nightmare that came sometimes when the pain was the worst.

Win lifted him and propped the pillows behind his back. Jack grabbed the brandy and poured it down his throat, oblivious of its fragrance, of its taste, of its burn.

"Lanark comin' soon?" Win asked.

"Yes." Jack touched his hip and gingerly slid his hand down his thigh. "I can feel a whole bushel of nails here." He lay back and tried to quiet his rapid breathing.

"You had another nightmare."

"And you were supposed to be gone from here until morning."

"Well, it is morning, Major. Heard the clock chime five times just before you woke."

"Ah! Then you enjoyed your evening?"

"Here now, this is no confessional." Win wiped Jack's brow with a damp cloth.

Jack felt the pain begin to subside. "So that is how it was? Sounds like the lady was pleased to see you."

Win handed him another glass of brandy. "Don't know where you got the idea there's a female, major."

"Look in the mirror, Win. Even by the light of a single flame, your grin shines bright as a coastal beacon."

Win gave a woof of laughter. "You have more wrong with you than iron in your sides and nightmares in your skull if you can make up something like that."

Kitty lurked near the stables until little Mary and her governess arrived for the girl's morning riding lesson. Miss Munstead, clearly showing her distaste, backed away from the mount as it was led out. Once Mary was on the pony and the groom moved off, Kitty shadowed the governess to a corner of the garden where she seated herself and opened a small volume to read.

Kitty hesitated a moment, then walked toward her, smiling. "Miss Munstead, a fine day, is it not?"

The governess looked up for only a moment before her gaze returned to the book. "Yes, miss, very fine."

"Are you enjoying a few moments of solitude?"

Her voice was prim and somewhat less than friendly. "Yes, in a way. Mary is having her riding lesson, and I am waiting for her."

"I see."

"I would never shirk my duties to sit here and read if she was in my charge."

Kitty responded quickly. "Of course you would not. It is just that I have seen very little of you and Mary."

"We have our own rooms—the schoolroom and our sitting room in addition to the bedchambers. I assure you we are well provided for."

"Do you take Mary to Her Grace every afternoon?"

"Oh, indeed not!" Again Miss Munstead looked up briefly, surprise in her eyes. "She sends word when she wishes to see us. Her nerves are delicate and she is subject to spasms. I cannot say more."

"I understand. One must certainly offer her every consideration." Kitty could hardly believe she was uttering such palaver. "I am sure her life is very difficult."

Miss Munstead did not respond.

Kitty suspected she would not talk about the dowager. After all, her position depended upon the dowager's favor.

"Have you cared for Mary a long time?"

"Yes," the governess murmured. "Since she was three."

"If might be so bold as to inquire, Miss Munstead, what happened to Mary's mother and father?"

"I do not know precisely. I understand they were traveling and met with a terrible carriage accident. Mary was an infant, the only survivor. Of course, she remembers nothing." Miss Munstead stopped and covered her mouth with her hand. "Oh dear, I fear I have said too much."

"On the contrary, you have said very little. But, no matter. Miss Munstead. I do not intend to report to the dowager."

Miss Munstead stood, clutching her book to her chest. "Thank you. I do not often—that is, I do not wish to incur the duchess's displeasure."

"You shall not, for my lips are sealed."

The governess glanced toward the house and muttered, "Unless she—someone—has seen us." She dipped a curtsy and hurried off.

Kitty walked back to the stable, her head full of conflicting thoughts. The governess seemed frightened. Would that be her own fate if she sought a similar position? To live in fear that a hasty word or reckless deed would cast one out on the street?

Up close, Miss Munstead looked much younger than Kitty had expected. Her life hardly seemed like one Kitty wanted to emulate. Yet her speech clearly identified her as of gentle birth. Until Kitty had the thought of striking out on her own, making her own way in the world, she had rarely given a second thought to the status of governess. Before she had gone to Miss Kirk's school in Bath, she and Bea had shared a governess, Miss Sterling, who taught them French and geography, in addition to overseeing their efforts on the pianoforte and with their needles and silks. Kitty wondered whatever happened to Miss Sterling. She probably had been much younger than Kitty had thought at the time. When you are ten, even five-and-twenty seems aged.

Kitty wondered whether she could ever accept being in a position like Miss Munstead's. Her Miss Sterling had been much more a member of the family, not shunted away to the attics. Or had she? Kitty knew her memories might be distorted by the years that had passed and by her fond attachment to her governess. To Miss Sterling's eyes, there might have been a quite different view.

Kitty let her thoughts wander to Mary. Why was she kept so sheltered? One could almost say imprisoned. Neither Bea nor Char had mentioned her, and Kitty doubted her mother even knew of the girl yet. The dowager was concerned with Mary's lessons and had her learning to ride. Perhaps Kitty could have Miss Munstead bring Mary to the cottage to learn the harp eventually. If the dowager could be convinced.

"You are three of the randiest scalawags in creation, you miserable whelps of the demons! Get out here and prepare to work like you've never worked before."

Jack stood in the door of the inn, watching the Three scramble to their feet in surprise, pulling their hands from the wenches' blouses or out from under their skirts. The three women giggled and hid their faces. Jack supposed it had only been a matter of time before he discovered them in compromising position, but the sight displeased him nevertheless. "It would serve you right if some angry brothers or fathers took after you with pick-axes, you wretched reprobates."

"Naw, Major," Yates said, tucking in his shirt. "We're jest having some fun, tickling and the like. No harm to nobody."

"There'll be harm to all three of you if I am not satisfied with your work."

"What'cha got in mind fer us?"

"I want you to pack up some brooms and rags and buckets. Bring soap and beeswax. Tell Mrs. Talbot I'll replenish her supply tomorrow."

"But we ain't much on cleaning. I don't have no skill with a broom, that's for certain."

"Then you will have to learn. Unfortunately, I do not have any maidens that require deflowering or gentlemen who want to be amused by your scurrilous stories, so you will have to do the jobs I find for you. Bring the supplies along to the cottage on the lane that leads to the Charsley Hall stables. I will expect you there within half an hour. So do not go back and finish what you were starting inside."

As Jack climbed back into the curricle, Win guffawed, hand clasped to his mouth. Jack gritted his teeth. "That will do, Baldwin. I am not interested in hearing your 'I told you so.'"

He picked up the reins and set the horses at a smart trot. Whatever was he going to do with the Three? Jack's land was productive, but needed no more farm workers, not that any of the Three had ever seen the back side of a plough. Or hoed a field or bundled hay.

Jack drove faster than he should have, and his shoulder and his hip screamed in protest. But he didn't slow down. The pain brought its own kind of satisfaction.

Just beyond the cottage, Jack saw Miss Stone hastening toward them. She wore an airy muslin gown, a tan spencer and a straw bonnet under a ruffled pink parasol, as delicious a sight in the morning sunshine as she had been last evening in the drawing room. His mood lightened and he reined in the team beside her.

Win jumped down and offered to help her into the curricle.

She shook her head. "No, thank you, Baldwin. If you do not mind, Major, I will just continue walking. It is such a short distance that by the time you turn the horses—"

"By all means. In fact, I shall walk with you. Win can take the horses back to the stable."

"Yes, sir." Win held the horses' heads as Jack lowered himself to the ground.

He winced as his full weight rested on his leg.

"Are you sure you ought to get down?" Kitty asked.

Jack grinned at her. "As you say, it is only a moment's walk. Not even as far as going from the Hall to the stable."

"Of course, you are right."

He tried hard not to favor his sore leg. "I have some keys for us to try, but Mr. Edgerton was not sure if any of them were correct. It has been years since anyone tried to enter."

"Do you know why? I would have thought the place could be of use to someone in the neighborhood. It has charming gardens that will need only trimming—considerable trimming, it seems—to look quite acceptable."

When they reached the front door, Jack tried the first three keys, none of which had any effect on the lock. The fourth turned with difficulty but eventually the door swung open, squeaking on its hinges and stirring a bit of dust.

Jack stood back to let her precede him inside. She went to the room on the right of the hallway and looked around, giving a little smile and nod of approval.

"This is lovely. The light is good, or will be once those windows are cleaned. There is plenty of room for my harp, and whatever furniture is piled under those dust covers."

"You will need a pianoforte, will you not?"

"I do not think I would dare ask for one. I am afraid it could cause Char a great deal of trouble."

"I may have one at Nether Acker, if it can be restored to use. There was a fine instrument there when I was a boy, and I have no reason to believe it has been removed by anyone."

"If it is no inconvenience, Major, a pianoforte would be wonderful."

Jack pulled out his notepad. "We need to make a list of things to be done. Ridding the place of cobwebs and dirt. Sweeping and dusting. Perhaps repairs to the doors and windows. Oh, yes, oiling the hinges."

Miss Stone nodded. "Washing the windows inside and out."

They looked into the other side of the cottage where the fireplace had been used for cooking. "Perhaps a chimney sweep," she suggested.

Jack wrote "chimney sweep" and followed her upstairs. In both bedchambers, the mattresses had been rolled up and the curtains folded beside them.

Miss Stone punched at one mattress. "I think these should be disposed of, and there's no need to replace them. No one will be sleeping here."

They went back downstairs when Jack heard the voices of the Three.

"C'mon, Bessie. Turn in here."

Jack opened the door to see Bart and Tommy pulling on the donkey's head, trying to keep it from nibbling at the long grass rather than drawing the cart toward the rear of the cottage. Yates sat atop the cart slapping the reins on the donkey's back and trying to get the animal to move.

It took another quarter hour to get the cart unloaded, to the lightly disguised amusement of Miss Stone.

When Jack read them his list of duties, Tommy and Yates looked glum. But Bart, Jack noticed, stared at Miss Stone with a look of dumb adoration, as though he stood before an angel.

Yates wrinkled his nose as though the instructions reeked of offal. "If ye don't mind my saying so, Major, this sort o' work is not what we're much good at."

"Then this job will give you a good taste of what it is like keeping up a house or cottage. That young lady you seemed to know so well a while ago might be looking for more than a man who can fondle her. She might like a man who could keep her house in repair and earn a living too."

"Ain't much call for winder washers, I don't believe."

"Perhaps not, but men who can repair walls and mend roofs might find plenty of work."

"C'mon, Yates," Bart said. "If Miss Stone wants this place cleaned up, I say we do it up proud fer her."

Jack grinned. "That's the spirit, men. Some of you can work outside tomorrow. These shrubs and bushes need cutting back. I'll ask the gardener to come by and show you the techniques he uses. Save you time and effort."

"Yessir," Yates muttered.

Jack looked from one to the others. "In a day or two, I am going to have a surgeon come and cut out some more metal fragments. I will be laid up for a few days, but I expect you to follow Miss Stone's instructions. She will report to me on your progress. Now get in there and show her what you can do."

Bart went with a smile and the other two trudged after him.

"I will be back in an hour or so," Jack told the men. "To check your work. It better be well done!"

When he and Miss Stone had walked out of earshot of the cottage, Jack heaved a great sigh. "I wonder if they will be able to accomplish much, Miss Stone. Please be sure they get the dirt taken care of, for I doubt any of the Three have much notion of cleanliness."

"I am sure they will do an adequate job. And I can always ask them to sweep more."

"And more!" Jack laughed out loud. "And more! May I walk back to the Hall with you?"

"Will that not cause you more pain?"

"Not particularly, if we move slowly. At the moment, I get little relief in any position. It is not comfortable to sit or lie down, either."

"Then let us proceed."

Jack tucked her hand in his elbow and began to walk.

She was silent for only a moment. "Perhaps instead of discouraging their attentions from the young women, you should promote them. Get those wedding bells ringing in the village chapel."

"Ha, the perfect revenge on them! Get all three of them hitched and let their wives deal with their nonsense."

"Settles several of your problems, it seems to me. Three of them, in fact."

"Miss Stone, you are quite the cleverest lady I know." Jack paused, then plunged ahead. "If I might be allowed the impropriety of commenting on His Grace's marriage, I thought you sounded much too sensible to appeal to him, Miss Stone."

"He spoke of me to you?"

"Last autumn, he said he was interested in a young lady. The way he described you, I pictured someone who would not take him or his habits easily."

He stopped to hear her reaction, but she only gazed straight ahead. He continued. "Your sister is a sweet chit, almost as pretty as you are, but she will make no demands on him. If you do not mind my asking, what happened?"

"Suppose I do mind?"

"Then I beg your pardon and will attempt another subject."

"If I tell you, I trust you will not share my version—"

"Never! The word of an officer."

"I had not quite decided I should marry Char. Honestly, I did not love him. To many people, our imminent betrothal was all but accomplished. No one imagined that I had reservations about marrying the Duke of Charsley. If he and Bea had not run off, perhaps I would have married him and tried to love him eventually. But it would not have been fair. He is a fine fellow and deserves a wife who cares deeply for him."

"So your heart was not broken?" He felt a curious delight at the thought.

"No. I knew he did not love me either. I thought he cared for me, felt I would be a creditable duchess. But I am sure he knew he was not hurting me when he succumbed to his passion, or whatever it was, and wed my sister."

"But there are many kinds of hurt beyond a broken heart. Living in London during the Season could not have been easy."

She gave a little laugh. "Let me say it gave me the oddest feelings ever. When I was assumed to be on the verge of being betrothed to the Duke of Charsley, people were kind to me, but I was nothing special. Yet when I became the aggrieved party in a scandalous elopement, I became one of the *ton*'s most sought after guests, invited everywhere, eagerly sought at soirees and the subject of endless speculation. 'Oh, my dear, we must keep you from repining too much, considering the . . . er . . . the unfortunate occurrence.'"

"So you continued to go about, Miss Stone?"

"I had little choice. The gentlemen were only too ready to offer their condolences, to spice up my life, to make me merry again."

"And you had to comply?"

"That, or be seen as overcome with sadness, Major. Which I was not."

"I see."

They walked on in silence for a moment, then she spoke again. "I could not say it to anyone, but I was actually relieved. I had considered marrying the duke mostly for family reasons. He is a wealthy man. My mother and sister would be provided for, you see."

"So there were financial considerations?"

"Exactly." She sighed. "It is no secret anymore. When my father died three years ago, we were left with little money. Father had considerable debts. The estate was run down. The title went to a distant cousin, but the property was not entailed. Mama did what she could do with her lot in life—took a house in town, and tried to marry a daughter to a fortune. Everything worked out exactly according to her plan. Just that the daughter who married was not the one she expected, thus causing delicious *on dits* for the *ton* to chew over. Mama had no options. She had spent every shilling we had to fit us out for the Season. If we had not been asked to come live at Charsley, she would have been forced to borrow or ask Char for money to take a house elsewhere."

"You mean she has no portion to sustain her?"

"Less than fifty pounds a year. And, to be honest, I have nothing. A roomful of beautiful gowns, slippers and reticules. Shawls and gloves. A necklace or two. But not a coin to call my own."

"You don't say!" Jack was truly surprised.

"Indeed I do."

"Extraordinary."

"Not at all extraordinary, Major. I knew of many other young ladies on the marriage mart who were looking for a fortune. And several men looking for an heiress. Sometimes I think it is more the case than not."

"I have always been pleased to live away from the affairs of town. I have spent my life in the army. The only reason I go to London now is to pester the army headquarters and members of Parliament. The only reason I attend a social event is to talk to a man I cannot otherwise reach."

"No ballrooms, Major? I think you would cut a dash in the ballrooms of the *ton*."

He gave a sardonic laugh. "A few ballrooms, Miss Stone. But very few. A bevy of useless fribbles, both male and female, populate the capital."

"And even worse. One man, who seemed to think I would welcome his attentions, wore so much hair pomade I called him The Eel, shiny, slimy and squirmy. He acted rather eelish, slithering around me, bumping me in all the wrong places. Slippery with apologies."

He shook his head. "Amazing fribbles, as I said." Jack did not want the conversation to end and gestured to the Charsley gardens. "Can we stroll a little longer?"

"If you are comfortable, Major."

They skirted the kitchen garden and walked toward a little bower where two stone benches faced each other across a patch of gravel.

"Shall we sit a moment?" he asked.

She perched on the edge and shook out her skirts. "Then there was the giraffe, whose head bobbed around at the top of a very long neck, so long I thought he must need two neck cloths to fill the area from his chin to his lapels."

"Now, that reminds me of one of our colonels, whose sloping shoulders and bobbly head reminded us of a heron fishing in the marsh. The marines who were in Egypt called him a camel. Either designation seemed entirely justified."

"I often see animals, especially birds, in humans," she said. "Sometimes I compare my mother's friends to parrots squawking away, while I think of my sister as a canary, twittering gaily."

"How did you characterize Char?"

She shook her head. "Oh, that I could not say."

"Why not? I shall never tell anyone."

"Oh, it is embarrassing. I should not confide these wicked thoughts to anyone."

"Wicked? I think not. I see you as a clever little robin, and I suppose you might see me as a flightless dodo."

"Indeed not. More as a falcon, I expect."

"And Char?"

"If you promise not to tell?"

He nodded.

She wrinkled her nose. "A preening peacock some of the time. Occasionally, one of those swaggering bantam roosters. But that was before I saw him with his mama."

Jack laughed. "So now we see him as a pigeon? Strutting one way and then another, taking off in sudden flight at the hint of danger. Then again, he might be a duckling, paddling along in the wake of his mother."

"Oh, dear," she said. "I do hope he learns to assert himself. I know he meets with the steward from time to time."

"Frankly, he does not have to do a lot more than that. The dowager has chosen an excellent man in Mr. Edgerton. And there are attorneys and men of business in London that look after Charsley's affairs."

"You mean if the dowager simply disappeared, not much would change?"

"Probably not. Would you like to resume our walk?"

"Yes, thank you."

They walked on through the rose gardens, now coming into glorious full bloom. How, Jack wondered, could Char have chosen anyone over Miss Kitty Stone, especially her silly sister? Kitty seemed the epitome of all that was admirable in a lady.

In the shadow of a tall yew, he stopped and pulled her around to face him. "Miss Stone, I must express my gratitude to you. For your kindness to Char and your sister. To my men. For your insight and your patience."

He stood near her, and lifted her hand to his lips. It trembled a little, and he followed his little kiss with a smoothing gesture, rubbing his thumb across her wrist. "You needn't fear me, Miss Stone. I mean you no disrespect."

She stepped back from him, her gaze lowered. The brim of her bonnet shielded her face from him. When she again looked up into his face, her eyes were luminous with unshed tears. "I understand, Major. And I appreciate your concern. I hope we can be allies as we try to improve matters for the duke and duchess."

He stared at her, forcing himself to keep his distance. The fire inside him built steadily, masking his pain, filling him with impulses he had not felt for years. He wished he could take her in his arms, feel her melt against him. He wanted to cover her hands with kisses, touch her cheek, press his lips to hers.

Instead he took out his handkerchief and dabbed at her cheek where a tear glistened.

She backed away. "I really have nothing to cry about. I want to make things right for Bea."

"Of course you do. And I shall do all I can to help." He thrust from his mind that her purpose for Char did not necessarily conform to his.

SEVEN

In the week Kitty and Lady Dunmark had been at Charsley Hall, the house had been curiously empty of visitors. When they asked Bea why there were no calls from the ladies of the neighborhood, Bea admitted she had received only a short visit from Char's relations.

On the morning exactly seven days after they had arrived, Kitty looked up from the yoke of the gown she embroidered with white rosettes. "Not another person has called upon you in more than three months?"

Bea set aside her sewing. "No one but Lady Euphemia, Char's great aunt, and her daughter, Miss Fanny Courtney."

"How very odd," Lady Dunmark observed. "I would have expected you to receive many bride calls, to welcome you."

"Is Lady Euphemia a close confidante of the dowager?" Kitty asked.

Bea picked up the fabric and frowned at it. "It did not seem so to me. They seemed very cold to one another. I thought I might like both Lady Euphemia and Fanny if I had an opportunity to know them better."

Kitty set another stitch. "Do you think the dowager has forbidden callers here at the Hall?"

Lady Dunmark gasped. "I cannot imagine such a thing, Kitty."

Bea put her stitching down again. "But I suspect that is exactly what has happened. To be sure, I admit I had not given it much thought. Yet what must the ladies of the neighborhood think of me? I will ask Char to order us a carriage this afternoon and to send a note to Lady Euphemia by one of the undergrooms. We need to ask her what happened."

"An excellent idea." Kitty joined in her mother's affirmative nods.

Kitty excused herself and went to fetch her bonnet. She would take a quick walk to the cottage to see what was going on there. But as she came down the staircase, Mrs. Wells called to her.

"Miss Stone. The dowager duchess wishes to see you."

"I shall return to the Hall in an hour—"

"She will see you now, Miss Stone. Immediately."

Kitty was momentarily tempted to ignore the summons, but thought better of it.

The dowager looked up from the small glass-topped table when Mrs. Wells led Kitty into her sitting room.

Kitty curtsied low. "Good morning, Your Grace. Mrs. Wells said you wanted to speak to me."

The dowager's dark eyes bore into her. "Miss Stone." There was not a hint of warmth in her voice. "I will come straight to the point. You want to use that abandoned cottage as a music room."

Kitty kept her voice matter of fact and even managed a little smile. "Yes, the one covered with roses, just down the lane from the stables."

"I forbid it. I will not allow it."

Kitty blinked in surprise. "What?"

"I said I would not allow it. You will have to find another place."

"But, Your Grace, I believe that cottage belongs to Major Whitaker, not to you. He has given his consent."

She looked stunned. "He what?"

"He has even offered to send over a pianoforte from his house, the house that is closed up."

The dowager grasped a handkerchief and pressed it to her lips. "But I must talk to him. It is impossible! I will not allow it!"

Kitty stood in silence and looked around the room at the cases filled with miniatures. She would have loved to study them, but with the dowager nearing the boiling point, this was obviously not a propitious time to ask.

Slowly the dowager summoned her self-control.

"Do you understand, Miss Stone? This is not to be allowed. I will not have that cottage opened."

"I think you will find that it has already been opened and thoroughly scrubbed, Your Grace. But of course, Major Whitaker will be the final arbiter of its use."

"Miss Stone, you have stirred up several things around here, and I want it to stop. Now."

"My mother and I have appreciated the duke's hospitality. His Grace has been most kind to us."

"You are dismissed, Miss Stone."

Kitty curtsied again. "You have a lovely room, Your Grace."

"Go!" The dowager held out a finger and pointed at the door.

Kitty hurried out and back to her own room, heart pounding now that she was alone. Maybe she should have told the old hag to go to the devil. But Jack liked her. He might accede to her wishes to close the rose cottage back up. That would be a pity, but if he chose to oblige the dowager, it was his business, not hers. Though she would be desperately disappointed. For the moment, she would not seek him out and plead her case, however. Nor would she tell her mother or Bea and Char.

That afternoon, Bea fumed without relenting from the moment she stepped into the open landau to the door of the dower house.

"Arranging for a five minute journey was intolerably difficult, almost impossible until Char demanded it done. The dowager would not give her permission, but when Char said he would go harness the horses himself, Randall relented and called for the coach. I would like to dismiss that butler without a reference."

Kitty exchanged glances with her mother. "My, Bea, you are showing a temper appropriate for a duchess of Charsley. Most suitable for your station."

"First you say I am too lenient of the dowager's harsh rules, and now you tease me for trying to assert myself. You cannot have it both ways, Kitty."

The horses stopped, and the footman lowered the steps as Bea made a face at her sister.

Kitty held her back in the seat and whispered in Bea's ear. "Watch your words. The dowager hears almost everything from her servants. Perhaps these, too."

Bea yanked her arm away. "I know. But I get so upset! We would not have had to make this trip if Lady Euphemia and Fanny felt comfortable visiting often at Charsley Hall. How could the dowager be downright unfriendly to them, her husband's kin?"

"That is," Kitty said with a smile, "precisely the kind of consideration a good duchess will show to others. Exactly, Bea."

The butler who answered the door bowed them into the foyer of the house, a handsome two-story structure of warm red brick covered with ivy below a steep pitched roof.

"The ladies are upstairs in the drawing room. They are expecting you."

Kitty followed her sister and her mother up the staircase and through the whirl of introductions.

Lady Euphemia, sister of Char's grandfather, set her bright eyes on Kitty. She was dressed in violet and black, and held a fat old pug dog, who slurped and snuffled as she stroked it. "Come here, child. You are a pretty thing." She stared at

Kitty a moment and then mumbled a few words, half to herself. "A quite likely lover for Jack, I think."

Without elaborating, she turned to Lady Dunmark. "Now, of course you, Lady Dunmark, are not enjoying Adelina's hospitality—the dowager, that is—and you have found out just how difficult she is. But you will help your dear daughter adjust, I am sure. Fanny and I find her a delight."

Kitty wondered if she had heard correctly. Had Lady Euphemia said a likely lover for Jack? Kitty could not imagine anything further from her mind. Or Jack's, for that matter. Least likely lover was more like it.

But it did remind her of a favor she needed to request. While Bea and her mama walked through the rooms with Fanny, Kitty stayed beside Lady Euphemia. "My lady, I wonder if it would be possible for me to use your stillroom once in a while. That is, until I am able to use the one at the Hall."

Lady Euphemia set the violet ribbons on her cap to quivering as she shook her head in disgust. "My, my, Adelina is more of a harridan than even I expected. So she has denied you her stillroom?"

Kitty nodded.

"Of course, my dear. You many use ours. Though it is small, I shall make my stillroom open to you always. Just come through the gardens at any time of day, and I will instruct the servants to take you there."

"Thank you. That is very kind of you."

"And what are you planning to concoct?"

"Willow bark tea for Major Whitaker."

"He is still suffering from his wounds?"

"He says he has pieces of metal under his skin that work their way out and cause him considerable pain, so Mr. Lanark is coming tomorrow to remove some of them."

"Ah, yes, I know the problem myself. My late husband had wounds such as Jack's and for years afterwards pieces, some of considerable length, worked their way out of his skin. And you think the willow bark tea will help?"

Kitty nodded.

"I agree. It is exactly what I made for Roderick. Several cups at a time."

"Thank you, my lady. I shall heed your advice."

"Now, my dear, you seem a practical gel. I had thought to tell your mama about this, but perhaps you will be a better choice. I am fond of your sister, for she is a sweet child, but a child indeed. Frankly I do not know what came over Char to do something as silly as marry her." She stopped suddenly and gave a little gasp. "Oh, my dear, I had forgotten. Please disregard the ramblings of an old woman. I do—"

"Think nothing of it, Lady Euphemia. I am glad that Char fell in love with Bea, for she worships him. But the opposition of the dowager makes it very difficult."

"I see that it does. But I suspect that Char never captured your heart, did he?"

Kitty shook her head.

"I can see that he did not. It is obvious to me, whatever others might think. He is rather a throwback to my brother, the sixth duke, you know, another fellow who tried to write poetry and drifted through life letting others do all the real work. In fact, that may be why his mother is so hard on him. She knew the old duke as her father-in-law. She saw what his lax attention to the estate did, and how her husband had to repair so much. Yet my brother was beloved among the tenants."

"I believe that Char is also held in high esteem. He is a man of great potential, but the way his mother treats him—"

"Yes, we see eye to eye on that matter. But let me tell you, Miss Stone, if you need something from Adelina, call on Jack to help. He is quite a darling of hers. If he asks, I do not think she refuses him anything."

"Thank you. I shall try that. But, tell me, Lady Euphemia, why does she has such a fondness for him, above her own son?"

"I do not pretend to know what Adelina thinks about anything, my dear. She has withdrawn from Society. She never goes to London, which I did until just two seasons ago when my joints made it too painful. Nor does she play a role in local doings. The squire's wife was out of sorts indeed when she tried to call on your sister and was rebuffed."

"But Bea said no one calls. It must be the dowager's orders to turn all away."

"Hmph. I did not think she would stoop that low. No wonder Mrs. Carter is upset."

"Mother, I have an idea." Fanny spoke as she, the duchess, and Lady Dunmark came back into the room. "I think we should undertake a few little gatherings, informal, of course, to invite some of the local ladies to meet the duchess. I believe many have been discouraged from making bride calls."

Bea clasped her hands together and cooed. "Ooh, that would be ever so lovely, Fanny. I would be greatly in your debt, Lady Euphemia."

The violet ribbons quivered again. "Why, of course, my dear. I should be honored to introduce you."

Bea went on enthusiastically. "Kitty and I have a wonderful idea, too, but Char is a little hesitant. We want to have a summer festival for the whole neighborhood."

"What an excellent idea. We used to celebrate St. James Day in July when I was a girl, but I know no one has done so for a long time. It is the beginning of the oyster season, which is the real reason. It is the feast, not really the saint, you know. Why is Char hesitant? Does he fear a row with his mother?"

Bea nodded.

"Then I suggest he enlist Jack in the cause." Lady Euphemia gave Kitty a little jab with her elbow. "That should help a great deal."

Bea launched into a muddled account of the events they might plan for the festival.

Lady Euphemia rose and beckoned to Fanny. "Dear, we will excuse you while you show Miss Stone our stillroom. She has a potion to make up."

With a smile and a nod toward Bea, Kitty followed Miss

Courtney downstairs and to the back of the house. Near the kitchen, the stillroom had a wall of shelves, most filled with jars of fruit preserves and corked flagons of tinted liquids.

"What do you need, Miss Stone?" Fanny asked.

"I wish to make up some willow bark tea. For Major Whitaker."

Fanny opened the door of a cupboard and contemplated its contents. "I collected some fresh new bark a few weeks ago, for I sometimes brew the tea for Mama when her joints are aching. Yes, here it is, well dried and ready to soak. How much shall we make?"

"Thank you, Miss Courtney. Major Whitaker will need several pots full when the surgeon comes."

"Please call me Fanny, my dear, and I shall call you Kitty. I far prefer to be informal with the family. As for Jack, I have it on the best authority that Mr. Lanark is indeed coming soon. The servants have a most effective system of exchanging information. Very little happens at the Hall that we do not hear all about."

"I hear nothing from the servants, except from our maid, Nell. Mrs. Wells seems to keep them under her thumb."

"Mrs. Wells is every bit the tyrant, just like the dowager herself. She came to Charsley with the dowager as a personal maid. She has spent her life guarding Adelina's interests, Kitty."

"That goes far to explain her attitude, except that I wonder why she is not more solicitous of Char."

Fanny took the bark and led the way to the kitchen. "We'll put some water on to heat, and I will try to explain."

When they were seated at a worktable, the kettle put to the flame, Kitty folded her hands and leaned toward Fanny. "I am eager to hear your story."

"I am of an age with Adelina, the far side of forty. Indeed it was through me that she met my cousin, the late duke. We were friends, and when she was newly married, I considered her a sister. I believe she felt much the same about me. But she changed over the years. Before Char, she lost a first son, born dead. How happy she was to have a healthy child when Char came along. But she protected him overmuch, almost made him into an invalid when he was entirely healthy, as far as I could tell. It got worse when she lost another infant."

"How dreadful for her," Kitty murmured.

"I'm afraid the losses affected her mind, and the duke took to finding his pleasures elsewhere. The worse she got, the more he strayed. The more time he spent with his mistresses, the more unbalanced Adelina became. And as Char grew older, he was not strong and active, did not take to hunting and shooting.

"The duke accused Adelina of ruining the boy and to some extent, he was probably correct. The seventh duke became a short-tempered man, tending toward dyspepsia and overindulgence. Adelina was not particularly upset when he died. She and his guardians did everything for Char, the new young duke. But what she wanted—and still wants—is for him to assert himself and show himself worthy of his heritage. Yet she constantly pushes him in the other direction, criticizing him mercilessly."

Kitty glanced at the kettle, just starting to steam. "I think I understand a little more. But can she not see what she is doing?"

"Both Mama and I have tried to point out the anomaly in her attitude and behavior. That is why we are not often welcome at the Hall."

"And where does Major Whitaker come in?"

"When Char was a boy, Adelina did everything to keep them apart. Naturally Char adored Jack, admired and tried to emulate him. Then Jack went away to the army. Whenever he came home, Adelina compared Char to him. Unfavorably, of course. It was very sad, and I imagine it continues."

"Indeed the dowager is very solicitous of Jack, or so I have heard."

"So make Jack your ally in anything you need from Adelina. Keep him on your side. And now, the water is boiling and we shall set the willow bark to steeping."

Kitty watched as Fanny poured the steaming water over the bark. So Jack was the key to helping Char and Bea. Now she hoped even more that this tea would increase his comfort.

Jack went to the dowager's apartment as soon as he received her invitation to visit, for it was unusual for her to summon him during the afternoon.

"I hope it will not be inconvenient for you if the surgeon comes tomorrow," he said.

"Not at all. Though I hate to think of you suffering, Jack."

"I will feel infinitely better once he has rid me of my unwelcome appurtenances. Believe me, once the incisions heal, I will be better than ever."

"I am glad to know that. But Jack, I am perturbed to hear that you have given permission for that disreputable cottage to be opened up for the use of Miss Stone. Aside from the fact that I disapprove of her setting herself up as something special—"

"Pardon me, Your Grace, but Miss Stone really does have an exceptional talent, as you heard a few evenings ago."

"Nonsense, she is nothing out of the ordinary. But no matter. I simply do not approve of using that old cottage. I am quite sure it is unsound and perhaps even unsafe."

"I have looked it over and had my men inspect it. There is no evidence of damage that we could find."

"Well, it ought to be pulled down. It is overgrown and a blot on the landscape."

"Perhaps, dear aunt, we will have to agree to disagree on its condition and appearance. I think it is quite charming with all those roses cascading over its walls."

"Why, Jack! How very plebian of you. Are you next going to tell me you are giving up your army career to become a hermit and move into someone's wilderness?"

He watched her face, a little surprised not to see the usual softening of her features. She usually looked quite sweet when she talked to him, different than she did when others were around. Apparently she felt strongly about that cottage.

"I assure you, Miss Stone will do no damage to the cottage. She can play there to her heart's content, far from your ears."

"But I do not want her there. Find another place for her silly harp."

"Why? I cannot think of a good reason, Aunt Adelina."

"Jack, I thought you were not like all the rest of them. I thought you cared about me."

"I do. I care about you very much. But unless there is a reason not to use it—"

"It is tumbling down. Dangerous."

"I assure you, it is not. Why you do not even travel that lane past the stables. I cannot imagine why it would concern you."

She narrowed her eyes. "I am very disappointed in you, Jack. I expected more from you, my favorite nephew."

From your only nephew, he almost said, but caught himself in time. "Now can I ring for some tea for you? Or bring you a sweet?"

"No! Just go away! You are just as bad as the rest of them. No consideration for me at all." She turned her back and walked to the window.

"You are being unfair, dear aunt, but we shall not allow a little disagreement like this to affect our mutual respect and admiration."

She said nothing, and with a respectful bow, Jack left the room.

Kitty sat alone in her bedroom gazing out at the midnight darkness. Clouds covered the moon and only a few stars showed to the east.

Jack Whitaker was both problem and solution. She hardly

knew what to think of him. He made no secret of his desire to return to the war. But even if he went tomorrow Kitty doubted the dowager's attitude toward Char would alter.

Then what was it old Lady Euphemia had said? That she was a likely lover for Jack? What a hum that was! Though her heart had pounded so hard that she came to tears when he kissed her hands, Kitty had no stomach for romance. Especially with one pledged to more fighting. She dared not risk her heart on such a man.

Whatever Lady Euphemia said, Kitty knew how to put Major Jack Whitaker in his rightful place as no more than a chance acquaintance, a person with whom to have a pleasant, harmless conversation, the relation of her relation.

No more than that.

EIGHT

In his brightly lit room, Jack clamped his teeth hard against the leather strap and strained to keep his body still. Drenched in cold sweat, he tried to concentrate on Win's bawdy song and the footmen joining in. Anything but the slice of the knife through his flesh.

"Hold him tight, men. Just a few more cuts." Mr. Lanark's voice rose above the lyrics. "Hang on, Major. The worst will soon be over."

Jack tensed every muscle to keep from flinching. The point pierced his skin in an agonizing burst of pain and a wave of nausea. The world went black.

It could have been hours or only minutes later when awareness slowly returned, consciousness he yearned to escape from again. Fire burned in a dozen spots, his throat was parched, his head throbbing.

He felt a cool cloth on his forehead and opened his eyes. In the dimness, the dowager leaned over him. "Are you awake, Jack? Mr. Lanark is downstairs with Char. He says you were very brave."

It hurt too much for Jack to speak or move. He closed his eyes again and heard her rinse the cloth, wring it out, and pat his cheeks. "I will be here, Jack, if you need anything. For now, go back to sleep."

He woke again later, hearing his own groans. The dowager was gone, but Win quickly offered him a swallow of brandy. Mercifully Jack faded into oblivion once more.

He heard the clock strike four as he again grew mindful of the stinging, the aches, the soreness.

Win offered him more brandy, lifting his shoulders and plumping the pillows. "Here, sir. You've had quite an ordeal. Mr. Lanark left you a handsome collection of metal he dug out."

"Hmm. I will treasure every piece. Has he gone?"

"Yes. He checked the bleeding an hour ago and pronounced you well on your way to fitness again."

Jack lay on the chaise, covered with a blanket and his head propped up with pillows. He had a brown shawl wrapped around his shoulders. "Good. I am always delighted to see him finish, much more than I am pleased to see him arrive with his scalpels and knives."

Jack took a second swig of brandy, ignoring the burning in his arm as he raised it.

"The newspapers have arrived from town. Would you have me read them to you?"

"Win, you are beginning to sound as starchy as the dowager's butler. But yes, I would like to hear the news, if you don't mind."

Before Win could seat himself, there was a knock at the door. He opened it and Jack could hear Kitty inquiring about his state, then there were a few whispered exchanges he could not make out.

"Stop that muttering over there. Come in, Miss Stone, and see for yourself that I am not completely done in."

"Miss Stone, may I assist you?" Win lifted a tray from her hands. When he set it beside the bed, Jack saw a teapot, a lemon and a jug of honey.

Kitty's smile was tentative. "I do not mean to disturb you. However, I have something I hope will help."

"I regret I cannot at the moment stand to greet you, Miss Stone."

Win backed away, and went into the dressing room.

"I see," Kitty said, "that you are indisposed. But that is why I came to bring you this willow bark tea. It has very good pain relieving qualities."

"I welcome anything that dulls the pain, Miss Stone, but this brandy also has such a quality."

"But later you may pay for the brandy's effects, while this tea has a bitter taste for only a few seconds."

"Why would anyone drink bitter tea?"

"It is an ancient remedy of the people, known for centuries but often overlooked by today's physicians. I think you will be favorably impressed."

"I am certainly willing to try it."

"I have some lemon and some honey to improve the taste. Would you like me to add some of either? Or both?"

"Not necessary. Let me try it undiluted."

Kitty poured a cup and handed it to him.

He sniffed the light brown liquid. "It looks like weak tea, but it has little aroma."

She nodded.

Wrinkling his nose a little, he took a sip. "Ugh, yes, it is bitter." He finished the cup and held it out for more. "If one cup is good, will two do twice the job?"

"Indeed, I believe that three will do even more."

She refilled the cup. With a look of distaste, he downed that one too.

"Rest now for a moment, major. I am anxious to see if you begin to feel a little better."

"Perhaps you will read to me. Win was just about to go over yesterday's newspapers. I think I far prefer your voice to his."

She nodded, picked up the papers and began to read, her tone soft and melodious. He closed his eyes and lay his head back against the pillows, listening without absorbing the meaning of the words. She spoke beautifully, making him warm and dreamy. It was, he assured himself, just the combination of the brandy and the tea, a lightening of the pain. Nothing more.

Kitty read on, even when the clock chimed softly. The major appeared to be sleeping. She read almost at a whisper for a few moments, then paused.

The tea had done its work, his face was relaxed now, the lines softened. His breathing was even, his chest rising and falling in rhythm. He was a handsome man, with his face in repose. His dark hair had a curl to it, and she longed to touch it.

She felt a smile spread across her face. What a foolish woman she was, attracted to this hardened soldier who longed to go off to war again probably to be killed as he almost had once before.

The silence lengthened. She knew she ought to slip away quietly instead of just sitting here looking at him. Win would return the tray downstairs later.

What are you thinking, you silly widgeon?

What she wanted from him was only indirectly personal: his help in getting Bea and Char into a better situation in regard to the dowager. Then, eventually, Kitty would be able to follow her own wishes without worrying that any moment she would be summoned back to Charsley Hall to help them again.

The major opened one eye. "I feel considerably better, Miss Stone. I believe your potion has worked."

"How very satisfying to hear. I will see to it that there is plenty more of the tea whenever you feel you need it."

"I am in your debt."

"Good. I am glad you feel you owe me a favor or two."

He opened both eyes wide in surprise.

Kitty picked up the tray. "I will tell you about a few ideas I have when you are feeling better." She turned to go.

"Wait. Set that down and tell me now, if you please. I am feeling much better."

"My little request can certainly wait for your complete recovery."

"Nonsense! Now that I am to become part of your plans, you must tell me what my duties are."

"But do you not wish to rest, to return to sleep? I assure you these little things can wait. I should not have mentioned—"

"Come now, Miss Stone. You bring me a pain-relieving potion, soothe me with your reading, then turn to teasing me? How very unfair of you!"

She felt the heat of a blush. "Now *you* are teasing *me*, Major."

"Just think of what an improvement that portends."

"Indeed I find your cheer very gratifying. But are you sure you want to talk about the mundane affairs of the household before you are up and about?"

"Miss Stone, I am beginning to think you are worse than a tease."

"All right, I shall tell you. But fair warning! You will find these matters very petty compared to your concerns."

He gestured for her to continue.

"You see, Major, I am afraid the way the dowager maintains control over the estate . . . you see, Char and Bea would like to bring back the age-old tradition of holding a summer festival at Charsley Hall."

"Ah, I see."

"But Char is concerned. That is, he thinks his mother will not agree."

"He is correct. She won't like the idea."

"But she is always criticizing him for avoiding his duties, for not taking any initiative. Would she not welcome this as a sign he is coming into his own? Of course.

"Now that I have been so indiscreet and said so many silly things, may I ask you a question or two, Major?"

"Yes, I will be happy to answer anything about which I

have knowledge, which unfortunately does not include a great deal of information on birds and their human counterparts."

"This is most indiscreet of us to discuss, but I am so curious. Why is the dowager so hard on Char?"

Jack shifted to an easier position. "It has disturbed me for many years, Miss Stone. Here is my assumption. What she says she wants and what she really wants are two different things. What she really wants is for Char to remain dependent on her, not stand on his own two feet. You see, once she acknowledges that he is capable of running the estate, she will be superfluous, will have no purpose to her life."

She touched her hand to her lips for a moment and stared off into the distance, then spoke slowly. "If that is true, she will never recognize his ability, no matter what he does. She will never help him to succeed."

"That is my opinion," Jack said.

"But that is dreadful for Char, for Bea. Unfair and vindictive."

He nodded.

"But she is kind to you and wants to help you mend."

"Yes. Aunt Adelina is good to me. I think she is genuinely fond of me, but mostly she finds me useful as a mark for her criticism of Char. I have tried to change her views, but Char has asked me to say no more."

"But can he just defy her and take over?"

Jack pondered his answer. "It is difficult to say. I am not sure he always wants to be in charge. Sometimes he would rather write poetry."

"That is true. Do you think he realizes what he must do?"

"More and more. We all must help him."

"But not nag at him," she said.

"Char simply has to take up his life and ignore his mother. He will never satisfy her as long as she feels endangered by his assumption of all the duties of his title."

"Then are you saying my idea of encouraging him to have a festival is worthless?"

"Not at all. I think it is a good idea. Just do not think that if the festival is a great success—and I can see that you will help to make it so—things will change. Even if the dowager sees that Char is an adept manager, she will not withdraw her criticism."

"I hoped," she said, "you would help the situation by convincing the dowager to agree to Char's idea of the festival—"

"Come now, Miss Stone, you mean *your* idea of a festival?"

She gave a rueful little laugh. "Char believes it is his idea now."

"I see. Very astute of you, Miss Stone."

She felt herself blushing. "I was only trying to help, though now that I have heard your views, I think I may be making things worse."

"On the contrary. You have a most useful idea. How can I help?"

"You mean you will convince the dowager to agree to having the festival?"

"I will do my best, though I cannot guarantee success."

"Oh, thank you, Major." Kitty stood and reached out to pat his shoulder, then pulled her hand back. "I do not want to cause you any more pain."

"Miss Stone, just seeing your happy smile and sparkling eyes is reward enough."

She looked down, embarrassed.

He moved and winced. "You know, the dowager duchess was not happy about the way you claimed that cottage."

Her heart quaked. "Is that what I am accused of?"

"I set her mind at ease. You need not worry."

"Truly? Then I have much more to thank you for. I will go immediately and see that more tea is brewed. I can see that is has a most salutary effect upon you." She went to the door, turned and smiled at him again. "Thank you, Major."

Jack closed his eyes and let the image of the lovely Miss Stone linger in his mind. He hoped he was not defeating his own plan for Char by falling into Miss Stone's web of purposes. Planning a festival for the local villages and tenants would distract him from convincing Char to take up his duties in the House of Lords next session. If Char became more involved with the affairs of the estate, not to mention the coming birth of his child, he would be less likely than ever to want to go to London for months on end. Yet Miss Stone had hit on a good way for Char to learn more about the workings of the estate. Perhaps that would be useful in the long run.

She seemed so earnest, so convinced of the value of her plan. He admired the urgency in her voice, the way she leaned forward and spoke with sincerity. He had not even considered turning her down.

She was right when she saw the dowager as an impediment to the happiness of her sister. The older duchess needed Char to be dependent on her, so she constantly harped at him for his inadequacies, faults that he easily compounded by hiding away and writing poetry instead of taking a more active part in supervising his properties.

Like Jack's estate, Charsley Park ran well under the direction of a capable steward and hardworking tenant farmers. Jack met with his men only a few times a year, and when he had been away, they exchanged letters from time to time. The dowager, however, met almost daily with Mr. Edgerton, and kept a close eye on every aspect of matters in the entire neighborhood.

It was not going to be easy to talk Char into going to London.

Kitty wiped the clippers with a scrap of cotton and placed them in her apron pocket. Among the three of them, they had filled four baskets with blooms and a fifth with petals shaken from blossoms already in decline. Bea and Mama were as hungry as she was, but the best flowers, their fragrance most intense, were picked early in the morning before the sun was high in the sky. Or so Mama always said.

Although these flowers might be dumped in a dustbin instead of carefully dried for sachets. The test was still ahead of them. Mrs. Wells would never allow it if they went directly to her. The housekeeper was as hostile as ever to Kitty and Lady Dunmark, and barely civil to the duchess. Mrs. James, the cook, on the other hand, was far more friendly and sincerely fond of Bea, eager to prepare food that appealed to the young duchess and reassuring about how soon she would regain her appetite.

Kitty had already talked to Mrs. James about using space in the storeroom adjacent to the stillroom to hang the flowers, heads down, for drying. Nevertheless, if Mrs. Wells ruled against it, the cook would have no choice but to accede to the housekeeper's directions.

Kitty picked up two baskets and squared her shoulders. "I think it is time to see if we can breach the defenses."

Lady Dunmark brushed a strand of hair off her forehead. "It is already warm, and I am eager for my chocolate, girls. So let us go inside and make our attempt."

Bea's apprehension was clear on her face. "I hope the dowager does not find out about this."

Her mother gave a little hiss. "We must start somewhere, Bea, if we are to make any progress toward establishing you as a voice in the running of this household."

"But . . . oh, dear!" Bea frowned, looking like anything but a formidable personage, her hair loose and her dress rumpled, her expression clearly showing her dread of a possible confrontation.

Kitty led the way into the house by the side door directly into the corridor leading to the service wing. The storeroom she had in mind was locked, but she knew it to be nearly empty.

When the three ladies, baskets overflowing with roses, came into the kitchen, three housemaids and two footmen sat at a table having breakfast. Mrs. James held a cup in her hand watching them eat until she spied them. Quickly she dipped a curtsy. "Your Grace."

The other servants quickly stood and bowed or curtsied.

Lady Dunmark favored all of them with a smile. "Good morning. The duchess, Miss Stone, and I need a place to hang these blooms for drying."

Mrs. James's glance met Kitty's and they exchanged a little nod. "Yes, milady, I shall find a place." She paused, as if thinking for a moment, though she and Kitty had already found the spot. "I suspect there will be room in that second storeroom. Davey, you and Zeke help Her Grace and the ladies."

She went to a drawer, took out a ring of keys, handed them to Davey, and followed him with a roll of twine. "You will need this. Davey can string it from one side to the other, and we will tie up each bunch of flowers separately. Will that do, milady?"

"That will be excellent." Lady Dunmark gave Kitty a sly smile. "Exactly what we need."

When most of the blossoms had been tied in small clusters and handed up to Davey, who stood on a stepstool, Mrs. Wells bustled down the corridor, her lips pursed in disapproval. Kitty had been keeping an eye out for her, sure that one of the maids would slip away from the kitchen to inform the housekeeper of the ladies' invasion of the storeroom.

"Good morning, Mrs. Wells," Kitty said, giving her a wide smile. "The duchess, our mother, and I have picked flowers for drying and we found this room exactly suited to our purpose."

Mrs. Wells gave the briefest of curtsies to the duchess. "Your Grace, ladies. Davey, do you not have duties elsewhere?"

Kitty held up a hand. "He has been kind enough to help us for a few moments, Mrs. Wells. Davey will not be deferred from his duties for more than a quarter hour. We found the morning perfect for gathering the blossoms. We have so appreciated his assistance."

Mrs. Wells's face maintained its usual sour expression. "This room is used for storing preserves and other fruits and vegetables. I fear there is no room for hanging flowers."

Lady Dunmark stepped forward. "But as you can see, Mrs. Wells, the duchess wishes to use just a little of the space to dry her blooms. The shelves are still quite accessible as long as we hang the flowers high."

Ms. Wells sputtered for a moment, then backed away.

Kitty poked Bea. "Now, tell her," she whispered.

Bea cleared her throat and clutched at Kitty's hand behind her back. "Mrs. Wells, take this smaller basket and have the flowers put in vases for my mother's room and my boudoir, if you please."

With all three of them staring at her and Davey paused in the middle of tying another bunch above, Mrs. Wells had little choice but to give another half-curtsy, take the basket and agree. "Yes, Your Grace." Her voice was brusque, her eyes hard.

Kitty gave Bea's hand a little squeeze.

Bea waited until they had their tea and coffee served in the morning room and the door closed behind the footman to express her delight. "Now I have done it, made that nasty housekeeper follow my directions for the very first time. I think we have made great progress."

Lady Dunmark sipped her tea. "Unless the dowager has something to say on the matter."

Kitty shook her head. "My guess is that Mrs. Wells will not even mention the matter to the dowager. It is relatively insignificant. Why should she admit she was unable to prevent it?"

NINE

Kitty had missed checking on the progress at the cottage for two days, and she hoped to be able to report to Jack that his three men had accomplished many of the tasks he had assigned.

When she neared, she could see Bart rubbing away at the front windows with a rather grubby cloth. "Good day," she called to him.

He whirled, dropped the cloth in the dirt, doffed his hat, and gave a little bow. "Miss Stone."

"Do you have enough clean cloths, Bart?"

"Yes, ma'am. I mean, no, ma'am."

"Those windows had not been washed in many years, I fear."

"Grimy they was, ma'am. Very grimy."

"Well, I thank you for your efforts. I am sure you will make them good as new." Not that the window glass was perfectly clear, she thought as she went to the door. It must have been very old, judging from the wavy lines and little bubbles in some of the diamond-shaped panes.

Inside, she could hear arguing from the kitchen side, so she quietly went into the music room, as she already called it. The rug was laid and the hearth swept. The furniture was distributed around the room and it looked almost ready for her harp. Three handsome chairs, a large table, and an ornate cabinet decorated with carved fruit. Rather fancy for such a cottage.

From the other downstairs room, Tommy's deep voice rose in fury. "I tell 'ee, we must finish scrubbin' this floor afore we start upstairs."

Yates sounded equally adamant. "Naw. Let that half dry—"

Kitty walked across the hall and stood in the doorway. "I do not wish to interfere."

Both men touched their foreheads and bobbed. "Miss Stone, what can we do to help you?" Tommy asked.

"I thought I would take a progress report to the major."

"How's he doing?" Yates asked quickly.

"I have not seen him yet this morning, but last night he was resting comfortably."

The men showed her upstairs where they had rid the rafters of the cobwebs and an old bird's nest. "We got the broken window out and took it to be fixed in the village. It'll be ready tomorrow."

"Very good."

"After we get it put back, we'll finish scrubbing these floors."

"But Miss Stone, there be no mattresses for those beds."

Kitty reassured them. "I doubt anyone will be sleeping here for a long time. It is really just for us to practice our music. The major will send over a pianoforte from his house, and the duke's men will bring my harp as soon as you are finished."

"Oh, then we just leave the bedsteads bare?"

"That will be fine. And I thank you for all your efforts."

Both men bowed again. Apparently having no more disputes now that the floor was dry anyway, they went back to their work.

The condition of the house was not quite up to her standards, but the worst of the dirt was gone. Two housemaids could polish up the furniture and give the windows another going over in an afternoon. The Three had done well by themselves, figuring they were fellows who had little or no experience in housekeeping. But as the major had said, she mustn't let them think they were just cleaning but repairing and updating. That made them more cooperative.

She went outside and walked to the tiny bower they had cleared, at least enough so that she could sit.

From here the cottage looked like a picture of rural neglect, still surrounded by overgrown bushes, tangled flowers and weeds run riot, and over all, the roses twining into the thatch. It had a considerable charm, much in line with some of the more outlandish ideas about creating an artificial wilderness in the garden she had read about.

Kitty had sent a fresh pot of willow bark tea up to the major's room that morning and she hoped it continued to give him some relief from his pain. He had assured everyone that he would be out of bed in another day, but she hoped he did not rush and endanger his recovery. He was naturally impatient, she mused.

A little later, after she had checked to see if the flowers were still hung in the storeroom, she would go back to visit him. She rather liked sitting by his bedside. It made her feel good to see the creases of pain ease from his face. But sponging his brow had brought her dangerously close to him.

Just thinking about him made her knees feel a little weak, her pulse quicken. How silly she was to let her sensibilities take flight without more than kindness, charm and a grin from the major, who just might be a practiced flirt.

Some of the officers she had met in London had perfected the art of flattery. But they never meant to engage one's affections. Kitty wished she had a developed a little more skill in flirtation herself. But after Char and Bea married, she had her hands full trying to discourage attention rather than polishing her abilities to attract gentlemen. They approached her out of curiosity. Or attempted to take advantage of her supposed vulnerability.

Jack Whitaker was definitely not interested in engaging her affections. The last thing she needed was an attachment to a man whose strongest desire was to return to the battlefield.

In the late afternoon, Kitty tapped on Jack's door. Win gestured her in, and made a sweeping bow.

"Your potion, Miss Stone, has proved quite efficacious."

Jack hooted from his bed. "Win, you fraudulent windbag! 'Efficacious,' indeed. Where did you ever come by that term?"

Win merely raised an eyebrow and went off to the dressing room without a word.

Jack chuckled. "Come in, Miss Stone, and please be seated. I assume Baldwin has stumbled upon a dictionary. You would never know the man came from a pig farm in Bedfordshire. He is developing his vocabulary and refining his speech to the point that I believe he is planning to apply to the Prince of Wales for a position." He turned his head toward the dressing room. "Is that not correct, Win?"

The answer came immediately. "Indubitably, sir."

Jack lifted both hands in the air and shrugged. "You see? I have taught him everything I know and he has become too good for the likes of me."

They both listened for another response, but there was none.

Jack shrugged again. In a low voice, he whispered, "I am very lucky. No one has ever had a better batman."

She nodded. "So it would seem. I came to bring you more tea. And to see how you are feeling."

"I am much better. I will be up and around by tomorrow, if the dowager can be thwarted. She wants me to stay inert for weeks. But I cannot. Not even to appease her."

"You must be careful, major. You do not want to—"

"Oh, I know, I know. I shall take care not to strain the incisions. By the way, Miss Stone, I have not fulfilled any of your assignments yet. When I next join the dowager and the rest of you for dinner, I think Char should propose the festival and I should endorse his plan before she has an opportunity to disagree."

"An excellent idea, Major. I do appreciate your help. And so will Char and Bea."

"Perhaps tomorrow evening."

"If you are up to it so soon."

"I had hoped to attend the review tomorrow in the village, but that will be impossible. I'll make the next one, I hope."

"I am sure you will. I have a report on the cottage. Your men have done a decent job, not perfect, but much better than I expected."

"Good to hear. Are they finished?"

"Not quite, but they will be tomorrow or the next day. Do you know, I was looking at the furniture there, and I admit I am puzzled."

"How so?"

"The pieces are of very high quality. There are chests and commodes upstairs that might fit in here at the Hall. And the music room has a fine writing table of rosewood, and the chairs are of excellent make, not new of course, but better than what one would expect in such a modest cottage. Do you know who lived there? Someone of consequence?"

"No. When I was just a boy, there was an old lady, someone pensioned off from the household, I would imagine."

"When they took off the dust covers, I expected to find rude benches and simple tables, but I was surprised indeed."

"I have no idea where the stuff came from."

"It is a mystery. By the way, Mrs. Wells told me I can now use the stillroom, but only for your tea." Since she already had the cooperation of the cook and could brew it in the kitchen, it was quite superfluous, but nevertheless a tiny step forward.

"When Aunt Adelina realized how much better the tea

made me feel, I scolded her a little about her inhospitable treatment of you and your mother. She blamed it on Mrs. Wells, of course, but I suppose she realized she ought to make some gesture."

Kitty poured him more tea and watched his grimace as he swallowed it down.

"I am glad to add some lemon and honey, and I am sure neither would detract from its—ah—its efficacy."

Jack smacked his hand over his mouth to keep from spewing tea until he managed to swallow.

"I am sorry, I did not mean to make you choke."

"Not at all. You are a treat, Miss Stone."

Not for many hours did the glow from his words fade. *Kitty*, she warned herself as she blew out the candle and settled into bed that night, *you are a foolish ninny and a skitter-witted dunce!*

"You would think it was a parade of the entire royal family, the King, the Queen and all the princesses, at a massing of the troops in Hyde Park," Bea whispered to Kitty.

They sat in an open landau with Lady Dunmark watching as Char, in full military uniform, led the dowager duchess to a large barouche. There followed the dowager's personal maid carrying a second shawl in case the breeze stiffened, Miss Munstead, and little Mary, dressed like a doll and moving just as jerkily.

"That poor child," Lady Dunmark said. "She always looks so woebegone."

Seeing his mother settled in her carriage, Char mounted his horse and the party began to move.

The drilling of the local militia, Bea had explained, took place once every month. Char, as the sponsor of the company, always attended, usually accompanied by the dowager as the group's patron.

Kitty found the event quite interesting, for she had never

thought of Char as having the slightest knowledge of things military. Char certainly looked the part in his scarlet coat adorned with bright gold braid and shiny brass buttons.

A good-sized crowd sat on the grass or settled onto benches outside the inn. A few more carriages of the local gentry lined the edge of the green. The dowager nodded to a few people, but apparently, Kitty observed, no one had the nerve to approach her. Even Lady Euphemia and Fanny, in a nicely turned out equipage, kept their distance.

Captain Peck, as Bea identified him, came up to Char and spoke with him briefly. Then the drums began, the men straightened up and began to march. Though less than half of them were in uniform and most carried wooden replicas instead of real guns, they tried hard to stay in formation. They marched from one side of the village to the other, then back again. The captain barked a series of orders and they formed into three ranks, then together backed one way and went forward another. They simulated aiming, firing and reloading on command, then to more drums, they marched back to the bridge and dispersed to widespread applause.

Kitty had seen more impressive military parades, but none that had the enthusiastic cheers of the young boys for their fathers, of the women for their husbands or suitors. As the marchers rejoined their families and friends, there was an air of celebration. Many gathered around some men across the road. Kitty was first surprised and then annoyed to see that the center of interest was Mr. Yates.

The dowager and Char were leaving, but Kitty asked her mother and Bea to wait a few moments.

Kitty climbed down from the landau and went closer to the group of people, staying the midst of the crowd, and watched as Yates held up a small bottle with a cork stopper.

"This is pure sand from the beaches of Portugal, from where our brave troops stepped on the shores to win such glorious victories. We have only a very few of these valuable and unmatched treasures. 'Tis only a few pence to have a reminder of our great troops! Straight from the strand in far-off Portugal." Yates scanned the crowd. His face fell when his eyes met Kitty's.

But it was not her presence, Kitty thought, that was spoiling his little scam. Though plenty of people surrounded him, no one was stepping up to buy. Instead caps came off and heads were scratched, men stroked their chins and looked amused, and women stuffed their hands deeper into their apron pockets. Though he repeated his spiel in ever more glowing terms, he made not a single sale.

Kitty stepped closer. "Mr. Yates, did you enjoy the militia's drill?"

Yates snatched off his hat and bowed to her. "Yes, ma'am. Can't say they was all keeping time. But, er, I guess they could stop a few Frenchies."

Once the surrounding folk realized she was obviously not going to buy any sand, they moved away.

Kitty watched them go, and then turned back to Yates. "I assume you did not find any takers."

"Naw, not a one. These folk are as thick and disbelieving as I've ever seen."

"Does the major know about this sand, Mr. Yates?"

"He, er, no, I suppose he don't."

"And would you wish to have me tell him about it?"

"No, ma'am, I hope you won't."

"Then I suggest you put that sand away, all of it. I do not expect ever again to hear of you trying to sell any sand, none of you." She gestured to Bart and Tommy who were lurking not far away. "Is that agreed, in exchange for my overlooking this little incident?"

"Yes'm."

"Then I shall see you tomorrow at the cottage. And I shall take your best wishes to the major when I see him later."

Yates nodded. "I thank'ee, ma'am."

Kitty could hardly keep from laughing out loud. Somehow the major's authority had transferred to her, it seemed. Or perhaps it was just a guilty streak in those fellows. Sand from Portugal? What would a farmer in Kent want with that?

Who knew what scheme they might come up with next?

That evening, Jack came downstairs to dinner. He admitted it had been difficult getting dressed; his wounds were still tender. "But I am tired of that bed, and I don't care to receive duchesses and other lovely ladies in my nightshirt."

The dowager favored him with a brief smile.

Char reported to him on the militia's drill. "Captain Peck was disappointed you were not there. He would appreciate your assistance if you could make the time, Jack."

"Really, Charsley, you should not encourage Captain Peck to pester Jack about local matters," the dowager said. As usual, her visage was grim.

Jack favored her with his brightest smile. "Oh, but I would be pleased to help him, Aunt Adelina."

She shrugged, but said no more.

When dinner was nearly over, Kitty feared the dowager would rise before Char posed the subject of the summer fête.

At last he set his wine goblet down and cleared his throat. "Mama, I thought today—with all the people gathering so congenially—we should reinstitute the summer fêtes you always used to sponsor."

Jack spoke before the dowager could react. "What a capital idea! Aunt Adelina, you always made those fêtes the highlight of the year for everyone. An excellent idea, indeed."

Kitty watched the dowager look from her son to Jack and back again. Across the table, Kitty could see Bea holding her breath, her eyes wide as she waited for the reply.

Char began to speak again, but his mother held up her hand for silence. "I myself had thought we might do something along that line. But perhaps not so soon."

"A few weeks seems like plenty of time to me," Jack said. "I cast my support to sooner rather than later."

"If you help, Jack, I am sure—"

Char interrupted his mother for the first time in Kitty's presence. "I will begin organizing this very evening."

To Kitty's surprise, the dowager said not another word. Nor was it mentioned over the tea tray, though Kitty was sure everyone but the dowager was bursting with eagerness to talk and plan.

When at last they went to their sitting room, Kitty and Lady Dunmark gave Bea a hug of victory.

"Now," Bea said, "we must see that it is a success. For Char's sake. And for mine."

"I know you are looking forward to this gathering, Bea. But you must be very careful." Lady Dunmark spoke with authority.

It had taken Lady Euphemia and Fanny only a few days to organize a tea at the Dower House for the Duchess of Charsley to meet the ladies of the neighborhood. If Bea followed Lady Dunmark's guidance, Kitty thought, she would make a favorable impression on all the local ladies.

Bea wrinkled her nose. "Why do I have to be careful? Despite what the dowager thinks, I am the Duchess of Charsley."

"That is exactly the reason," Lady Dunmark said. "You are the Duchess of Charsley. You will set the standards for the residents of this estate and the neighborhood. At the moment, I think they are all confused, not knowing how to go on because the dowager does not do her duty by the local society."

"But what am I supposed to do?" There was almost a whine in Bea's voice.

"My dear, you act just as I have always taught you. Be gracious and respect everyone, no matter what silly things they might say. They are curious about you, and eager to know you. I suspect they're all pleased to have you to replace the dowager. In a way, she insults them by taking no part in their affairs. But, I warn you! Do not let a word of criticism of the dowager pass your lips, no matter what any of them might say. If you do, they will leap upon it and discuss it over and over. It is sure to get back to the dowager eventually, via the servants' gossip."

"Mama, you make me feel like I am about to enter a pack of wild beasts in a menagerie who will try to eat me alive."

Lady Dunmark clasped her hands together. "Oh no, my dear, nothing of the sort. I hope that among the ladies you will find some who can be your friends."

Kitty watched the emotions on Bea's face. She was barely eighteen and knew little of the world. "Do not fret, sister, dear. Just be yourself and smile."

"That will be easy enough for you, Kitty. You can say and do anything you want."

Kitty silently counted to ten. Bea had no idea what London Society had been like for Kitty, not an inkling. She summoned a smile. "I promise not to embarrass you by comparing any of their faces to horses I have known, or their clothing to the washerwomen of my acquaintance, or their voices to the squawking of Squire Daniels' scrawny old parrot. Will that do to keep me in your favor, Your Grace?"

Bea giggled merrily. "You are always a lady, Kitty. You must have absorbed every lesson Mama taught you while I was daydreaming." Bea wore a pale blue pelisse and a matching bonnet adorned with white silk roses. A fringe of her golden curls showed around her cheeks and called attention to the exact match of her ensemble to her wide blue eyes. She was the perfect picture of English loveliness.

Lady Dunmark retied the ribbon on her bonnet. "How do I look? Presentable as the mother of a duchess?"

Kitty shook her head. "Much too young and pretty to have a daughter in such an exalted position." Kitty was dressed entirely in shades of cream and ivory, other than her pink parasol.

Once at the party, Kitty accepted a cup of tea and managed to fade into the sidelines. To her relief, no one here seemed to know of her former connection to the duke. They knew only that his marriage had been quite sudden, which increased their curiosity about Beatrice. But no one cared much about Kitty, and for once, she enjoyed being something other than a center of attention.

Kitty was glad her mother stayed beside Bea, avoiding all attempts at separation. *Perhaps Mama and I have too much experience of London society*, Kitty thought. These ladies hardly seem like the predatory types from Almack's. But it did not hurt to keep Bea aware of how some might want to hurt her.

"I am pleased to make your acquaintance, Miss Stone."

Kitty turned to find a kindly-looking lady in a black ensemble at her side.

"I am Mrs. Driver."

"Of course, how very nice to meet you." Kitty was surprised. When she had seen the vicar at church he had looked rather young to have a wife of this lady's age.

"We welcome your sister to our little circle here in Charsley and Ackerbridge. Mr. Driver cares for both parishes, you know."

"I did not know that. He must be a busy man."

"The Charsley parish is by far the larger."

"I see."

They were joined by three ladies whose names Kitty promptly forgot. One of them confided that she was the mother of Miss Amanda, who was speaking with the duchess at that moment. For the next hour, time passed slowly, but not unpleasantly. The conversation among nice rural ladies was little different than that of London ladies—local affairs, the exchange of children's antics, fashion, and the weather.

When most of the ladies had departed, Fanny Courtney beckoned to Kitty, who excused herself and hastened across the room.

Fanny whispered in her ear. "Mr. Driver has come to fetch

his mother, but before he does, I would like to introduce you."

Kitty smothered a giggle. Apparently the lady she had thought was his wife was his mama.

Fanny went on, oblivious of Kitty's amusement. "Mr. Driver is a widower, Kitty, a most obliging gentleman, and I am sure you would enjoy his company."

Kitty suppressed a little squirm of embarrassment. Why would Fanny, herself a spinster, try to bring a man into Kitty's life?

Fanny led her outside where the gentleman waited. "Oh, Mr. Driver, here is Miss Stone."

He cast her an indulgent smile and bowed low. "I am pleased to make your acquaintance." He turned to Fanny. "Miss Courtney, how may I be of service to you?"

"Miss Stone has expressed a wish to see the family plot at the church. I thought perhaps you might be willing to show her around while your mother finishes her tea."

Wonderful, Kitty thought. A tour of a cemetery, just the perfect thing to cap an otherwise pleasant afternoon.

Mr. Driver nodded to Kitty and offered her his arm. "I often escort the dowager duchess to visit her dear departed. I am happy to tell you anything you want to know about the ancestors."

"Thank you," Kitty murmured. She could have throttled Fanny for getting her into this, but after all, Fanny was only exercising the right of all females to perform a time-honored ritual: introducing a lady to a gentleman. But, oh, how she wished she had been able to avoid it.

Mr. Driver pointed out the gravesites of several local families as they walked down a crushed gravel path among clipped yews.

It was, Kitty thought, not much different than the plots behind the church at Dunmark Manor, a solemn place set off from the village lane by a stone wall.

". . . and the Whitaker family is gathered here on the little rise." Kitty was not surprised to see several elaborate marble monuments, typical of the last century or even earlier.

A small bench was placed near the largest marker and Mr. Driver indicated that she should sit. But Kitty wanted to stay on her feet. If he launched into a long account of the exploits of the dukes, it might deter him if she kept moving.

Fortunately, he took out his timepiece and looked at it before he got very far along in the history of the barons who held the first manor. "I regret that I cannot tell you the whole story because I have promised to confer with some parishioners after I see Mother home."

"That is fine, Mr. Driver. I am planning to read some of the family history in the Hall library. If I have any questions . . ." She let her voice trail off. Was fibbing to a vicar a more grievous sin than to a less exalted personage? Kitty hoped not.

"Then I shall take you to the seventh duke's grave." He gestured to the left and she preceded him to a simple stone a little whiter than the others.

1759–1794 were the dates. That meant Char had been duke for fifteen years, since he was a boy of ten. And had he been bullied all that time by his mother? Or was her treatment of him more benign before he came of age?

She began again to listen to Mr. Driver. ". . . he was a fine example of his class, taking excellent care of his flock. I myself owe him a great deal. I will tell you just one little story . . ."

Kitty managed a sickly smile.

TEN

Jack reluctantly mounted his curricle for the trip to check on the Three at the Cross and Bell. He was tired of using a vehicle of some sort, but it was too soon after his surgery to get back in the saddle. His muscles were not only tight and sore, they seemed to have lost much of their strength.

Jack felt the pull of the reins in his shoulders and winced at the pain, then determined to put the matter from his mind. He could not afford to waste time lolling in bed any more. It was time he got moving again and his wounds would heal just as fast under a few layers of clothing, or so he had decided. Anyway, he had to make sure Bart, Yates and Tommy were behaving themselves.

The lane led past the dower house on the edge of the village, beside the church. Usually, the churchyard was quiet and deserted, but he saw a pink parasol and instinctively slowed the horses to a head-tossing dancing walk. Yes, he could see it was Miss Stone . . . with a man in black.

He glanced back at the road and slowed the horses even more. When he looked again toward the church, he recognized Mr. Driver, the vicar. Mr. Drivel was what he ought to have been called, Jack thought. Drivel was what his usual sermons consisted of, pure, unadulterated drivel. And what was he doing with Miss Stone? Or more accurately, how had she gotten herself caught up with him, of all people?

He loosened the reins and the horses stepped out, back to their preferred spanking pace.

Deuce take it! It was well known in the village that Drivel was looking for a wife, someone besides his mama to care for his motherless children. But what kind of a man would commence a courtship among the gravestones in a church-yard?

He was tempted to swing the team around and rescue her. But an hour in Drivel's presence and that of the shades of generations past would give her an accurate impression of the man. Nothing Jack said could more correctly character-ize him.

Surely Miss Stone would perceive that he was a pompous and shallow fellow.

Surely Drivel would not appeal to her, a lady of taste and culture.

Surely Jack could see to that before the day ended.

In front of the little inn, he climbed down gingerly and tossed the reins to Win, looking forward to a bite to eat. Mrs. Talbot, the proprietor's wife, was always good for a fine, well-aged cheese and fresh, crusty bread. He heard a burst of laughter, then another from inside, and felt his good humor drain away. What were they up to this time?

Taking care not to draw the attention of any of the men clustered around a table in the taproom, he stood quietly in the doorway and observed the scene.

He could hear Yates's London pitch above the others.

"Now look 'ee here. This pea goes under the thimble in the middle. Then I jest move 'em around, from here to there and back. Now every one of you should know where it is, right?"

As one man pointed, then stepped back, Jack got a glimpse of the three thimbles sitting on the table in front of Yates. Quickly he switched them around.

"Now, where is it? Two pennies for a look."

Tommy put two pennies down and pointed at a thimble.

The other men—Jack counted five—nodded or shook their heads as their opinions registered.

"Anybody have another guess?" Yates said.

A burly lad in a brown smock drew two pennies from his pocket. "I go with you." He nodded to Tommy and put his pennies on the table.

"Any more?" Seeing no response, Yates lifted up the thimble the men had bet on. There indeed was the pea.

The men all laughed. Yates took four pennies from his pocket and slapped them on the table. "Two winners take me for tuppence each."

"Now shall we go again?" Yates recovered the pea with the thimble and moved them around. Jack was not close enough to see if there was sleight of hand involved. Now they had one winner, he felt sure Yates would manage a string of victories for himself, hiding the pea in his hand or in some other crafty way making sure that only a very few would identity the correct thimble. But as Jack watched, most of the men shook their heads and drifted away from the table.

Yates had no takers.

Jack stepped into the room and walked over to the Three.

"Best of the day to you, Major," Yates said with a crooked grin. Tommy and Bart looked surprised and vaguely sheepish.

"Afternoon, all." Jack pointed at the thimbles. "Been at it long?"

"Naw, these beggars are much too cheap for a real good game."

Jack looked directly at Yates. "Or they know a scam when they see one?"

Yates stuck out his lower lip and shook his head. "Don't seem likely, Major."

Jack gave an elaborate shrug. "Once I saw a few of these worthies give a good sound thrashing to a fellow who tried to take them with some trick or other. They took every cent he'd filched from them and plenty more. Don't believe I've seen him around here since."

"Izzat so?"

"You might keep that in mind, Yates."

"That I'll surely do, Major."

Jack sat at the next table. "Now, Mrs. Talbot, I'll have a slice of your freshest loaf."

When he had a tankard of ale and had finished a hunk of the delicious bread, Jack sat back and looked at the Three. "I have some more work for you men, though I doubt you'll be up to it. It's not exactly what you have had experience doing."

"Wot d'ye mean?" Bart sat up straighter. "We is able to do most anything."

"Well, in this case, it means repairing the roof of a stable."

Tommy gave his wide grin. "You tell us what to do and we'll figger a way."

Jack sighed. That was exactly what he was afraid of.

Kitty marched along the garden path toward the Hall. She tried to shake off the feeling she had been a complete hypocrite. She had fibbed to Mr. Driver, a man she hoped to keep her distance from in the future. Then she told Fanny she had appreciated seeing the graveyard, another plumper. And finally, she had pleaded the need for fresh air when she told Bea and her mother she chose to walk home. Actually, the path through the dower house gardens to the edge of the Charsley Hall gardens was both more direct and quicker than taking the road in a carriage. But what Kitty really wanted to do was sit for a time, hide away down some empty path all alone. She needed to rid herself of the remnants of Mr. Driver's solicitous and overbearing attitude.

She realized, belatedly, that Fanny truly thought the vicar might be a good match for her. It was a horrifying notion, spending more time with Mr. Driver. His extreme solicitude alone was enough to keep her from enjoying his company, not to mention his bad teeth, receding chin, and straight, drooping hair. And how he clasped his hands together in an exaggerated way that seemed to mock piety rather than reflect it. When she recovered her aplomb, she strolled back to the Hall, more convinced than ever that in a few months, she would go far away from Charsley.

She joined Bea and their mother in Bea's boudoir.

"I suppose I have to thank the dowager for barring guests to visit us."

Bea looked up and gaped at Kitty. "Whatever do you mean?"

"While you were making your good-byes to the guests, I had a personal tour of the churchyard graves from the vicar himself, Mr. Driver."

Lady Dunmark spoke very cautiously. "Did you find him, ah, interesting?"

Kitty shivered. "Decidedly not. Quite the contrary. I am only relieved that if he tries to call on me, he will be turned away, as all others are."

"Oh, dear." Lady Dunmark looked crestfallen. "Fanny was hoping you might enjoy his company. He is a learned man, she says, and has a fine living. He is a widower with four lovely children."

Kitty pursed her lips and raised her eyebrows. "So, Mama, you also had a hand in this scheme?"

"Well, dear, I did not discourage her. He seems like a perfectly amiable man. He certainly presents a creditable appearance."

Bea squealed. "Mama, I do think you are in need of spectacles."

The three ladies broke into laughter.

Kitty pressed a hand to her chest. "Spectacles, indeed. I do not think you have been listening to him in church either, if you call him amiable."

Lady Dunmark gave a last little chuckle. "I shall be sure to tell Fanny that her mother was correct. Lady Euphemia predicted that Mr. Driver would not meet with your approval."

Kitty pushed the stems of the roses into a better position and stood back to admire her handiwork. The bouquet looked exactly as she had intended, a combination of pale pinks and creamy ivory roses set off by a few blossoms of deeper shades. An occasional leaf of shiny dark green peeped through the velvety petals. Was anything, she wondered, more ideally suited to make a room look perfect than a vase of flowers?

She loved the beautiful ambiance of the music room of the rose cottage. The old harpsichord Jack had sent over as a surprise was painted in pastel scenes of Italian lakes and tranquil pastures, set off by intricate gilded scrolls in the manner of the early years of the last century. Jack's pianoforte was elegantly made, one of Broadwood's finest instruments. Her harp, shimmering in a shaft of sunlight, always gave her a thrill of momentary awe when she beheld its graceful shape. That she had learned to bring music from its strings seemed almost a miracle to her.

She hoped that Jack would stop by this afternoon to see how the cottage had turned out. Day before yesterday, she had thanked the Three and sent them back to the inn. It had taken just a few hours for a pair of housemaids to give the furniture a final polish.

Kitty took a song sheet from her own pile of music and sat down at the harpsichord. She loved the sound of the instrument, a sort of combination, a midway point between the lilting voice of the harp and the power of the pianoforte. If there was not a collection of traditional tunes among the sheets in the music cabinet, she would have to send to London for one. Somehow the traditional tunes sounded better on the harpsichord. When she had a little more time, she would sort through the music that filled that delicate cabinet made of a particularly lustrous satinwood.

After a last chord, she went next to the little bench beside the harp and ran her fingers over the strings, then launched into one of her favorite melodies, the sprightly Mozart tune that came from one of his operas, though she could not remember which one.

She lost herself in the music, closing her eyes and letting her fingers see for her.

When the last sound died away, she opened her eyes. Jack leaned against the doorway, a smile on his handsome face.

"Do not let me disturb you, Miss Stone. I'm glad you were playing, and I could not make myself listen outside. Somehow the sight of you at the harp makes the music more . . . more complete."

Kitty could feel her cheeks warm in a blush. "Why, you are certainly exaggerating. I begin to think you might be one of those London dandies!"

"Ah, too cruel, especially when I only speak the truth."

"Please, Major, if you will forego more overblown compliments, I invite you to come in and sit down."

"Thank you, though I am crushed you find my true appreciation of your art to be unpalatable."

Kitty could not stop her little giggle. "Now that is exactly the kind of remark I find preposterous, kind sir."

"I speak only the truth." His grin belied his words. "You will have to excuse my attempts to express myself according to the dictates of polite society rather than the blunt talk of the soldier."

She made a gesture, as if pushing away his words. "Please, do be seated, Major. How are you feeling today?"

He went to a chair, limping only slightly. "Much better. I drink your tea by the gallon, and I almost feel like dancing a jig. I must say, Miss Stone, to take the conversation away from my various afflictions of the body and of the tongue, you have made this cottage quite lovely. And comfortable."

"As I told you, the furniture is of a high quality, surprisingly so. And the harpsichord and pianoforte make it perfect. The room is fully furnished without being crowded. I must thank you again for sending over the instruments from your house."

"I was astonished to come across the harpsichord, but once I did, I remembered that my mother played it from time to time. The pianoforte was almost new when she died. I remember it mainly because I had many years of lessons upon it. My father insisted that I learn, though I fear I have forgotten everything."

"No, I am sure you have not. Once you sit down and run your fingers over the keys, it will begin to come back."

"I doubt it."

"Well, let us try."

"Perhaps in a moment. First I would like a little tour of the cottage."

They walked to the other side of the ground floor where the other half of the cottage held a table and a hutch with a few kitchen items. "This is perfectly suited for preparing a luncheon or tea. I thought Nell might accompany me here from time to time and do some stitching while she waits."

"Where did you find those pitchers?" Jack pointed to the row of white milk jugs in the shape of cows lined up above the hearth.

"Are they not quaint? They were wrapped up in a box." A discussion in an old kitchen seemed an odd setting for the quickening of Kitty's heartbeat, the heightening of her senses. Jack looked anything but romantically aware as he examined the various hooks and hobs at the open hearth. Until he looked up at her and their eyes met. A tremor shot through her and she could not turn away.

She felt her fingernails press into her palms and forced her hands to relax. Jack's slow grin, spreading from his lips to his eyes, melted her heart.

Kitty swallowed, forcing herself to speak. "Would you like to go upstairs?"

"Yes."

She twirled around and almost dashed to the stairs, trotting upwards as fast as she could without tangling her legs in her skirt.

The narrow hall separated the two bedrooms, the larger one above the music room. The tall tester bed, without mattress or hangings, looked rather forlorn.

"As I told you, I was surprised to find such lovely furniture here," she said.

He walked past her and ran his hand over the marble-topped console. "Yes, it is not what one expects."

"Though," she added quickly, "I hear cottages are quite the style among some circles these days."

Jack laughed. "I suppose that puts you in place as a fashion leader."

She joined in the laughter, swishing the skirt of her simple sprigged muslin. "Oh, quite. You can see how very *au courant* I am, sir."

He stepped a little closer. "I think you are quite lovely." He reached for her hand and lifted it to his lips. "Quite lovely indeed."

The touch of his very soft lips spread a warmth up her arm to the center of her being. But she managed a light laugh. "Oh, kind sir, you are a shameless flatterer."

"Why, I am shocked, Miss Stone, at your accusation. How can you so cruelly impugn my motives?" The twinkle in his eye told her he was anything but serious.

She led the way out of the room and waved at the smaller bedroom. "There is little to see, just a small chair and a wardrobe."

In the music room once more, she summoned all the composure she could find but had not another word to say.

Jack sat down and looked around once more. "I would say you have a knack for house decoration, Miss Stone. Would you be willing to come and see my house at Nether Acker? I want to open it again, but my father always used to say that the whole pile ought to be demolished so we could start over."

Kitty's pulse raced and she drew a deep breath. "Yes, I would like to see it, for I love old houses."

"Then perhaps we could go in a few days. I want to start riding horseback again soon, and I have promised to take Mary for a little trip someday. She does well on her pony."

"I once asked the dowager if I could ride with her, but she would not allow it."

"Then you can join us someday, as long as I am fit for it."

"Thank you. I wish you could also bring Mary here, so that I could teach her to play the pianoforte."

"She would love that. And I think I can get Aunt Adelina to agree, if I am very, very sly."

"I hope you can. And now are you ready to try your hand at the pianoforte?"

He shook his head. "Would you favor me with a piece on the harpsichord first, and then on the pianoforte? I want to hear if the tuner got them right."

"I think you are behaving like the little boy who postpones his practicing until he is called to dinner, Major."

"I have no secrets from you, Miss Stone."

She went to the harpsichord and again played the tune she had used to try it out a while earlier. "What do you think?" she asked when she finished.

"I think it sounds superb. Your ability is such that I would not know if the tuner was skilled or not."

"Oh, major, you are incorrigible."

He grinned, looking not the slightest bit contrite. "Sorry. I seem to be unable—"

"Nonsense. I will play for you, but then, I shall impose a lesson upon you and order you back every day to practice, just like a naughty lad."

"It will be my greatest pleasure to come here daily."

She sat down and tried to cover her embarrassment as she leafed through her music. Why had she invited him to come so often? What kind of fool was she? Hadn't their brief brush upstairs a few moments ago been bad enough?

When she brought her breathing back to normal, she selected a rondo and played it quickly, leaning into the keyboard and hiding herself in the notes. She kept her eyes either on the music or closed them to keep out her view of him sitting across the room. When she was finished, she stared down at her hands.

He applauded and walked over to the pianoforte. "Bravo, Miss Stone."

She leaped to her feet and moved away from the bench. "Here, Major, sit down."

"I would rather face a line of French artillery. You must sit beside me, give me confidence."

She looked at the narrow bench. If two sat there—

He reached for her hand and pulled her down beside him. "Now, then, remind me where I place my fingers."

She shivered at the press of his hip and shoulder to hers, then gritted her teeth and promised herself she would not be flustered. "Begin with your right thumb above middle C." She pulled out a simpler song and placed it on the music rack. "Try this."

She could feel that his eyes were on her, not the music, but she refused to acknowledge it though the tingles that ran up her spine threatened her composure.

"What next?"

"Look at the music. Do you remember what key on the pianoforte that represents?" She pointed at a note on the page, representing E above middle C.

He paused for a moment, then struck the correct key.

"Excellent," she said, trying to edge away from him and still keep her balance.

"But I cannot remember the next one." There was the sound of mischief in his voice.

She grabbed his forefinger and hit the A with it, then the B-flat, then back to the E. "Now repeat that sequence by yourself, if you please."

She kept her eyes strictly on his hands though she could almost feel his gaze warming her cheek, her neck.

He repeated the musical phrase.

"Faster," she said.

He played it again. And again. "Now I think I am getting the idea."

She turned toward him with a smile. Too late she realized her mistake as she met his clear blue eyes directly. In an instant, his finger lifted her chin and he pressed his lips to hers.

This was exactly what she feared.

This was exactly what she desired.

* * *

A memory to treasure forever. If I never have another kiss, if I end my life as a spinster governess, I will always have the memory of Jack Whitaker's lips taking mine.

Lost in reverie, Kitty studied her reflection in her dressing table mirror. How wonderful! How embarrassing!

She knew her initial reaction to his kiss had been pitifully lacking in decorum, for she had kissed him back with all the emotion he stirred in her, though with little skill or knowledge of the appropriate technique.

She had been kissed before, once or twice, but this was the first time she wanted to bestow a kiss, not just receive one. So when she had stayed close against him on the bench, leaning into his chest and letting her mouth do what came naturally, she gave away her eagerness. And her inexperience, she supposed. For it was the major who had gently pulled away from her, not the other way around.

He had murmured sweet words to her, calling her his "dear Kitty" and imploring her to call him Jack. She, like a complete ninny, had simply gazed at him, dumbstruck, unable to say a word.

She had been in that trance until the moment she sat in her bedchamber and contemplated her own radiant face.

What was she to do? She should not become attached to the major, to Jack. But they were together often, and had made plans for further meetings, none of which she could avoid, even if she wanted to.

Before long, he would leave England and go back to the war as soon as he was able. She would leave Charsley Hall and make a new life for herself someday. There was no future for the two of them together.

She could think of no path other than to continue her very undignified series of deceptions and pretend it had never happened. The memory she would store in her heart, but the next time she saw Jack, she would not say a word.

ELEVEN

Jack found the frustrations of the next few days rivaled even the most chaotic moments of preparation for battle. Kitty was never alone at the cottage, always having Bea or Nell nearby so he never had a private moment with her. At the Hall, she almost ignored him, as if she did not remember their kisses.

He was not healing as fast as he wished. Riding caused him excruciating pain.

The dowager summoned him each time her son's wife edged a little more onto the dowager's terrain. Secretly, Jack admired the tactics of the young duchess, her sister and her mother. They were ingratiating themselves with the local ladies and had even visited the family of Charsley's largest tenant farmer. Among the complaints of the dowager, the crowing of Beatrice, and the straightforward, impersonal account of Miss Stone, he learned that Mrs. Croft had welcomed her seventh child, who now wore a cap embroidered by the duchess's hand. The family had received a fine plump ham and a basket of bread and pies, along with an afternoon dominated by insignificant twaddle, or so the dowager had characterized the visit.

But if he tried to add up all the complications among the

competing interests of Miss Stone and himself, of the young Duchess of Charsley and the dowager, Jack found the most crashing headache assailed him. And that was even before he tried to sort out the intentions of his cousin, the duke, who seemed immune to Jack's entreaties on behalf of Wellesley's troops.

Jack's only accomplishment was to bring Mary to the cottage and start her pianoforte lessons with Kitty. The dowager had reluctantly agreed when he spoke to her of the child's loneliness and her longing to learn to play. Months ago when he had come to the Hall to recuperate, he had found Mary more lonely than even he had been as a boy. Mary had neither mother nor father, the dowager as her guardian was distant and remote, and her governess was a sober, stiff figure.

At her age, about ten, Jack's situation had been far less acute, for he had a father, however cold and aloof; a cousin, Char, with whom he had a few adventures whenever Char could escape his mother; and he had the village boys with whom he played games and got into mischief. Yet he had been very lonely. How much worse was it for Mary, who had no parent at all and seemed to associate with none of the nearby children?

Mary was very shy, as could only be expected from her sequestered upbringing. But as he had engaged her in conversation, he found her bright, well versed in geography and history, able to speak a little French, and an accomplished sketcher. He developed a real soft spot in his heart for the lonely little girl and now hoped Kitty would too.

Ah, Kitty! How he wished he could forget about going back to Portugal! She made him want to dismiss his aspiration. For the first time in his life, he felt more for a woman than lust or vague companionship. Kitty Stone made him think of sharing not only a bed but breakfast and dinner. Even having children. She made him yearn for the things he had never before desired. Things he found himself daydreaming about no matter how he tried to put them out of his mind.

But instead of allowing himself to waste time lingering over dreams that could never be, he worked at getting back into the saddle. In the meantime, he needed to show Miss Stone the house, Nether Acker. If he had it opened and got started on repairs, at least he could put some space between the affairs at Charsley Hall and himself.

After Sunday services, Jack escorted the dowager duchess, swathed in black, out of the ducal pew in the church. Everyone made way for them, bowing to the dowager, hardly daring to speak. For years, she had rarely attended, but when she did, the people deferred to her in the most toadying fashion. She did not smile nor did she acknowledge anyone.

The vicar—Drivel to Jack—hastened to her side as they came through the door, but not so fast that Jack missed seeing he had been talking to Kitty. Miss Stone, his four children, their grandmother, and Lady Dunmark were still clustered together across the path. Kitty had crouched down to talk to the youngest boy, and though her face was turned away from him, Jack could tell that she was smiling. He wished he could shake off the dowager and run over to drag Kitty away.

When he had once questioned Miss Stone about her meeting with Mr. Drivel in the graveyard, she had shivered with repugnance, bringing Jack a chuckle. But might not the children sway her? Drivel babbled on and on to the dowager, bowing and scraping until Jack wanted to shove him in the shrubbery.

To make matters worse, Mary and Miss Munstead joined the other group, and Mary, too, seemed captivated by the little Drivels. However unfair it might be, Jack wanted to haul Mary and Kitty away, prevent them from becoming caught up by the children. Could Kitty be claimed by the needs of those boys even when she did not care for their father? Could she come to tolerate the father—or much, much more—if she loved his four sons?

Since he had kissed Kitty, there in the cottage, and she had so eagerly kissed him back, those questions had grown more and more important. Jack stood beside the dowager and fumed inside, and his consternation grew as they rode back to the Hall. He had lost track of Kitty. He only hoped she was not experiencing another tour of the graveyard on the arm of Drivel.

When they arrived at Charsley Hall, a messenger had come with a letter for Jack.

"He will await your reply," Randle said.

Jack took the letter, and excused himself. "I will join you later, Aunt Adelina."

When she had gone to her rooms, Jack settled in the library and broke the missive's seal. It came from Lord Pearson. Due to the importance of the recent victory and the tragedy unfolding among the British forces on that North Sea island, Lord Pearson was assembling a group of men on his yacht in a few days for a short sail. The men aboard would talk over the situation and discuss alternatives. Could he count on Jack to come and would he bring Char?

Jack let the letter fall to the floor. With the fête only a few weeks away, how could he convince Char to go sailing far from home?

As he drove Miss Stone toward the bridge in the curricle, Jack apologized. "I know I promised you your first glimpse of Nether Acker would be from horseback, Kitty, but I feel we must get started on the house and I am still not quite up to riding. The proper approach for the most scenic vista is to ride over the hills and down to the river, crossing at the ford. From there, the house shows to its best."

"I am sure the view will be lovely from any direction," Kitty said.

"You are kind to say so. But I wonder if you will simply laugh at me when you see it and try to imagine me wanting to live in such an old place. Compared to the magnificence of Charsley Hall, Nether Acker seems insignificant. But the house is most unusual, built up and out from its original walls in diverse styles, none less than a hundred years old."

"Jack, I am sure I will like it. I prefer houses with character."

At this first time spent alone with Kitty since they had kissed many days ago, he realized they had naturally fallen into a habit of calling each other by their given names, while they had addressed one another more formally in the presence of others.

"My father always talked about the need to replace it and build anew, but somehow the work never got done. It has been years since I had even thought about unlocking the doors and entering it. And now I am almost embarrassed to be taking a young lady of taste to look at it."

"I assure you, I will be honest, but I am quite partial to old houses, the older, the better."

As they drove nearer, the stones of the building glowed with a reddish tinge in the morning sun. Shiny green ivy covered part of the wall near the entrance. A wave of memories overcame him as they entered, for the house, even after a dozen or more years, still smelled the same. How could that be? he wondered.

He tried to steer Miss Stone away from the old hall, the heart of the house centuries ago, but now an old-fashioned relic of the middle ages. But she insisted on seeing it, with its carved screen shielding the entrances to the old buttery and kitchens, long ago altered into servant's quarters.

To his surprise, she claimed to be awed by the dark hammer-beamed ceiling, the small windows, high gallery. "Why, Jack, this house is wonderful. So ancient and so well preserved."

"My father thought it ought to be pulled down."

"Oh no! It is a great heritage. Just think of the feudal lord sitting here at his high table, the floors strewn with rushes, eating the grand feast."

Jack gave a little laugh. "I rather expect it would have been a foul-smelling place with flocks of chickens pecking around, and great slavering hounds slouching among the people looking for a bone. Or, for all I know, this is merely a replica, built after the Restoration when some families needed to pretend they came from the barons of the Norman nobility."

"You really do not know when it was built?"

"There were Ackers here by the time of the Tudors, whether the family was named for the river or the river named for the family. The Whitings were on the other side for a long time also. Come along to the drawing rooms, which are a little more up-to-date, not more than one or two centuries out of style."

One drawing room opened into the next, one with square Jacobean paneling, the other with linen-fold paneling.

She looked about as if thunderstruck. "Oh, Jack, this is breathtaking."

"You don't say. Do you really like this old stuff?"

"Look at the mullioned windows and the planked flooring. I do not know about the authenticity of that Great Hall, but this part is certainly Tudor."

"This was my mother's favorite room, as I remember."

"How old were you when she died?"

"Nine. Almost ten."

She smiled and ran her hand over the panels. "And she must have been very beautiful."

"Oh, yes. There used to be a portrait of her someplace, but everything has been put away. Except in the dining room."

Jack realized why the moment he entered. The length of the table would make it impossible to move, though it too was draped in white as were the side chairs, more than a dozen of them.

Kitty went to the window and looked out on the remnants of a decorative parterre. Jack joined her to gaze at the outlines of the design still in evidence, though the topiary had grown into odd shapes never intended by the gardeners who once clipped them.

"Tell me, Kitty, do you think the place is worth opening up?"

"Why, there could be no question about it. These rooms are quite lovely, and I am sure the furniture would match their fashion. You say the roof is sound?"

"My steward assures me this section is intact. There are several bedchambers above. The wing on the other side of the hall is in poor condition, but I have a notion to let the Three loose on it. They might learn something or they might just knock it to pieces. Either way, it would not matter to me."

"Really, Jack, you should not be so cavalier with this house. There might be a great history behind that wing. Where are the estate records kept?"

"The steward has the current papers and the old library is full of antique volumes gathering dust. There might be some family history to be found in those."

"I think you should find those documents and learn all about the house. Let me supervise the Three cleaning up this section, and we will get these rooms in order for you. They did not do badly on the cottage."

"But I do not wish to take you away from your harp now that you are so cozy there."

"Please leave that to me, major."

As they drove back to the Hall, Kitty heaved a great sigh.

"Is something wrong?" he asked.

"Oh, it is just my worries about my sister. She does not believe she has made any progress in stopping the dowager's unfair criticism of the duke. It is very frustrating for her, especially when she sees the dowager being partial to you, Jack."

"I believe the dowager is entangled in what is known as a vicious circle. The more she criticizes him, the more she convinces herself—and Char—that her role in running the duke's affairs is essential."

"But if she would just let him meet with his steward, supervise his men of business, meet with his principal tenants, and do these things without her interference . . ." She paused in mid-sentence.

"I do not believe the dowager duchess would see it that way, but of course he is capable if she allowed it. I have tried to suggest a few changes around here, but she does not hear me."

"And if she does not pay attention to your suggestions, then she will not listen to anyone. You are certainly her favorite."

"And that is why I have not pushed her harder. I do not dare endanger my influence by going too far."

"Probably a wise decision."

"But I am more interested in turning Char's thoughts to governmental matters than just what happens in this little corner of Kent."

"What do you mean, Major?"

"He needs to think about the future of his country, not just his fields and orchards. If Napoleon has his way, there won't be any Charsley beef or apples or hops."

"But, Major, if Char is not sure of himself at home, confident he is doing right by his wife and family, by his dependents all over his estates, he will never be comfortable in governmental circles."

Jack shook his head. "I cannot expect a female to understand," he muttered.

Kitty bristled. "I hear that remark. But do you not see? If more men took the time to see their households operated well and their loved ones were secure, they would be able to guide the government with more confidence. Perhaps even keep from getting bosky every night as well. So much drink certainly cannot add to the reasonable and rational nature of conversations."

Jack reined up and walked the horses. "I can see it will do me little good to try to discuss this with you. But——"

Kitty did not wait for him to finish. "Just look at the Duke of York. Here he is, out of office, and why? Because he could not stay away from a silly female. If he was going to keep company with her, he should have had the sense to see that she was provided for sufficiently. Then the poor woman would not have to take money from officers seeking his favor, looking for promotions."

"You cannot have any sympathy for Mrs. Clarke, can you, Kitty?"

She heard the incredulity in his voice. "As a matter of fact, I do. She had children to take care of and an expensive household to run for the duke's pleasure. He was entirely a nip-cheese when it came to giving her money. If he had been generous, perhaps she would not have become involved in questionable activities."

"I am amazed at you, Miss Stone. I would not have believed you would defend such a person as Mrs. Clarke."

"I do not approve of what she did, of taking money to give him a little list of names to take care of. But it was the duke who listened and followed her suggestions. If he had not been so susceptible to her in the first place . . ."

"So now you are trying to change human nature?"

Kitty sounded quite indignant. "I do not view it as human nature to say that gentlemen well beyond the age of understanding need to buy the pretended affections of young women who shamelessly flatter them and indulge their dissipations."

"Why, Miss Stone, I believe you have the makings of a crusader."

"To me, punishing the mistress is letting the real miscreant escape unscathed. As far as I know, the Duke of York has a wife he keeps hidden away instead of trying to make something of his marriage."

"Expecting any of the princes to be faithful husbands is probably the most fanciful thing you have yet implied."

"And is that not a sad commentary on the state of our monarchy? This could not be the example you wish Charsley to follow."

Jack rolled his eyes. "I surrender. You have won this skirmish, Kitty. You are the victor in all regards."

Kitty bit her lower lip to keep from grinning.

"Perhaps it is you and not Charsley that I ought to be wishing to London to argue our case."

Kitty laughed. "But you know there are many women who do have influence with their husbands. Or with other men, though I will not speculate on just why."

"No, please do not. I fear you would shock me to the core."

"I rather doubt it."

Later, thinking back on their spirited exchange, Jack realized he had thoroughly enjoyed himself, even when the sparks glittered in her eyes. In fact, especially when the sparks flew. But what would she say if she knew he was about to spirit Char away for a week? It did not bear thinking about.

Jack placed his hand on the duke's shoulder as they stood to let the ladies precede them from the dining room.

"Wait a moment, Char. I'd like to discuss something with you for a quarter hour."

Char looked at Jack in surprise, then nodded. "We will be along shortly, Bea."

Jack drew him toward the terrace doors before the dowager turned back to chastise them.

A footman followed them with their refilled wineglasses on a tray. Jack took his and leaned against the balustrade. When they were alone, he motioned Char to a chair.

"What is this all about, Jack?"

"There are several things we need to talk about. I like the idea of the fête, Char. It will signify the passing of the control of the estate to you and your wife."

"What? I do not think that Mama—"

"Char, you know how fond I am of your mother, even when she is at her most overbearing and difficult. She has been kind to me and I certainly owe her my return to health."

"Yes, you do, Jack. That is true."

"Even so, I think she has taken on far more than she should."

Char looked dispirited. "I know I am a great disappointment—"

"The devil you are! May I speak frankly, Char?"

Char's expression now reflected a sense of bewilderment. "Of course you may, Jack."

"You have asked me not to interfere and I have tried not to, though sometimes I have to bite my tongue. I love Aunt Adelina, but her criticism of you is too much."

"But, Jack—"

"Look here, Char. Your mother is hard on you for many reasons. One of them is that if you take over running the estate, what is left for her? As long as you hide away, writing poetry and allowing the dowager to intimidate you, she remains important to the operation of the duchy and its estates. I know she would not see it that way, but to me, her attitude is based on the fear of losing her usefulness."

"Never thought about that." Char pulled at his earlobe. "You could be right."

"Especially since you brought home a wife—a wife not chosen by the dowager, correct?"

Char nodded, his lips set in an expression of exasperation. "But what can I do about the situation?"

"I wish I had a ready list for you. The fête is a start. But I think you have to go further than mere household and village matters."

"What do you mean?"

"I am not the only man in London who wishes you would take your seat in the Lords next session. We need your support for the troops in Portugal."

"I do not understand most of the subjects they talk about. I went once. After sitting for hours, I could not have repeated a single thing that was said."

"Yes, much of the work is mundane, tedious. But we need you, Char. The French—that damned Napoleon—they threaten all of us."

"Thought they were no longer massed at Boulogne ready to cross the Channel and invade."

"You are right. They marched away and trounced our friends. The French threaten all of Europe. Not a single army has been capable of standing up to them—the Austrians, the Prussians, the Russians. I believe Sir Arthur Wellesley, with whom I served, is the only hope, both for England and for Europe. If Napoleon rules the Continent, you can't imagine he would overlook England, can you? He would be sure to return to his invasion plans."

"I don't understand. Thought Wellesley had an army in the field already. You see, Jack, I am dense when it comes to these things."

"Balderdash! You are not dense. You are like most members of both Houses, Char. They assume that Horse Guards will send sufficient troops, all the supplies they need, ammunition, horses, money. But unless we keep a close watch, this peer or that member will have some pet project to divert resources from our purpose. Some regiments were sent off to capture another port, someplace in the low countries. But the effort has bogged down in the swamps of Walcheren Island. Half the troops have been stricken with fever and are useless. Sir Arthur needed those men and supplies. His efforts in the Peninsula are our best opportunity of delivering another blow to the French, as we did at Vimeiro."

"Where you were hurt, right, Jack?"

"Yes. The real tragedy was the lack of following up, a pair of weak generals—no use going into it now. But I want you to know, Char, that we need you. Having the Duke of Charsley as one of us in the House of Lords would be more valuable than I can say."

Char shook his head, as if disbelieving. "Very flattering, Jack. Very good of you to say so."

"I mean it."

"But I cannot be away from Bea while she is, er—"

"Of course not, Char. Though she has her mother and her sister."

"And Mama."

"Yes." Jack could not say more, though both he and Char

were probably thinking about how the dowager might try to interfere in Bea's confinement.

Jack clapped Char on the shoulder. "You underestimate yourself, Char. I do not think your mother means half of her criticism."

"Don't know about that. But we must get to the ladies now."

"Indeed, in a moment. Lord Pearson has invited us to sail on his yacht next week. I hope you will come, Char. Just a small group of men to take the sea air. You can get to know a few of them better."

"See what Bea says."

As they went inside, Jack's dissatisfaction grew. He would have to do more convincing, because he needed to have Char on that yacht, needed to have him part of that group. It was only a start, but it would help to accustom Char to the idea of being more active in the government.

"Jack!" Kitty practically spit his name. "How could he take Char away now?" She stalked from one end of the duchess's boudoir to the other.

Bea sobbed into her hands and then threw herself across the coverlet. "It is so unfair!"

Lady Dunmark drummed her fingers on the table. "What is the purpose of this journey?"

Bea sat up and wailed anew. "Ooooww, they are going out on a yacht. They are going sailing! And the fête is just three weeks off."

Kitty wondered how Jack had convinced Char to go. She remembered that Char had once expressed an aversion to sea travel long ago.

It would serve Jack right if she had the Three yank out that lovely paneling in his house and burn it. But then, he did not fully appreciate it anyway.

"Tell me again, Bea. What did Char say."

"Oh, I am so distracted! I cannot remember. He could not understand why I was so upset. He says everything is already taken care of, but I can think of a thousand things that could go wrong."

Kitty excused herself, marched up to Jack's room, and banged on the door.

Win was surprised to see her. "Why, Miss Stone!"

From within, Jack spoke. "Please come in, Kitty, if you will excuse my shirtsleeves. I believe I know what you are here about."

She stood just inside the door, rigid with anger, but suddenly bereft of words. Jack stood before the mirror in tan breeches and white shirt, arranging his neckcloth. She could see him in the mirror watching her, and she looked like a witch, hair in disarray, face twisted in fury, hands clenched before her as if she was about to swing at someone. And she wished she could have, if she only knew how.

Jack favored her with a crooked grin. "You have heard about the—"

Suddenly her words poured forth. "Jack Whitaker, how could you be so selfish as to take Char off a-sailing? After all we have done to make him more responsible, now you go off on a pleasure trip at precisely the wrong time. What if you are becalmed in the middle of the Channel? Or run aground in the fog? We cannot postpone the fête. And though we could certainly have it without you, Major, the duke's presence will be required! It is the most empty-headed, childish, downright stupid trick I can imagine."

"Are you finished, Miss Stone?"

"No!" She could see the reflections of both Jack and Win trying to suppress their grins. "No, I am not finished! I will not be finished until you come to your senses and postpone this jaunt."

Jack turned slowly to face her. "It might interest you to know that the purpose of Lord Pearson's party is to bring together a few men who may back the needs of the army and speak up for Wellesley. It is precisely because I am helping Char to learn and to accept his responsibilities that I wish to have him present."

"He would be a great deal better off if he left London politics to others for the time being. It seems to me he will have his hands full running Charsley and tending to his family. But it is just like men to run off and pretend they are talking about important matters when they are simply taking the sea air and indulging in—in whatever men do on a ship. Drinking, I presume."

Jack stared at her calmly, but Kitty could see the exasperation begin to heighten his color and quicken his breathing. "Miss Stone, I also presume a few bottles will be uncorked aboard the yacht. But our purpose is serious, perhaps more serious than you are capable of understanding." He turned to Win. "I'll have my coat, if you please."

Kitty stood her ground and watched his batman help Jack into a jacket of deep blue. "If we are talking about understanding, it is certainly not I who lacks comprehension of what is wrong around here. It will not be fixed by running off to sea, Major. I must say I am deeply disappointed in your actions." Kitty whirled around and left the room, slamming the door behind her.

TWELVE

"I wish they had not gone. Char should be here helping me plan the fête." Bea sniffed, then leaned toward the mirror to adjust a curl.

"Nell said that the dowager has forbidden the servants to assist us," Lady Dunmark said. "I cannot imagine what kind of vitriol runs in that woman's veins."

Kitty nodded. "She is truly a dragon. But you have Lady Euphemia and Fanny, and you have all the ladies of the neighborhood. I think you will show the dowager just what you are made of, Bea."

"I hope so. But I would rather have everyone's help."

"Mrs. James will assist you as long as the other servants do not know. Meet with her here, in your boudoir. She is very pleased about the oysters."

Bea blanched. "Oh, oysters! Ugh."

"The beginning of the oyster season on St. James Day is one reason the festival is in late July. Mrs. James told me the Whitstable oysters have been famous since Julius Caesar conquered Britain. In fact, some people think those delicious oysters were the reason for his interest in our little realm."

"Ugh," Bea repeated.

"Perhaps you should avoid them, dear, in your condition." Lady Dunmark smiled at Kitty, who caught her meaning.

"But be aware, sister, they are quite the delicacy, all the rage, at London dinners."

Bea looked up. "I might try one."

Kitty smiled to herself. Bea had a spirit that would serve her well someday. In fact, Kitty suspected Bea might become one of those great duchesses who set the styles in fashion as well as in political and social circles.

Later, as she hurried toward Nether Acker, Kitty laughed out loud at her sister's determination to make the fête memorable. No mere dowager duchess was going to stand in her way. How typically paradoxical that the dowager's very opposition was growing into Bea's greatest incentive.

Kitty knew the Three were about to finish the outside work on one wing at Jack's house.

Tommy first saw her approach. "Miss Stone, did you walk here again?"

"Why yes, it is a brisk walk, but I enjoy the exercise."

"But we fixed the stable. We live there now, upstairs. The stalls are all swept and ready if you want to ride over."

"Why, thank you, Tommy." Kitty knew she could save a great deal of time by riding Diamond to Nether Acker and back.

They went inside and Kitty looked carefully at the drawing room walls. She had studied several books from the Charsley Hall library about Tudor domestic architecture. She was determined to make these rooms as perfectly authentic in décor and furnishings as possible, given that comfort must also be considered.

"Now, Bart, what you need to do is rub this beeswax hard into the wood and rub and rub and rub some more. Then take another cloth and polish it. That's it, Bart. Very good."

Kitty paused to let Bart bask in her appreciative smile. She wanted them to do their utmost to complete work on the major's house before he returned from his week at sea. For the past several days, as they brought the house alive once more, Kitty could not help noticing Bart's puppylike devotion to her. He followed her around, heeding her every wish, even spending most of his evenings polishing the brass chandelier and the silver serving pieces discovered in the dining room cupboards.

"Now," she said, "all the paneling in this room needs polishing. And in the next room, too. That old oak will be beautiful when it is cleaned and polished. Tommy, come with me. We shall do the same thing on the staircase. I figure it will take you at least two days to finish this before we can wash the windows, unroll the carpets, and uncover the furniture."

Yates had that look on his face, clearly trying to think of a way to persuade someone else to do his share. But not even the village maidens were vulnerable to his begging any more.

At noon, when Kitty brought them hunks of cheese and fresh-baked bread from the Charsley Hall kitchen, the Three had made significant progress.

Jack wished he knew what Miss Stone had put into that pain-relieving tea. On the third day of their yachting party aboard Lord Pearson's twin-masted yawl, Char had yet to make an appearance above deck due to a miserable stomach malady. The poor fellow had begun casting up his accounts only an hour after they set sail. He had been unable to participate in any but the first of the talks the seven men aboard had over dinner, over port, or as they sat on the deck. Pearson's yacht had not encountered anything but a tranquil sea, but Char had felt queasy from the first night.

Char's seasickness had nothing to do with the swell of the waves, nor was it caused by something he imbibed. Jack was convinced it had more to do with Char's memory of a difficult Channel crossing when he was a boy. His wife had been no help. Bea had cried and wailed when Char told her he would be away for a week. She had begged him to stay home, arguing they had far too much work to do on the fête for him to be away.

Now Jack wished neither of them had come. Lord Tifton, the other young peer Lord Pearson had hoped to persuade to support them in the next parliamentary session, was far more interested in games of chance, wagering too many reckless bets, even playing at dice with some of the crew.

Lord Pearson was disappointed, but not defeated. He planned to make a further attempt to engage the duke, but this time on dry land.

"I never knew Char was subject to seasickness." Jack sat in the main saloon of the ship, drinking more of Lord Pearson's fine brandy.

His host shrugged. "We will just have to work harder at another time, Jack.

"I was hoping that Wellesley's success at Oporto would stimulate the interest of both Charsley and Tifton. Sir Arthur attributed much of their victory to a combination of French ineptitude and negligence. As well as plain old luck."

"But you know better than I do, Lord Pearson, it takes competence and fortitude to capitalize on fortune and an enemy's blunders."

"Wellesley is wily, and though I suspect he sometimes overstates his anger in dispatches, he has a level head and thinks carefully about his strategy."

"I can attest to his coolness under fire. And his astute mind."

Jack sipped his drink and stared out at the dark sea. He wanted to be there, at Wellesley's side in Portugal. Or following the French into Spain, which was probably where the army was today. But here he was, sailing in the Channel, tending to his ailing cousin. Even worse than trying to get Char out of his sickbed were the dreams and daydreams about Kitty Stone that haunted him.

It was the sight of her standing in the graveyard with Mr. Driver that haunted him. Or actually it was the thought of

Kitty's soft spot for the vicar's children. Would she accept Drivel's suit to become the mother of four little orphans? Then what if she wanted more children? With that pious fool? The thought made Jack's stomach quake. And brought an ache to his loins. The idea of Kitty Stone in a nightgown caused visions he fought to chase out of his head. If she went to any man's bed, Jack wished it could be his own.

He could not bear to think of Drivel standing near her, much less touching her. Jack was far away from home. But even if he were there, what did he have to offer as an alternative? Could he say that someday, assuming he survived the war, he would come back to her?

He recalled the conversation he and Kitty had about Drivel and his motherless children. Now he thought of all sorts of brilliant remarks he could have made. At the time, he had been so upset, he probably made little sense at all. But what did it matter? He needed to forget about Miss Stone and her pretty ways.

As Kitty waited for Mary to arrive at the cottage for her lesson, she idly strummed the harp, thinking about the list of entertainments the ladies had drawn up. The three-legged races were to be held in the early afternoon with several versions for children, ladies and men. Only after they had decided upon the three categories did Kitty realize that Mary would have no partner for the children's race.

Miss Munstead would certainly not enter. So if the girl were to participate, Kitty would have to go with her.

When Mary was seated at the pianoforte and Miss Munstead had gone to the kitchen to take tea with Nell, Kitty gave her student a warm smile. "Would you like to try to run with me in the three-legged race, Mary?"

The girl hung her head. "I do not know how."

"Neither do I, to be honest. I have not tried it since I was a girl of your age. Should we have a go, and see how we do? Practice, I mean?"

Mary looked up, her eyes bright. "I would like to try," she said solemnly. "I would like to see if we could do it. I watched a three-legged race once, and it seemed to me that the best ones worked together. Most everyone fell down on the ground."

"Were they laughing?"

"Oh, yes, Miss Stone. Laughing very hard. But when they fell, you could see the petticoats of the girls."

"Then we must sew a pretty flounce of lace on our petticoats, Mary, in case we fall."

At this Mary's eyes grew wide and she covered her mouth with a hand. "What?"

"Well, if someone gets a glimpse of our petticoats, we will want them to be the prettiest, will we not? Even if the spectators are a long way off?"

Mary paused for a moment, then gave a little smile. "Yes. The very prettiest. But Miss Munstead would never approve."

"Then you bring me a petticoat and I will see to it. Later this afternoon, we must practice working together."

"I will meet you in the kitchen garden this afternoon, about three, when Miss Munstead takes her nap."

Later, Kitty found a length of cloth and brought it to their meeting. They walked to a secluded lawn and Kitty tied their ankles together. She wrapped her arm around Mary's shoulders and had the girl put an arm around her waist. "Now we step together, starting very slowly."

With many stumbles, they managed to walk carefully onto the grass.

Kitty counted. "On one, we move our tied legs. On two we step on our outer legs. Can we do that?"

"Yes, I think so."

After a quarter hour, they had developed a rhythm and slowly increased their speed. "Remember not to watch the other couples racing. Some will run very fast at first but they get all tangled up and end in a heap. We have to be like the tortoise racing the hare, steady and sure, and we will get to the finish line on our feet. And if we look away at others, we endanger our counting."

They went farther and farther, faster and faster until they could run together, not as fast as if they were alone, but ably enough.

"One, two, one, two." Kitty increased the speed of her counting and they moved faster and faster. Kitty tripped and they went down on the grass, their skirts billowing about them.

Mary giggled. "This is harder than I thought."

As they tried to get up, their legs tangled and they again ended up in a heap.

Mary giggled again. "How do we get up?"

Carefully they tried again and got to their knees and from their knees to their feet.

"Whatever are you doing?" Jack called from a distance.

"We are practicing for the three-legged race. What does it look like?"

Jack grinned as he walked across the grass, limping only slightly. "It looks like you are practicing for the three-legged race. But as I walked up, it looked like you were out here on the grass wrestling."

Kitty and Mary scrambled back up on their feet.

"Major Whitaker, I thought you were not due back until the day after tomorrow."

"We ended our cruise a little early. Char had a touch of *mal de mer*."

"What is that?" Mary's voice held concern.

Jack grinned. "Seasickness. It stopped as soon as he stepped onto dry land. Now, tell me about what you two are up to?"

Mary clasped her hands together. "Can you help us? Watch and see if you can tell us how to improve?"

"I should be happy to."

They set out again, this time with Kitty counting softly.

As they went they picked up their pace and managed to stay
on their feet for several yards, they stopped and slowly turned
around.

"What do you think?" Kitty called back to Jack.

"I think you have to be faster. And you have to learn how
to go around the post at the end and head back. The way you
turned just now will dump you on your bottoms if you try to
do it quickly."

They practiced for another quarter hour before untying
their ankles and heading back to the house with the major.
They promised to repeat the practice tomorrow.

Kitty felt quite distracted on Monday morning. Yesterday
after church, Mr. Driver had drawn her aside and offered to
tell her the story of how the church had been used as a ref-
uge during the Civil War. Though she was interested in the
local history, another hour spent listening to Mr. Driver's
nasal voice would have driven her to distraction. She had
made her escape by inventing an urgent duty at the Hall that
afternoon, but he offered to put himself at her disposal at any
time she wished.

She had warned Bea and Mama to say nothing about the
cottage to the vicar. If Mr. Driver knew she was there part of
every day, he might stop by and then she would be in the
soup, subject to one of his long and boring discourses.
Maybe she needed to sit down and concentrate on coming up
with a way to discourage him. Instead, she played a few
songs, but needed something more challenging to keep her
mind occupied. Perhaps, she thought, there would be some
music in that cabinet she could try.

Like all the cottage furniture, the cabinet was beautifully
made, with intricate inlaid designs in various woods cover-
ing every surface. She lifted out the music and thumbed
through the pile. In between the leaves, she found a packet
of papers, presumably letters, and set it on the table. Had
someone lost them among the sheets of music? Or had they

been hidden here, safe in this secluded place from the eyes of others?

She reached for the packet and turned it over in her hands. A piece of blank vellum had been wrapped around it and tied with a yellow ribbon in a plain knot. It was not a pretty bow, which might have indicated a girl's sentimental attachment to the material. But neither did it look like a man's business correspondence.

It would be simple to slip off the ribbon and sort through the writings inside. Perhaps they were not letters at all, but a diary or a sheaf of poems. The package did not look very old, but certainly not new enough to be Char's work either.

Kitty's curiosity made her tingle at the thought of what might be inside, treasures of old information or just a collection of kitchen receipts, bills for furniture, or invoices for anything, from farm animals to velvet draperies. Perhaps instructions for a hat maker.

Yet the more she wished she could see the contents, the more she hesitated. Did she have any right to read these papers? Would she be disappointed in their mundane content? Or excited to see the accounts of parties from long ago, perhaps descriptions of the lady's gowns or the attentions of a particular gentlemen?

Her fingers itched to open the package, yet she did not. Instead, she went to the harp and played a series of glorious arpeggios, Mr. Driver completely forgotten.

A knock on the door interrupted her chords.

She stopped playing. "Yes?"

Jack came into the room. "Excuse me, Kitty. I am sorry to interrupt you, but I want to be certain my men are cooperating with your wishes at Nether Acker. Are they doing their work to your satisfaction?"

"Why yes, they are . . . ah . . . very helpful."

Jack grinned. "Yes, I see that they are most attentive. I am sorry if they offend you in any way."

"They make up in amusement value what they lack in ability."

He laughed. "To change the subject for a moment before I leave you to your playing, I want to tell you that your misgivings about the voyage with Lord Pearson were entirely justified."

"They were?"

"As it turned out, our time was not well spent."

"Because Char was seasick?"

"That was only part of the problem. But I think you would be quite justified in gloating."

"I should indeed not! But I appreciate your acknowledgment of my judgments, even though they were given in utter anger."

He leaned against the chair. "You were most impressive in that anger."

"Pooh."

"And while I am interrupting you anyway, may I ask how you can reach for the correct string so quickly when you make that lovely music?"

"Why, that is how one learns to play the harp, just as you move your fingers to the correct keys when you play the pianoforte."

"Somehow it seems much less secure than hitting a key."

"Would you like to try sometime, Jack? There might be some beginner's exercises in that stack. I began to look through the music, but I became diverted by that packet of papers."

He looked over at the stack and shrugged. "What are they?"

"I do not know. I must admit I was very tempted to take a look, but I could not bring myself to indulge my curiosity without asking if you know anything about them."

"Me?"

He picked up the packet and looked at them, turning them over in his hands.

"You claim ownership of the cottage, do you not, major?"

"Why yes, it is on my property, but I have not seen it inhabited. You know, Kitty, there is nothing written on the outside."

"Which only makes it more intriguing."

"Who would have used this cottage? I cannot recall any-one here. Though I was away more often than not." He shrugged again. "There is an easy way to solve this little mystery." He slid the ribbon off the packet, unfolded the paper wrapper and rifled through the stack. "They appear to be letters, about fifteen or twenty in all."

"Are they very old?"

He set down the pile and picked up the top letter and read the first few lines. "It merely says Thursday, with no date."

He read the rest of the page, a smile breaking across his face. "We have here, Kitty, a love letter from a lady, a rather passionate letter, in fact."

"How delicious! I wish you could tell how old it is. Would it not be fun to think of this little cottage as a love nest for a forbidden couple?"

"Perhaps it was." He turned the letter over and read a few more lines, before looking up, his face suddenly sober. "This is indeed a devil of a coil!"

"Truly?"

"Yes. I will have to read the rest of them to be certain, but it seems these are from the dowager duchess."

A hundred thoughts flashed into her head. "You mean . . . not to her husband?"

"It does not appear to be her husband. She writes of the restrictions of the need for secrecy. If she were meeting the duke—I hardly need say more."

Her initial elation faded. "Perhaps we should wrap them again and put them back where I found them."

"And pretend we never knew?" He frowned, looking over the page once more. "She says she must go away for a time."

Kitty felt her heart twist and her shoulders slump. "My instant suspicion is . . ." She paused, unable to put her thoughts into words.

Jack nodded. "Yes, I am thinking the same thing. Why does a woman withdraw from society for a few months, go abroad, and return with a child as a ward and a story about a carriage accident in the mountains that killed off the child's parents, people no one ever heard of?"

Kitty sank onto a chair and tapped her chin with a forefinger, wrinkling her nose as she thought. "If our speculations are true, this is a coil indeed. However can we ascertain the best way to proceed? For the benefit of Mary? To protect her or to protect the dowager? And the recipient of the letters?"

Jack shook his head. "We have gone this far. Now we must read the rest of the letters, confirm our suspicions. Then try to see who Mary's father might be."

"The way you phrase your statement makes me see you have little doubt about the main points. You do not think we have jumped to an erroneous conclusion?"

"I have read—and that very briefly—part of only one letter, but what else could these things mean? The rest of the letters will have clues to the timing and the identity of the man involved, do you not think so?"

"But do we have any right to read them?"

"As you pointed out a few moments ago, Kitty, everything in this cottage is legally mine."

"The dowager could not know her letters were here."

"No, she did not want the cottage opened up, but if she had known about the letters, she would have come and taken them. Probably ages ago. It must have been her lover who misplaced them among the music sheets."

Kitty did not want to admit the thoughts that flitted through her mind about getting the dowager to leave Charsley Hall. Instead, she wondered about the dowager's life, what motivated her. And poor Mary.

"This might explain why the dowager is not active in London society. She has the means to be a reigning hostess or a patron of the arts in town. Instead she has closeted herself away, seeing few persons except her ward and her staff."

Jack looked thoughtful. "Exactly."

"Until we know more, it is futile to speculate. But I admit my mind spins with possibilities."

"Yes, I see many too. I will leave you now, and go to my rooms to read the letters and try to sort it out. I will see you later, at dinner, and let you know what I learn."

When he was gone, she sat in silence, thinking about the changes that might lie ahead. If Jack's reading of the letters confirmed their suspicions, they held the key to greatly reducing the ability of the dowager to rule everything, to manipulate Char and Bea.

But how could they manage such a change? Using the letters as blackmail seemed too cruel. But, unless the situation with the dowager was resolved, Bea would be forever miserable. Therefore Lady Dunmark would be miserable. And Kitty would be forever called back to soothe their nerves and calm their souls.

If she was ever to have a life of her own, whatever that might come to be, she needed to set the stage for the happiness and contentment of her sister and her mother at Charsley Hall. Which meant shushing the dowager.

But how could they use the letters without exposing everything and destroying her? As much as she wished the woman to go far, far away, Kitty was not so heartless as to wish her crushed. And what would happen to Mary? She deserved to have a happy life without the stigma of bastardy.

Thank God, Kitty thought, she had not read the letters first. Jack was in a much better position to decide what to do with them.

THIRTEEN

"Apparently the only thing the dowager likes more than berating her son and his wife is receiving the obeisance of her neighbors and tenants," Lady Dunmark observed. She and Kitty sat in a landau beside Lady Euphemia's carriage and watched the dowager nod to the assembled villagers and workers as her barouche approached the platform at the edge of the green. The dowager lifted one hand, not quite waving, as she nodded from side to side, the barest hint of a smile playing on her lips.

Kitty sat back and sighed. What a performance! Other than Jack, not one other person at the gathering knew the duchess's secret. They pledged their silence for the time being. When he had time, Jack wanted to investigate who might have stayed at the cottage, but for now, everyone for miles around was in the mood for celebration.

The dowager had two long white plumes waving above her bonnet that made her seem to tower over the duke as he helped her down and led her onto the platform where the two of them acknowledged a great cheer from the throng. Bea remained in the duke's curricle, though she had argued she ought to be on the platform too. It was only Lady Dunmark's caution that the dowager was likely to snub her in front of everyone that convinced her to let Char and his mother open the fête at noon.

Kitty could hardly hear the dowager's brief words, but she was sure they were all that was correct, if delivered without a smile. Char read his poem, which was, in Kitty's view, a few stanzas overlong, just enough to cause a rustle in the crowd. But they cheered again when he finished, for indeed they knew whose largesse was providing for their day away from work as well as the food and drink.

After she and Mary won third place in the three-legged race for women, Kitty felt like she drifted through the festival in a daze. She could not rid herself of mental arguments and counterarguments over what to do about the dowager. The idea of sending her away for good to allow Bea and Char their chance at full happiness was very tempting. But that was intimidation. And downright blackmail as well.

Sometimes a little voice in her head said, what difference does that make? The dowager browbeat her son for years and years. Why not make her to go away and leave him to his wife and child? Another little voice would remind her of Christian charity, of a woman with at least two broken hearts. Did she deserve to be punished again?

The third voice repudiated both its comrades in argument, saying the dowager could go away quietly, not too far, and pledge to stay out of Char's affairs.

Kitty wandered without watching where she was going among the booths and tents set up on the lawn, turning these arguments over and over in her mind. She did not smell the delicious aromas wafting from the meat pies nor hear the cries of the cider seller.

But passing the west lawn, where many were assembled to watch the early rounds of the tug-of-war, she heard a familiar voice.

"Guaranteed to give you added strength and power. Brings your muscles to full might. Cures the most distressing catarrhs, the deepest coughs, the lowest of moods. Gives you health and vigor and fortifies all your body parts!"

Kitty could not believe her ears. Here was Yates, trying another crazy scheme to extract money from the locals. She walked toward the group gathered round him. Bart lurked at the edge of the crowd.

Kitty grabbed his arm. "What is your role in this quackery, Bart?"

"Me? I don't know nothing."

"Fustian! You are here to promote potential buyers."

"Well, that's what Yates wanted me to do. But I won't."

"Really?"

"Miss Stone, I don't think that stuff oughta be drunk by anybody."

"What is it?"

"Well, it give Finnegan's dogs the flux."

She pressed her lips together to keep from laughing out loud. "Who made it?"

"Yates. Mixed gin with somethun that tasted terrible."

Yates' voice rose again. "Peckover's Famous Tonic. Widely used in Scotland by Edinburgh's leading doctors. Usually sold in London for two shillings, here a special price of one shilling sixpence. You'll want more than one bottle, my friends."

Kitty watched the men and women around him.

"Special qualities make your eyes sparkle, and your hair grow thick and glossy."

Kitty nudged Bart again. "I do not see anyone buying it."

"Naw, not yet. Yates spent more money going to town to have the labels printed than the major paid him for all the work we done at Nether Acker."

Kitty smiled to herself. Perhaps she needn't worry about these people falling for such an obvious waste of money.

"Bart, you tell Yates and Tommy that the major will be boiling mad if he finds out about this."

"Yes, ma'am. I'll tell 'em."

She went in search of Jack, but saw nary a trace of him. Inside the house, everything was in readiness. The dining room was quiet now, but a corps of footmen were poised to serve the food being prepared in the kitchens.

Several dozen gilt chairs stood in rows in the drawing room in preparation for the concert that would follow the dinner and precede the dancing for the neighborhood gentry. Char had brought in a group of singers from London to perform favorite arias from the most admired operas of the last few seasons.

The orchestra would follow the singers with a short interlude while the footman moved the chairs to open the floor for dancing.

Kitty was pleased with the setting. Lady Dunmark had guided Bea every step of the way. Char, with Jack's advice, had worked with his bailiff and the men from the village, and things seemed to be going smoothly. The dowager had looked around that morning, sniffed, and grudgingly said it would do.

Kitty heard voices from the morning room and went in that direction, stopping before she came into the view of the speakers. She stayed quietly around the corner.

"I understand your concern," Jack said.

"No, Major. I don't think ye do."

Kitty had no idea to whom Jack was speaking, but she had a sinking feeling she knew why. The man went on, his voice gruff. "My wife is sore upset and cried all day. My boys are ready to tear 'im limb from limb."

"But what is the answer you want? If the man is such a scoundrel, do you want your daughter to marry him?"

"He's a discredit to the human race, a worm of the worst kind."

"So if you have forbidden your daughter to see him again, what more can I do?"

"I may forbid 'er, but she got a mind of her own, that 'un."

"So they have been together again?"

"That I can't say. Sal don't speak to me. You tell him to leave her be."

"And of course if we both do that, try to keep them apart, we only make the romance more tempting, is that not so Mr. Green?"

"Yes, I s'pose so."

"And is she not already, well, ah, so to speak . . ."

"You mean ruined? Several times over, I 'spect."

"And is not their affair widely known in the village?"

"Jest like Sal to make a spectacle of herself."

"Then, Mr. Green, I do not see any reasonable alternative than to marry the pair."

There was a pause. Kitty could almost see the farmer stroking his chin and thinking.

"My wife won't like it," Mr. Green said at last.

"But she would dislike even more a ruined daughter who is the laughingstock of the neighborhood. Am I not correct?"

"I'll talk to her."

Kitty decided that Jack had enough concerns, and slipped away down the corridor and back outside. She did not know which of the Three had compromised Sal, but Jack did not need the tonic sales pointed out to him at the moment. He would learn about them soon enough.

As she stood on the terrace of the Hall and looked across the lawn at the tents with their flags waving in the breeze, the crowds of festive people, she felt a curious loneliness. Of everyone here, she did not fit in. In a few months she would be far away living a completely different kind of life.

So would Jack. He might well be back in Portugal by Christmas if he continued to improve at the present rate.

Before she succumbed to tears, Kitty went back outside to watch the tug-of-war, the most highly anticipated event for most of the neighborhood. Several teams had formed after the fête was announced. It was an old custom at Charsley, but no one could remember just how the teams were made, so groups put together their own. A number of the grooms, a few footmen and the estate blacksmith were acting in the name of the Hall.

"Do not be foolish, Char," the dowager had said when he declared his intention of joining the team. "It is bad enough that we will have the lawns torn up without you making a cake of yourself."

But as far as Kitty observed, everyone else thought of the

tug-of-war only with excitement. Here were children and wives cheering, and the grandfathers had formed a betting pool.

As the afternoon wore on, the contest narrowed down to two final teams. To Kitty's surprise, one of them was the group from the Hall, including Char. In fact, his presence seemed to be a stimulus to the other men, as they managed to drag the other final team closer and closer to the crucial mark. Bea yelled with the other women, restrained only by her mother's steady hand.

When, with a final heave, the Charsley team towed the others across, Kitty found herself jumping up and down in glee. The victorious team hoisted Char to their shoulders and paraded through the crowd. As she followed them, holding Bea's hand, Kitty saw Jack shaking a finger in Tommy's face. Whether the subject matter was the tonic sale or the bride-to-be, Kitty could not tell.

Though not a single woman in the area had neglected to bake a pie or two, the stars of the crowning feast were the cartloads of oysters brought from Whitstable, the first of the season and a cherished delicacy long favored by the local folk and gentry alike. When Kitty and Bea left the fête to change for dinner at the Hall, even Bea had dared to try one cooked on the open fire outside, where lines of people clamored for their share.

It was almost time for the concert when Mr. Driver, his mother on his arm, offered effusive congratulations to Kitty. "A most excellent dinner, Miss Stone, far beyond what any of us could possibly have expected. To bring in the freshest oysters and the specially smoked hams! The dishes were indescribable. Ah, the buttered oysters!"

How Kitty wished that were true. But he went on.

"The butter here at Charsley is superior and greatly complements all the dishes. It is said to be the result of very superior grasses in this part of Kent, which in turn is the result of superior soil. Of course Mama is particularly partial to the creamed oysters, is that not true, Mama?"

Mrs. Driver nodded.

"She has a most discriminating palate, Mama has, and she loves the squabs too, is that not correct, Mama?"

To Kitty's relief, the major strode up and made a bow to Mrs. Driver and to Kitty. "I beg your pardon, Miss Stone, I have need of your counsel on an urgent matter regarding the concert."

"Oh, by all means, do take her off to insure a perfect completion of our very finest fête." Mr. Driver completed his statement with a sweeping bow.

Kitty was halfway across the room before she realized Jack was only pretending. "Major, you are being so very rude," she said with a smile. "Poor Mrs. Driver."

"That man Drivel is amazing. He can make a simple statement of thanks into a lecture."

"Or a compliment to the cook into a list of ingredients and their sources. I do thank you, however, for extracting me from an awkward situation. It is almost impossible to get away from Mr. Driver once he starts to talk."

"So I have noticed."

"Did Her Grace enjoy the oysters?"

"As much as she enjoys anything. When we get to the bottom of this mystery, Kitty, I think we will find that all her afflictions stem from a broken heart."

Kitty sat beside her mother in the second row to hear the singers Char brought from London. Though she had spoken with a number of the guests at dinner and entering the music room, she still felt as though most of her mind remained far away from the festivities. The same ideas chased each other around in her brain, occupying more of her attention than anything going on before them on the little stage. If the dowager moved away . . . if Char took over the reins of the estate . . . if Jack helped him become a presence in London circles . . . it all came down to whether Jack would stay in England. And he had never mentioned that he would consider that possibility.

Not until her mother elbowed her to join in the applause did she realize the program was well underway.

She tried to keep her attention on the singers, all three

from Italy, a man and two females, dressed in elaborate costumes. The orchestra of eight musicians played a rather long introduction during which the three pantomimed a lover's quarrel. Eventually one of the ladies sang a mournful farewell to her lover, and the other two joined in a rapturous duet.

When the applause began again, Lady Dunmark leaned close to Kitty. "Are they not wonderful?"

"Yes, Mama. Quite superior."

But when the music resumed, Kitty found her thoughts drifting away again. Jack, who was somewhere in this very room, saw the world quite differently than she did. And sometimes, his self-sacrifice made Kitty feel selfish and petty. He was talking about the very survival of England and its way of life in the face of Napoleon's conquests. She tended to think merely of the happiness of her mother and sister. The ironic thing was that Jack probably did more for the welfare of the British army in Portugal by staying here and keeping the issues in the forefront of political maneuvering. But he burned with the desire to fight again with Wellesley.

Again she applauded when she saw her mother begin to clap, but she could not have claimed to hear anything but some background accompaniment to her tortured thoughts.

Kitty would never have predicted two months ago when they arrived at Charsley Hall that her days would have been so filled with activities that she had no time to embroider caps for Bea's baby. She had expected to ration out each day to keep herself from becoming bored to flinders. A morning ride, a session practicing on her harp or the pianoforte, a little reading and then many hours stitching with Mama and Bea. Instead she had arranged a cottage, decorated an old mansion, helped to plan a fête for the entire neighborhood, taught a young girl, and abetted her mother's efforts to make Bea into a proper duchess. And in her head she had a scheme, so far unmentioned to the gentleman, of restoring the major's parterre garden outside the windows of the main rooms of Nether Acker.

But never very far from her mind was her plan for her

eventual departure from Charsley Hall to establish her own independent life. For the moment, she lived as a guest of her sister, like her mother. And she knew that no one expected her to harbor ideas of changing her circumstances.

But she had to go. She did not want to live at the Hall indefinitely. Nor did she want to entertain a courtship by Mr. Driver. Or anyone else.

Especially Major Jack Whitaker. There was the real danger, the danger to her heart and soul. She liked him far too much. When she was near him, her entire body betrayed her, attuned to his every word, his every move.

She feared the pain of heartbreak, a condition she had carefully avoided for her twenty-two years. There was no way around it: getting closer to Jack Whitaker certainly meant heartbreak, whether it came from yearning for his love or from waiting for word after each battle in a distant land.

She was already on the verge of hurting herself by thinking far too much about him. That he moved her more than any man ever had, that he made her want to melt into his arms whenever he was near, that he caused her to imagine the most intimate of loving acts . . . all those things gave her cause to throw caution aside and flee.

Not that she had any place to go. She had only a few shillings in her reticule. She had a string of pearls, some ruby earrings and a few gowns she could sell, but they would bring only enough to last a few weeks. She could seek a position as a governess or a companion, neither of which brought her a swell of eager anticipation. A better option might be to find a school needing a teacher of music for very young students. Kitty knew the limits of her abilities, but she also knew she had a bright mind and might be able to augment her limits by teaching geography or history. At a school, her connection as the sister of a duchess might appeal to a proprietress.

As soon as the fête was over, perhaps tomorrow, she would find time to write to a few schools, perhaps in Bath where there were a number of female academies.

FOURTEEN

Outside the breakfast room, Char pulled Jack aside and spoke into his ear. "I need your help."

"Anything, Char."

"Can you put up Maestro Salsini for a few days? I have engaged him as a singing teacher for all of us, and I am hoping he can stay at Nether Acker with you."

Jack was not sure he had heard his cousin correctly. "Salsini is staying here, but you want him at my place. And what is he staying for?"

"Mama is always carping about how we need to do better at singing, so I talked to the fellow and he will stay here and give us some pointers. All of us."

Jack had all he could do to keep from laughing out loud. "Did Aunt Adelina put you up to this?"

"Of course not. She won't like this idea any better than the others I've put forth, Jack. You know that."

"Where is he now?"

"I put them up at the Red Lion, but I cannot expect him to stay there while he is teaching us."

"Why not?"

"It is too far away. Someone will have to run him back and forth."

Jack shook his head. "I have only one bedroom fit to be used in my house and that is mine. I could put him up in the stables, but he would have to share the space with my three men, the ones who keep causing so much trouble around here. They are fixing up another wing of the house, but to say they are indifferent workers is to give their abilities a compliment it does not deserve."

"You mean you have no place for Salsini?"

"Not unless you think he could put up with Bart, Tommy and Yates."

Char shook his head. "That would never do. But now I am in a terrible fix."

"You have miles of corridors with bedrooms on either side in the Hall. Use one of those."

"But what will Mama say?"

"Char, I am losing all patience with you. You are the duke. You have just staged a successful fête for your whole neighborhood. Every one of your servants is paid in your name, and every one of them would be loyal to you if you let them. With the possible exception of Mrs. Wells, who might think she was betraying your mother by following your instructions."

"But what could I say to them? They rely on Mama for all their instructions."

"Then now is the time to change all that. I will go with you."

Char actually wrung his hands as they walked to the Hall and summoned the head servants to the morning room.

Jack whispered to him as the butler approached, "Just be firm and say what you want."

"You called for me, Your Grace," Randall said.

Mrs. Wells hurried along behind him, a look of surprise on her face.

"I, er, I want you to prepare a room for Signor Salsini, the singer. He will be staying a few days . . . er, at least a week."

Mrs. Wells made a crooked curtsy. "But, Your Grace,

none of the rooms are ready for more guests. I will have to consult with the dowager duchess."

"Yes, er, I see."

Jack gave Char a poke.

Char cleared his throat. "That will not be necessary, Mrs. Wells. And Randall, please see that footmen are available to help if they are needed to prepare the room."

Mrs. Wells frowned, but apparently she would not directly disobey the duke.

Char cleared his throat. "You had better get started."

Jack spoke for the first time. "We should go along to your mother's rooms, now, Charsley."

"Thank you, Your Grace." Both servants bowed again and left.

"But I was hoping to avoid—"

"We will not be asking her, Char. We will be politely informing her of your decision."

To Jack's great satisfaction, the dowager did not object, though she was clearly displeased. He hoped Char was learning that he could succeed when he was firm with his mother and allowed no questioning of his authority with the servants.

Later, he found Kitty playing her harp in the cottage. "A singing teacher!" Jack spat out the words as if they were bitter in his mouth. He shook his head, paced across the room, turned to her and raised his hands and almost started to speak, then dropped them and slumped into a chair in silence.

Kitty waited a few moments to see if he would elaborate on his statement, but eventually he sat, with exasperation in his expression, and gave a tiny shrug.

"You do not want singing lessons, I take it?" she asked.

"Ha! Hardly. But that is not the problem."

Kitty felt sure she knew why Jack was so upset. Perhaps by telling her, however, his irritation might be blunted and begin to fade. "I do not see what has you upset, Major, unless you do not want the maestro's advice."

"Oh, the devil with him. It is Charsley, not that Neapolitan wine merchant." Jack absently massaged his knee, a clear indication his mind was far away.

"But the duke only wants to please all of us."

"And that, Miss Stone, is exactly the point. He is not looking beyond the mundane, the silly little concerns of . . . of . . ."

"Of my sister? Of the dowager?"

Jack stood and after initially favoring his sore knee, paced firmly across the room and back. "Yes. Between preparations for the festival and now singing lessons, he hardly pays any attention to—" He stopped and let his gestures express the frustration he felt.

"You must be very displeased that he is not interested in your concerns."

"Exactly! It would take little of his time, just a few days next month, then an occasional visit to London."

"What exactly do you want him to do? Speak in the Lords?"

"Precisely."

Kitty blinked in surprise.

Jack shook a finger at her. "He is quite capable of it, you know. The way his mother treats him sometimes, you might think he was . . . excuse me, Kitty. I did not mean to draw you into this again."

"Jack, you are quite right about Char. I understand the importance of what you ask from him, but let me ask you this. Of what value is it to have a man do your bidding when he is distracted by concerns of his wife—or his mother—or more precisely of the two ladies not getting along well together? Of what value could it be to have a man whose home life was in disarray try to suggest ways out of international difficulties?"

"But if what you infer is even partially true, how could most of the men involved in government do their work? I rarely meet anyone who is perfectly content with his arrangements at home."

"Precisely. That is exactly what I mean. It is no wonder our affairs are a bumblebroth."

Jack looked at her quizzically, then broke into laughter. "I think you may have the right of it, Kitty. Indeed you might."

She smiled at his agreement. "I had a thought after the success of the fête yesterday. Once Bea has her baby, she will want to be presented to the Queen. Perhaps even reside in London for part of the Season."

Jack nodded. "Go on. This could be quite promising."

"Young women enjoy balls. They like to dance. And even give parties themselves. And one needs to invite guests to have a party."

Jack broke into a broad smile. "Tell me more."

"Oh, the youthful Duchess of Charsley will not become a great political hostess in a few weeks. But if you want to entice Char to London, she might be your ally, not your foe."

Jack pulled Kitty up from her stool and wrapped his arms around her. "And all this time, I have been praising Sir Arthur for his strategic thinking. I did not realize how clever you are, Kitty."

"Pooh. Far from it, Major."

"We long ago agreed to Jack and Kitty."

"But when you have your arms around me, I find myself worried about—"

He brushed his lips across hers, effectively putting an end to her words.

Despite Jack's misgivings, Char insisted they all meet with Maestro Salsini two hours before dinner. Char had informed his mother they would be having lessons and if the noise bothered her, he would gladly call for a carriage to take her for an airing.

Bea came reluctantly, sure the Italian teacher would find her voice too thin or too warbly.

"You have listened too much to the dowager," Kitty said.

"I hope you are right."

"And she achieves her purpose by making you nervous, and then you are shakier than ever." Though Kitty would have loved to assure Bea her own home here at Charsley Hall would someday be rid of the dowager's pall, she could not. She and Jack had pledged not to reveal their discovery of the dowager's old letters. But Kitty sincerely hoped that somehow, the dowager would be gone from Charsley soon.

Signor Salsini carried a large velvet box of music. He took out a few sheets and distributed them to Kitty, Bea, Char and Jack.

"This is a very simple little song we will all sing together." He sat at the pianoforte and played it through, then asked them to sing, nothing special. "Just let your voices be natural."

"I am not interested in learning to sing for the stage."

"Of course not, Signor. I do not teach you for the opera. For if you and your friends were to attract a big audience, what would be left for my friends, we poor refugees from Italia? No, I want to help you sing a little better when you are with your friends."

Jack gave a little shrug.

Char cleared his throat. "But do we not need to warm up, sing scales or something?"

"Your Grace, this is how I like to warm up, with little songs. Scales are so very boring, though good to learn breath control."

Kitty decided the man must know what he was talking about. And amazingly, the hour went quickly, with praise for all participants. She learned quite a bit more about her lungs than she had ever known. And how breathing properly and deeply gave more power to her voice.

She noticed her mother had slipped in while they were singing and watched the lesson from across the room. When the group broke up to prepare for dinner, Lady Dunmark lingered behind to talk to Maestro Salsini.

* * *

Jack went to the dowager's apartment to share a glass of wine before dinner. Now that he had read her letters to her lover, he was amazed she had not put up more of a fight to keep them out of the cottage. It must have been her love nest. She certainly could not have known the letters were there and after many years, she apparently thought her secrets were safe—or at least would not be revealed by anything in the cottage.

As usual when he entered, she was bent over a case, polishing her miniatures, studying and rearranging them.

"Good evening, Aunt Adelina." He made his formal bow to her, noting with satisfaction the lessening of the aches in his side. Every day, he was regaining strength and overcoming pain.

"Jack, you are looking well."

"Thank you, I am improving steadily."

"Will you pour us a glass of sherry?"

He lifted the heavy crystal decanter and filled two small glasses. As far as he knew, she never drank more than one before dinner.

"I trust the singing lesson did not disturb you." He handed a glass to her and took a sip from his.

"I was not pleased, but no one cares about my feelings any more."

Jack strolled over to look at one of her cases of miniatures. "Where is the one I brought you from Lisbon? I never thought to ask if it was of any worth." He peered more closely at each small and carefully framed face.

"It is here, Jack, in this case beside my chair. I have sent for a book from London which might tell us more."

Jack leaned over and squinted at the case's contents. "Ah, yes, there she is."

"I have studied the signature on the rear and I think the artist is French, from the sixteenth century."

Jack's eye stopped on a man's face in the far corner of the case. He looked familiar.

"There were a number of very fine painters at the court . . ."

Why, Jack thought, that looks very much like my Uncle Joshua. "Aunt Adelina," he began, then paused. Uncle Joshua?

"I may have another example from an artist Mr. Bronson told me was . . ." She went on, oblivious to his confusion. Good Lord, Jack thought, Uncle Joshua Cannon, brother of the long dead Madeline, Jack's mother, had certainly been here, or over at Nether Acker, for quite a long time after Jack's father died. He made all the arrangements, handled estate matters, closed up the house according to Jack's wishes while he had been abroad with the troops. Uncle Joshua and Aunt Adelina?

". . . hope to learn more if my man ever locates a copy of that book."

He stole another glance at the miniature. No doubt about it. That was the face of Joshua Cannon. "Why, yes, the information would be most valuable. I hope it turns out exactly as you wish."

"You are always—well, almost always—exactly true to my wishes, Jack." She took a last sip of her sherry and set down the glass.

As Jack tucked her hand under his arm, he took a surreptitious glance at her face. Yes, he thought, it was possible, even probable the rose cottage had been the site of lovers' trysts between the Duchess of Charsley and Joshua Cannon, his uncle, who had used his urgent business interests as an excuse not to visit Jack since he returned from Portugal. Jack could not wait to talk about it with Kitty.

Kitty expected dinner to be a quiet affair after all the excitement of the previous day, but she had not reckoned with the presence of Maestro Salsini.

He exclaimed over every dish, described how various foods and wines affected one's vocal abilities, and kept them laughing with his stories highlighted by a charming melange of Italian and English words.

Kitty was surprised to see her mother gazing at the maestro with soft and melting eyes. She thought that initial attraction would have worn off overnight.

"The red wine, it is bene . . . bene . . . beneficial to the voice." His mixture of Italian with English delighted them all, other than the dowager. He was handsome, not particularly tall, but well built, with dark hair and flashing white teeth. He seemed to be of middle age, though when he sang, he sounded youthful.

The dowager retired immediately after the meal, without explanation, but she had shown her disapproval of the Italian guest, which was no surprise to Kitty.

Lady Dunmark moved to an empty sofa when the men came into the drawing room, and the maestro immediately sat down beside her.

Kitty whispered in her sister's ear. "Psst, Bea. Have you noticed Mama?"

"Why, of course I have noticed her, Kitty."

"I mean how she and Signor Salsini—"

"Is that not sweet, Kitty? I think she has rather developed a *tendre* for him."

"Do you really?"

"She told me after he sang at the concert that she had never heard such an angel."

Bea moved off to play cards with Char.

Jack caught Kitty's eye and gave a little shake of his head. He stepped out of the room, and in a few moments, she followed, noticed by no one.

They met in the shadowed corridor well out of earshot of the others.

Jack grabbed both of her hands. "Kitty, I have discovered the identity of the dowager's lover."

Kitty drew in her breath with a sharp little gasp. "Who is it?"

"This is amazing. It is my Uncle Joshua, older brother of my mother. I saw his miniature in the dowager's collection, and it all became clear."

"Jack, tell me all about your uncle. This is fascinating."

"He has always been a bachelor, devoted to my mother when I was little. A solicitor who deals in imports and has numerous business connections. A most conscientious fellow." He gave a little laugh. "Though now I suspect he had more reasons to stay here and finish the details of my father's estate than just getting all the papers and finances in order."

Kitty nodded. "In my imagination, I can see them falling in love. She was a widow whose husband had not been true to her, he a lonely bachelor. They filled that little cottage with lovely furniture, and probably kept their romance a secret from most of the people in the neighborhood. But I do not understand why they ended it. If, as we suspect, she was already in an interesting condition, why did they not marry?"

Jack shook his head and shrugged. "Perhaps she did not know when she sent him away. Or he had told her of other plans he had, and she was afraid if she revealed her condition, he would reject her. Even in love, the dowager would want to have the upper hand."

"Yes, and she probably wanted to protect the interests of her son, the little Duke of Charsley."

"She is a proud woman, perhaps unwilling to foist her problems on anyone, even a man she loved. Though you know we may be jumping to conclusions about Mary's parentage. Is it possible that story about the carriage accident is true?"

In unison, they shook their heads in denial.

She pursed her lips. "We do not know if she ever told him about Mary."

"True. If she did, I would have thought a man like Uncle Joshua could never have abandoned his child or its mother. We have a bit of an enigma on our hands."

"Could you write to him? See what his feelings are?"

"Even better. I will go to visit him. Char and I are going to a houseparty in a week or so, to combine our political talks with the summer meet at the Greatapple racecourse. Before I go there, I will drive over to Bristol and see what Uncle Joshua has to say."

Kitty bit her lip. "Oh, Jack, that will be a difficult conversation."

"On the contrary, I expect it to be illuminating. After all these years, if he does not know about the child, he might even volunteer some information."

"How do people manage to make their lives so difficult?"

"Kitty, my dear, you and I are hardly immune." He took her in his arms and hugged her to him.

She pushed against his chest. "Jack, if anyone should see us—"

"Yes? If anyone sees us, we might have to become betrothed instantly."

She gave a little giggle. "Unless it is the dowager walking in her sleep. I cannot imagine she would ever believe you might embrace the likes of me." She stepped back, away from him. "Jack, I know you have a very different sort of relationship with the dowager, different then mine, or Bea's, or even Char's. Do you find her . . . well, ah . . . loveable? My perception is limited, I know, but she does not seem to be a woman of . . . er . . . passion, the kind of woman who fell into a—"

Jack broke into quiet laughter. "My dear Kitty, for centuries the poets have tried to define the qualities that lead to love, especially the sort of love that causes a person to lose his—or her—head."

Kitty joined in his laughter. "You are correct. I should not even try to speculate."

Jack moved closer again and took her hands in his, lifting them to his lips. "Perhaps instead of speculating, Kitty, we should let ourselves feel that wonderful emotion ourselves."

He kissed her hands again, then brought them around his waist, moving his arms to her shoulders, caressing the nape of her neck with one hand.

She leaned against him, murmuring, "I think I know what it is, Jack. Could that cottage be haunted by the shade of long-ago lovers who spread their happiness to every couple that enters?"

"Ah, Kitty, let me sample those lovely lips first, before I answer. You do not have to convince me, for I am sure it is some supernatural force that drives my feelings for you."

"Sh-h, Jack." She drew his head to hers and kissed his lips, like the soft touch of a feather at first, then with more force until his mouth opened over hers and their kisses deepened until they were breathless and trembling.

"What does it mean, Jack?"

"It means we want, we need each other, Kitty. We cannot turn away."

"But you are going away soon, Jack. I cannot wait for you . . . I could not give my love and then have to wait until the war ends." She gave a deep sigh. "But Jack, I could come with you. I know that—"

"Do not even mention it, Kitty. You have no idea what it is like to travel with the troops. And waiting in Lisbon is not any better. No, that is no solution."

She stepped away from him. "Good night, Jack."

"Good night, Kitty."

The aches he felt as he walked to his rooms had nothing to do with old wounds.

FIFTEEN

Jack drove a phaeton borrowed from Char's collection of carriages. He handled Char's team of dapple grays with gentleness, making sure they rested frequently. At a small coaching inn on the Bath road, he put up for the night and enjoyed sitting before the fire after dinner, listening to the conversation in the taproom.

A burly fellow with long hair harangued his companions on the need to back the navy, the pride of England, he said. It was after he rose to stomp to the bar for another tankard that Jack realized he had a wooden leg. But before the old tar could sit down again, another grizzled fellow shouted the praises of Wellesley. It warmed Jack's heart to hear the forthright support and he took out his notepad to jot down the particulars to send off to the general.

After a night's sleep, he drove on, his mind now occupied with the visit ahead. He had sent a note informing his uncle of his imminent arrival, but he still had not decided how to broach the subject of an old affair. It had seemed easy when he was back in Kent, near Kitty. But now he wondered just how a man asked another about such a matter.

He was surprised at the bustling streets of a prosperous Bristol. He had not been in the city since he was a child and he remembered little, only a busy waterfront crowded with boats of many sizes and shapes that had fascinated him. Just one stop for directions was needed before Jack pulled up in front of a large house set in elaborate gardens.

A footman must have been watching for he came out immediately, followed quickly by a groom to take the horses. Obviously Uncle Joshua was still wealthy and had a well-trained staff.

Joshua greeted him with a warm embrace. "How are you, my boy?"

"Improving markedly, Uncle Joshua. Every day I grow stronger."

"I am delighted to hear it—and to see you."

Joshua escorted Jack into his library and they settled in deep armchairs. "Now before you go upstairs, I want to hear all the particulars from Portugal, and your views on the conduct of the war."

Jack talked for half an hour, taking time out for an occasional sip of the finest claret he had ever tasted. Joshua listened intently without comment.

"And so," Jack concluded, "I intend to go back in a month or two."

"Hmmmm. You are determined, I suppose. It is a mark of all the Cannon men. Your mother had a dose of it too, you know, for though she was not strong, she had an iron will."

"I wish I had known her longer. Better."

"Her loss was a terrible blow to me, and to your father. But worse for you, my boy. Yet she would be proud of you and what you have made of yourself."

Jack took a larger swallow of the wine, pushing back the lump in his throat. "You know I have been recuperating at Charsley Hall, resting under the care of Aunt Adelina."

At the mention of her name, Joshua looked off into the distance. "Ah, yes. Is Her Grace in good health?" He continued to stare at nothing.

Jack plunged ahead. "I believe she misses you intensely."

Joshua's gaze turned abruptly to Jack and his voice grew gruff. "What do you know of that?"

"I found a packet of letters."

"What?" He started to rise from his chair, then sank back and covered his eyes with a hand. "Devil take it, I had almost convinced myself I had burned them, as I promised her. Where were they?"

"In a little cottage on the edge—"

"What the deuce! I never thought to look there. I promised Adelina I had thrown them on the fire, but deep down . . . I suppose she despises me."

"She does not know I found them."

He laid his head against the back of his chair and took a deep breath. "When she said she was going away, I thought she was going with someone, another man. But I never heard that she married."

"And you never tried to contact her again?"

"Never. I respected her wishes."

"But do you not wonder at her feelings, whether she still longs for you?"

"I do not dwell on my feelings, Jack."

"But this lovely house! It is almost as if you had it built for her."

"I did." Joshua raised a hand and gestured around him.

"Uncle Joshua, why do you not come to visit me? You can give me advice on rebuilding the old hulk at Nether Acker. It's been shut up since father's death, and I have just opened a few rooms in one wing."

"What do I know of fixing houses?"

"Probably far more than I do, if truth be told," Jack said. "If Aunt Adelina does not welcome you, you can stay away from her. She has become somewhat reclusive, but I know she still cherishes your miniature."

"I will think about it. I admit I have never stopped loving her. Never."

"I must go to Greatapple on the way home. I have

promised to try my hand at some political manipulation on behalf of Wellesley, something well beyond the creation of titles for him. But I will look forward to receiving you in two weeks or so."

"I will consider it, Jack."

"You must go to the Ruchester's houseparty, Kitty." Lady Dunmark sniffled delicately in her hankie. "I cannot imagine where I caught this chill, but I would be of no use to Beatrice like this."

Kitty blanched. Only last week had she turned down the invitation to accompany Char and Bea to their first house-party. Two of London's most insipid gossips would be there, Lady Pontarch and Lady Clarissa, both of whom had taken delight in asking Kitty over and over at every occasion how she was faring after the duke and Bea eloped. Both were annoyingly effusive on the subject of how admirably Kitty was holding up.

Kitty had survived one particularly horrendous encounter only by pasting a smile on her face while envisioning at least seven methods of causing Lady Clarissa to expire. The drowning scene had been particularly vivid, complete with a monstrous octopus waiting to drag Clarissa down to the depths and have her for lunch. As Kitty recalled, snakes and spiders had also figured in her secret schemes for the woman.

But now she would be with these two gossipmongers and a half dozen others just as catty for seven days of torture. She would also have to try to keep her impulsive and hen-witted sister from making error after error of propriety, which all the ladies would delight in spreading through the *ton*.

Bea implored her to go. "I cannot face it alone. If Mama is too ill, you must come, darling Kitty, or I shall give it up too."

"They will watch us like falcons circling in the sky over their prey, Bea, waiting to dive down for the kill. Every word we utter will be studied for an indication of trouble or envy.

If you so much as breathe a word of your frustration with the dowager, within days the *ton* will turn it into a contest to rival that of the Prince of Wales and his wife, Caroline of Brunswick."

"Char is already there with the horses he will enter in the Greatapple races. I want to go, but I cannot face it alone. I hate the thought of being the focus of their gossip. And I do not want anyone to know I am—ah—I am in a family way."

"But why not? Are you not excited?"

"Yes, of course I am thrilled. If I am careful to choose my fullest gowns, I do not think anyone will know."

Kitty thought nothing of the kind, for Bea's full figure looked decidedly rotund. "I predict everyone will suspect, Bea."

"Oh, no."

"Curiosity will make them try to ask, but we do not know any of the ladies very well. I think we can say nothing. Let them draw what conclusions they wish. If anyone asks me directly, I will say that is between you and the duke. If someone asks you, just smile sweetly and change the subject to the rain or the sunshine or whatever is happening outside."

"Yes. And Jack will be there, you know. He is off on some business or other and will meet us at Ruchester House."

Kitty sighed. If she saw Jack there, she would hear what he had learned from his uncle much faster. "If I go, Bea, we should have plans, pastimes to keep us occupied during the idle afternoons while the men are out doing whatever it is that they do. Fishing or billiards."

"But I thought they were going to the races. We all are."

"That will be only a few days. It is the rest of the time I am concerned about."

"What can we do, Kitty?"

"Perhaps we could take Lady Euphemia's dog. The pug, the one who wheezes and slobbers, so that no one will come near you."

Bea made a face. "I cannot bear that animal."

"Neither can I. So if not a dog, what?"

Lady Dunmark gave a sniffle. "You could always loosen the clasp on your bracelet and let it fall. But that will only work once or twice at the most."

Kitty cast a glance at her mother. Just how bad was that cold? "A sketchbook is good."

"But I cannot draw. If I sit and make little pictures, no one will recognize the subjects. They will laugh at me."

"We shall have to write a lot of letters. Pretend letters, perhaps."

Again, Lady Dunmark gave a little cough. "You must take along a needlework project, preferably one with many colored silks that you can untangle and retangle every day. Then you will never have to show off your stitches."

After the flurry of packing, Kitty was glad to settle back in the carriage the next day. Nell and the baggage followed the comfortable chaise in which Kitty had first arrived at Charsley Hall, a few months ago.

Bea looked out the window and idly twisted her fingers in the fringe of her reticule. "What do I say when someone asks me about you, Kitty? I am trying to think of the right things to say before I get tongue-tied."

"Bea, everyone knows the facts of the case. Char courted me for months and everyone expected he would propose marriage, including me. But I am glad he did not. I am glad he fell in love with you."

"You are?"

"Yes, because I would have married him. But we would never have been in love, not the kind of love you two share. You adore each other. I liked Char, and I was willing to marry him. But I knew he did not love me. And I was not in love with him."

"Will people not understand that?"

"Oh, Bea, no one expects us both to be happy with the situation. Either I am supposed to be prostrate with grief at having been jilted—almost—or you are supposed to be the sacrificial lamb who was carried off by the nasty duke. Or they will try to learn if we are in constant competition for the duke's attention."

"But that is ridiculous."

"Not in the eyes of the gossips and tittle-tattlers. They want to make it a scandal, and the more we say, the more they try to twist our words and make it into a very big thing."

Kitty took Bea's hand. "I found out what people are like in those months in London. Every place I went, people tried to give me counterfeit comfort, or pretended to sympathize, or tried to get me to say you and Char were positively evil. So I learned to say nothing. Whatever I said, people would misinterpret my words. But, we must face the truth. Many will try to get us to talk about the duke. If one of us frowns, they will have us in a spat, or worse."

Bea said nothing for a long time. Just when Kitty assumed her sister had fallen asleep, she sat up straight and spoke. "All right. I have thought of three things to say. One, my sister is a great help to me when I try to improve my skills at the pianoforte. Second, my sister is an excellent rider and knows more about the far reaches of the estate than either the duke or I do. And third, I depend upon my sister for advice about dealing with London society, for she is a perfect lady and knows just how to deflect remarks that verge upon the rude or improper."

"How I wish that were true," Kitty said.

"I will say my sister is an angel."

"Then, Bea, I should say my sister has the perfect disposition to be the duke's wife. They are exactly right for one another. I am far too sharp-edged, too cynical for him."

Bea's smile was wan. "Oh, Kitty, I fear I will be too nervous to say a word."

"Excellent. Just smile shyly and pretend not to understand."

When they arrived at Ruchester House, the housekeeper showed them to their rooms. Kitty's, done in fashionable shades of Nile green, had a huge feather bed with heavy brocade hangings.

"If I do not emerge some morning," she told Nell, "come in and dig me out for surely I will be smothering in all those pillows."

When they were refreshed and changed, they went to the Red Salon, where the ladies were gathered. Once the introductions were made, the explanation of Miss Stone's substitution for the Duchess's mother voiced, and the current activities of the gentlemen enumerated, Lady Ruchester conducted them on a short tour.

"Our little home is modest in comparison to what I hear about the magnificence of Charsley Hall." The Countess of Ruchester was pleasantly plump, nearing forty, it appeared, and seemingly quite self-satisfied in her role as the wife of an earl, Kitty thought, a lady of generosity with a measure of ambition.

"The house is baroque at the core, but has many features from the time of Anne, then two wings in the neo-classic style of sixty or seventy years ago." She led the way through ornately decorated salons, one leading into the next. Kitty almost gasped when she saw a pair of Van Dyke portraits in the East Parlor where the walls were paneled in golden oak.

When she saw Kitty stop and stare, the Countess made a sweeping gesture. "As you might imagine, the founders of the earl's family were supporters of the monarchy. Van Dyke did those portraits when the Baron Ruchester was rewarded with an earldom. If you look closely, both the old section of the house and the chapel bear the pockmarks of the Roundheads' bullets."

Kitty felt Bea give a little shudder.

When they returned to the Red Salon, Lady Clarissa sat beside Kitty.

"Why, Miss Stone, how very nice to see you. Have you been enjoying your visit to your sister's estate?"

Kitty could hear the real queries behind Lady Clarissa's words. Such as, *Do you find it difficult to share a residence with your former suitor and your sister?* But the woman gave voice only to the most innocuous of questions.

There were other little digs. To Bea, Lady Clarissa exhibited her most simpering smile. "You must enjoy living at Charsley Hall. I hear it is a showpiece of furniture and art from the last century. Not that it is out of date, I do not mean to infer any such thing."

Oh no, Kitty wanted to say. *We are quite up to date at Charsley Hall. Why, we have a wilderness with a hermitage in the garden. And I am the hermit!* But she smiled and said nothing.

Bea did not change expression. "Mr. Adam's designs are exquisite. I would never think to change a thing and risk marring his perfection."

Kitty patted Bea's hand. She was definitely going to rise to this occasion.

Over the next two days, the gentlemen went from the fishing streams to watching the grooms exercise the horses to the billiard room. The ladies spent most of their time sitting together, and only by inventing a sisterly tournament of dominoes did Kitty and Bea manage to pass the time without participating in endless gossip in which the other ladies eagerly indulged.

But eventually, the inevitable moment arrived when Lady Clarissa trapped Kitty alone in the garden. She took a seat on the opposite bench. "Is it not close this afternoon, Miss Stone?"

"I have found it quite cool and comfortable here in the shade," Kitty said.

Lady Clarissa took out her fan and waved it before her face. "I prefer the cooler months, but my Charles would insist on bringing his new filly to try out."

"I wish them the best of fortune."

"Thank you, I am sure she will perform well, but I certainly hope a fortune is not involved. Charles is usually a cautious bettor, thank heavens." She continued to fan herself.

Kitty glanced down at her book, but considered it too rude to resume reading while Lady Clarissa was present.

Eventually, Lady Clarissa posed the subject Kitty had been expecting. "How very, er, unusual it is for a sister to reside with . . . well, I do not mean to pry."

Yes, you do, Kitty wanted to say. *You want me to say something shocking about Char or my sister, something that you can run to your friends and repeat.* Instead she forced a smile. "No, I imagine everyone is curious, but we find it quite comfortable for the time being."

Lady Clarissa said nothing, obviously waiting for more details, but Kitty remained silent.

Eventually, Lady Clarissa rose. "I think I will go dangle my fingers in the fountain. Mayhap that will cool me."

"What a very good idea." Kitty said. "If I find the heat oppressive, I shall do the same."

When Lady Clarissa had gone, Kitty gave a big sigh. It was so aggravating to hold back when what she really wished to do was tell the woman that some things were none of her business. But she could do that only inside her head.

Before dinner, Kitty sat near Bea, on the satin cushions of a wide sofa. Lady Clarissa seated herself on Bea's other side, a sly smile on her face—the smile of a predatory fox viewing a plump hen entirely unaware of danger lurking.

"Duchess, you are looking very much a happy bride."

"I am that," Bea said, wrapping a bright blue strand of silk around a small spindle.

Kitty kept her eyes on the page of *La Belle Assemblée*, an article, appropriately enough about the elopement of two members of prominent London families, the Pagets and the Wellesleys, thinly disguised with names from mythological legends for the publication. Only that morning, she had overheard a vociferous discussion of the scandal. But at the moment, Kitty had to strain to hear Lady Clarissa's soft tones.

"What are you working on, Duchess, if I may be so bold as to inquire?"

"Oh, it is to be a garden, but like the blooms in a breeze, the colors get tangled."

"I am sure it will be perfectly lovely when it is finished."

"I have so little time to work on it." Bea gave a little giggle. "I am better at looking at flowers rather than trying to stitch them."

Lady Clarissa clasped a hand to her chest. "My dear, you are charmingly droll."

Bea went on. "I am particularly fond of roses. Though the primroses are always so welcome in the spring. They are also among my favorites."

"I see," Lady Clarissa said.

"And at Charsley Hall we have some very lovely tulip beds that I greatly admired. But they have all died back now. Is it not sad, Lady Clarissa? Flowers have such a very short life."

Kitty almost laughed out loud. Perhaps Beatrice would be better at the social game than either of them had anticipated.

"But they make up in beauty for their very short tenure on earth, do they not? I think of the roses, but I do try to save the petals and preserve their fragrance."

"How interesting," Lady Clarissa said.

But her voice did not sound as though she was the slightest bit interested, Kitty thought with considerable glee, silently urging Bea to continue in the same vein.

". . . and sometimes we add several kinds of roses together, the darker red with the pinks and some with small petals, and then I can also mix varieties. What are those long-stemmed flowers we like to pick, Kitty?"

Kitty feigned a lack of attention to the conversation. "I'm sorry, Bea. I was not listening—not really."

"Oh, it does not matter. I am afraid I was boring Lady Clarissa with my ramblings about flowers."

Good, Kitty thought. Now Lady Clarissa will be forced to

demur, although it was exactly what Bea was doing. On purpose.

"Why, Duchess, how could you think you were not fascinating me in your views?" Lady Clarissa replaced her hand over her heart.

Bea gave a very sweet sigh. "Just look at these silks. What in the world have I done to them, Kitty?"

Kitty moved closer to Bea and gave her a secret wink. "Let me see what I can do."

For the next few minutes, the sisters did little more than stir the silks around, having them neatly wound being the very last thing either of them wanted. When three other ladies entered the room, the conversation began again, and at last, Lady Clarissa moved away.

To the others, Bea only smiled and nodded, offering little. Kitty, too, uttered only pleasantries. She was more than willing to be labeled "mousey" than to take a chance of being either the subject of or the participant in gossip.

Kitty found she yearned for Jack's arrival, which came on the fourth day, just after the first visit to the races. Her first opportunity to speak to him came after dinner when Char and Bea were immersed in conversation about the exciting victory of one of Char's horses that afternoon.

Jack followed Kitty onto the terrace under a starry sky.

"I am bursting to know what your uncle said."

"He held back nothing, as far as I could tell. He is completely unaware of Mary's existence, but otherwise he was very open about the affair. Uncle Joshua is eager to see the dowager, once I assured him we would support his suit."

"His suit? You mean he wishes to court her, perhaps eventually marry her?"

"He has never stopped wanting to marry her."

"I am thunderstruck, Jack. It is beyond anything I imagined."

"Yes, I know it is hard to fathom. Indeed they used the rose cottage as their little love nest, and he has never forgotten a moment of their time together. He worships her."

"Tell me more about the conversation."

"At first he was shocked I had found the letters. Then he convinced himself it was fate having a hand in his future."

"And he said nothing about Mary?"

"Oh no. And I did not give even the slightest hint. When Aunt Adelina sent him away, he feared she had another lover. In my view, anything about Mary would be for the dowager to reveal, if she ever does."

"Of course. We could not interfere in such a matter."

"I suspect he has no idea of the child's existence."

A burst of laughter preceded the emergence of a half dozen people onto the terrace and ended the conversation between Jack and Kitty. But the possibilities it raised made Kitty's sleep particularly more comfortable that night.

SIXTEEN

The final morning of their visit to Ruchester House followed the high-stakes race at the Greatapple race course. Char was disappointed in his prize stallion's third place showing, but Bea had forgotten the horse's name and had her bet placed on the winner.

"All by accident," Bea assured Kitty as they walked into the gathering of the ladies in the morning room.

Mrs. Faspan was the eldest of all the guests, at least seventy years of age. She reached out and pulled Bea down next to her on the sofa.

"We have all been wondering, and I am the only one with the nerve to ask. I probably should not, for you will see me as rude and overbearing, but I must. Such inquiries are the responsibilities of the old ladies. The elderly, you know, are allowed to be more forward and to stand in for all the mealy-mouthed gels who are too terrified to state their questions."

Bea tried to rise and move away, but Mrs. Faspan had a tight hold on her wrist. "Tell me, Duchess, does your sister not regret—I should not go so far as to suggest resentment—your marriage to the duke? Was she not expecting an offer from him any moment when the two of you dashed off to the altar?"

Bea's eyes were wide, her expression shocked.

Kitty summoned her most docile expression. "Perhaps I might be allowed to answer Mrs. Faspan's question. As I told several people who wondered about this in London just after the duke and Bea were wed, the assumption that the duke was calling upon me with an eye toward making a match was erroneous from the start. Although I enjoyed his company, no seriousness of purpose was ever expressed, nor did I assume one."

"Wait, Kitty." Bea's voice had a ring of authority.

Kitty watched her sister stand and draw herself up to her full height, chin tipped upward, and eyes steely. Bea looked from Mrs. Faspan to Lady Clarissa to each lady in turn.

No one said a word until she again spoke with a regal bearing and a clear voice worthy of a duchess. "I have had quite enough of the whispers and the innuendo. What do you expect Kitty and me to say? What would satisfy those to whom you wish to spread your stories? What would you say to hearing that we all three climb into bed together?"

There was a quick gasp from several of the ladies, including Kitty.

Bea was not finished. "Is that falsehood shocking enough to satisfy your eager audiences? Would that make an appropriate *on dit* for your next dinner engagement?"

No one said a word, frozen into silence by Bea's righteous anger. She looked around the room once more, giving each lady present a straight, if momentary, stare.

"I do not wish to hear another word on the subject after this afternoon, nor do I expect to hear that any of you have engaged in further elaboration upon my remarks. My sister, Kitty, has always had gentlemen callers, one of whom was briefly the Duke of Charsley. But they found they did not suit. She has numerous other suitors and will probably take a rather long time to make up her mind to marry any one of them. I, on the other hand, fell in love with the first gentleman whose gaze happened to meet mine, after he and Kitty decided to go their separate ways. For me and for Charsley, love was sudden. My sister is a more careful and perhaps more discriminating lady."

Kitty wanted to jump up and applaud her sister, whose performance was stunningly effective.

After a few more moments of quiet, the others burst into voice. Of course they had known such was the case, that no one had broken a promise, that no one had been jilted, or was broken-hearted. How well they understood, how eager they were to quash any other stories, to set others to rights.

Mrs. Blake came to sit beside Kitty. "Your sister did herself proud, Miss Stone."

Kitty nodded. "Indeed she did. It may not be the end of the story, but I expect we will hear little more about it by autumn."

Bea was overflowing with self-praise for her confrontation with the ladies at Ruchester House when she returned home. Kitty watched her mother's reaction and found Lady Dunmark only partially listening to Bea's excited version.

Kitty placed her hand on her mother's arm. "Really, Mama, Bea was most courageous, speaking out so bravely."

"Is that so, dear?" Lady Dunmark smiled absently.

"Mama, I wish you had been there to see it," Bea gushed. "The looks on the faces of Lady Clarissa and Mrs. Faspan were wonderful, as if someone had dumped a bucket of wash water over their heads."

"I see." The smile on Mama's face was that of a contented woman not in the slightest concerned with her daughters' affairs.

Half an hour later, Kitty followed Bea to her boudoir. "Sister, dear, I suspect our mama has become involved with that Italian singer."

"Aha! I thought she was rather vague this morning, but . . . Maestro Salsini?"

"I daresay she would not admit it, but I suspected before

we left that she was not really ill, just did not want to go away. From him."

"My gracious, Kitty, you can not be serious. Mama? Playing with the truth, just as she always warned us not to do?"

"But where love, or should I say *amore*, is concerned—"

The sisters broke into whoops of laughter.

Kitty wiped her eyes with a lacey handkerchief. "Mama is certainly old enough to know her own mind, and if she is enjoying a dalliance, I do not have any objection."

"But what if people find out? Will she not be embarrassed?"

"If I needed to choose any place less likely to draw attention than Charsley Hall, I could not think of a place. Mama knows few ladies in the neighborhood."

"But what of the dowager? If she learns of a romance under the roof of her own house . . . could she not order Mama to go away?"

"I think it unlikely. I suspect Char's mother would not dare to approach Mama on a matter of the heart."

"I would not put anything past her."

"I believe Jack could deal with it."

"Oh, yes. Jack can do anything with her. And speaking of Jack, Kitty, what is your feeling about him? He seems to be paying you a great deal of attention."

Kitty held up a hand. "No, Bea, he is a fine gentleman, but his attentions are entirely focused on the war, getting healthy enough to return to Portugal, and in the meantime, building support for Wellesley's army. That was the real purpose of his visit to Ruchester House. Not to see the horse racing. And certainly not to spend time with me."

"Are you certain? I see him looking at you sometimes and I wonder."

"We are only friends, Bea, nothing more."

"You know, Kitty, that is exactly how Char and I, er, got started. We were friends. Oh, I should not even bring that up. I apologize."

"Do not fret, Bea. I do not mind."

* * *

Jack looked around the drawing room at Nether Acker and walked into the dining room. Kitty had done a fine job with her suggestions on moving the furniture about and removing the old draperies from the windows overlooking the formal garden. As the light faded and the candles were lit, the room would be even lovelier, the mellow paneling now rubbed to a soft shine with beeswax.

Uncle Joshua joined him in looking around the two rooms. "This is a fine old house, Jack. Shame to have had it shut up so long."

"Yes, you are correct. But there has to be someone to live here. Otherwise why keep it open?"

"True."

"Perhaps it is just the place for you and the dowager?"

"Talk about rushing your fences, m'boy. I have not even seen her yet."

They heard the carriage wheels crunching the newly raked gravel and listened to Baldwin escort Aunt Adelina and the others into the drawing room.

Jack kept his eyes on the dowager's face when she saw her old lover. Unless he was completely mistaken, a watery brightness filled her eyes as she clasped a hand to her bosom. "Joshua," she breathed.

The others, not knowing what an important moment was occurring, moved past her into the room, exclaiming about the furniture, the look of settled comfort.

Jack listened with less than half an ear to their praise, reserving his attention for the dowager and his uncle. Joshua stepped forward, seized her hand and lifted it to his lips. "Adelina, you are as lovely as ever."

Strangely, Jack thought, she did look lovely, the sour expression she usually wore replaced by an eager smile and high color.

Bea had pulled her mother and Kitty over to the paneling, which they admired enthusiastically.

Bea trilled her admiration. "I love old wood. So very Elizabethan."

Lady Dunmark was not to be outdone. "Distinguished, I call it. Only in the finest, most venerable homes. And families."

Kitty smiled indulgently, brushing off their exclamations of how cleverly she had supervised its cleaning and restoration. "It was merely beeswax and lots of polishing."

Char was as startled as his wife at the transformation of the setting. "Think you might do well without many changes. Good room as it is. Changes not necessary."

Baldwin offered a tray of glasses of sherry. The dowager took one without taking her eyes from Joshua.

Jack saw Kitty surreptitiously smile as she watched the dowager and Uncle Joshua. They managed, after a few sips of sherry, to enter the general conversation, all the while exchanging melting glances. Lady Dunmark had not noticed. Nor had Bea and Char. To think they might be aware of anyone else seemed beyond consideration.

While Lady Dunmark and Bea admired the painting above the fireplace, Mr. Cannon whispered a few words to the dowager, and the expressions on her face ranged over a variety of emotions, surprise, adoration, struggle for control.

Char broke into the couple's whispered conversation. "Mama, and Mr. Cannon, I want you to see the portrait I discovered in Jack's attics, a picture of our ancestor, Lady Anne, who married the first duke of Charsley. Do you think there is any family resemblance? You know," he continued speaking rapidly and in an excited voice, "I was the one who found this, when Jack and I and Miss Stone were upstairs looking through old trunks—"

The dowager was glassy-eyed, too stunned to make much response. "That was nice, Charsley," she murmured.

"I say, you made a valuable find," Mr. Cannon said.

When dinner was announced, they walked into the dining room informally, with the dowager taking Jack's arm and sitting beside him. Mr. Cannon took the place at the other side.

Lady Dunmark pulled Kitty aside. "What has come over the dowager? Is she not well?"

"I did not notice anything," Kitty fibbed.

"Open your eyes, my dear. I think she is about to have palpitations."

"Do not concern yourself, Mama. I think she is fine." And when they took their places at the table, Kitty looked closely at the dowager who had a beatific smile on her face, then nodded to her mother, who shrugged as if to say she must have been mistaken.

The dinner conversation centered on Jack's accomplishments at Nether Acker, but the dowager said hardly a word. Instead of her usual references to the shortcomings of those in her family, she smiled and nodded as if she had been struck by a sudden mood-altering sunbeam of happiness.

After dinner, Jack suggested a promenade around the grounds, which he had lit with flambeaux to show the way among the newly sheared yews and past the work in progress at the rose garden.

Here he stopped and waited until they all had caught up and were gathered around him. "As you can see, it will take a season or two more to make this a creditable display. However, I found something very interesting." He gave a little whistle and in the distant darkness several more torches came into flame, lighting a white marble statue on a back plinth.

"Oh," Bea cried. "That is lovely, Jack."

"Yes, Duchess, and I have you and Char to thank for finding it." He turned to the others. "They spotted it deep among the twisted vines and overgrown branches. We have decided it must be Venus, or Aphrodite, if you prefer her Greek name. The man from London who came out to clean it said he thought it was well over a hundred years old, so we thought perhaps it was a gift from the first duke to Lady Anne who grew up here and brought all this property into our family."

As they walked back to the house, Kitty tried to see that

the others allowed the dowager and Mr. Cannon to fall back and speak only to each other.

After they had their tea and the gentlemen had gone out on the terrace to smoke, the party for the Hall prepared to depart.

Jack and Mr. Cannon waved them off, but not before Kitty spied a last little wink for the dowager from Mr. Cannon. Could they have been making plans to meet later? Where would it be?

In the carriage, Bea praised the beauty of the house and the excellence of the dinner.

Lady Dunmark whispered in Kitty's ear. "It would have been much nicer if Jack had invited Maestro Salsini."

Kitty had to press her hand to her mouth to keep from giggling.

Just a few days later, Jack and his uncle talked over breakfast. "You and Aunt Adelina should spend your lives together. You say you still love her. She is lonely and—"

"Yes, but Adelina is troubled by her situation. She is devoted to Char and to her coming grandchild, but she fears the estate will not prosper if Char takes over its supervision. She says he does not have a head for practicalities."

Jack chose his words carefully. "Naturally I respect her views, but I think she underestimates her son. Char is a poet, a dreamer much of the time. But he has the capacity to learn, to grow into his role."

"Are you saying that Adelina has kept him on too tight a rein?"

"My observations would confirm such a possibility."

"I thought as much. She is a compassionate woman, but—" He paused.

Jack almost laughed out loud. Compassionate was one of the last terms he would apply to the dowager. But then Uncle Joshua was looking at her through loving eyes, was he not?

"Adelina has a strong sense of history, of her duty to her husband's family. Though I sometimes wonder why. He was not a good husband. The seventh duke kept mistresses in town and lavished his attention on them, while Adelina was left behind here at Charsley."

"I hope neither of you tell Char," Jack said, "for I do not know how he would take to hearing criticism of his father."

"Ah, no, of course I would not say this to Charsley. Neither would Adelina. Poor lad. If he had more of his father's attention, he might have . . . oh, well, why speculate?"

"Yes, it accomplishes nothing to try to recast the events of many years ago. You should be looking to the future."

"I have a fine house in Bristol, a handsome fortune stashed away, and I want to take Adelina there to live. And I want to take her to see the continent once the wars end. She has never been to the Alps or to Italy."

"I applaud your plans, Uncle. But you do not mean to tell me the dowager is resisting such an offer?"

"Not resisting, precisely, but worrying about how Char will manage without her."

Jack nodded, but thought that it might be the best thing that ever happened to his cousin.

Joshua went on. "You see, the only decision Char has made without Adelina was to marry Beatrice and, needless to say, that was not a decision of which Adelina approved."

Indeed, Jack wondered how it had happened at all. How had the dowager let him spend so much time in London, to allow him to court Kitty, then run off with Bea?

"So I have a proposition to you, Jack. I know you intend to return to Wellesley and the army in the Peninsula."

"Yes. It is my hope to go soon."

"But I also take it that Wellesley wants you here, working on his behalf. Is that not correct?"

"Sir Arthur seeks the support of many men, not just me."

"Then why do you not respect his requests? Take an active role in the government? You are in an ideal place to stand for Commons. I have some influence over a seat from Bristol, if you agree."

Jack sighed. It was the third seat he had been offered, safe seats, any one of which would give him an excellent position from which to persuade others—but what was he thinking? He was a soldier, not a man of politics.

"I can see that you are not going to agree to my request without more consideration, Jack. But keep it in mind. And if you were here, close by, I do believe the dowager would be much more likely to fulfill my wishes." He paused and a smile spread across his face. "Yes, much more likely indeed."

With his astonishment showing in his voice, Win informed Jack that the dowager duchess had arrived at Nether Acker alone in her coach. "She awaits you in the drawing room."

Jack was as surprised as his batman. He could never remember Aunt Adelina coming to him instead of summoning him to her.

He was equally surprised to see her dressed in a gown of pale pink and looking so fresh. "Aunt Adelina, you look pretty as a picture."

"Thank you. Joshua tells me you are responsible for bringing him back to me, Jack."

"He did not take much convincing. He admitted he had never stopped loving you."

"Nor had I ended my love for him."

"Aunt Adelina, I regret to tell you that Joshua has gone into Canterbury on some business matter."

"I know. I almost went along. But I need to speak to you in confidence, Jack."

She stood and walked to the window, taking a handkerchief from her reticule. "There are complications. Complications that could stand in the way of Joshua's—and my—desire to be together for the rest of our lives."

Jack watched her peer out the window at the soft mist rising from the river. "Few complications cannot be overcome."

"That is why I need your advice, Jack. First there is Charsley. I worry about leaving him to—to tend to the estate. I have done a poor job of training him."

"Aunt Adelina!" Jack spoke decisively. "Char is entirely able to run his estate. He will do what is needed in his own way, but he is certainly up to the responsibility."

She shook her head. "I wish I agreed with you. He needs someone who will be a strong adviser, Jack. If you are here at Nether Acker, he can count on you. But if you are gone—"

"You have excellent advisers, Aunt Adelina. And they will be here for Char, too. And I can write to him from wherever I am."

"But that is not the worst problem." She drew a shuddering breath. "Oh, Jack, I have a terrible confession to make, and I cannot bring myself to do it."

Jack realized with a start that he had never seen her in tears before. He went to her and led her to a sofa. "Here, dear aunt, please sit and dry your eyes."

"But what I have done is unforgivable, Jack. Beyond redemption, I fear."

He patted her shoulder and waited.

"You see, when Joshua and I were so in love, Charsley was barely fourteen, at such an impressionable age. I could not . . ." She paused and looked at Jack with tears rolling down her cheeks.

"Go on."

The story poured out of her, the love affair, the secret pregnancy, the banishment of Joshua, the trip abroad, the birth of Mary, the story of her non-existent parents. "I was wrong to lie, Jack, but once I started, I could not stop."

"Why did you not tell Joshua then and marry him?"

"I should have. But I was thinking of Charsley, and how he needed me."

Jack listened as she berated herself, a litany of self-reproach.

"And now," she said, "even now, I cannot bring myself to tell him we have a daughter. I am all mixed up inside."

"Aunt Adelina, nothing you have done is unforgivable. Uncle Joshua will be delighted he has a child."

"But how can I tell him what I have done? Will he not despise me for keeping it a secret? I have lied to her for her entire lifetime."

"I know you love the child, Aunt Adelina. I, too, want the best for her, just as you do. Could you not wait a few more months before you tell her, before you tell Joshua? Once the two of you have married and lived together as man and wife, you can tell him in a way that will bring him great joy. In the meantime, Mary can stay at Charsley Hall with Miss Munstead. She already is excited about the duke's coming child. And the duchess will love having her around to amuse the baby. Miss Stone is quite attached to Mary, you know."

"I should not abandon her."

"But you will not be all that far away. She will be surrounded by people who love her. She will be happy here and you can make decisions about how to tell her later. In the meantime, she can come to visit and Joshua can get to know her."

"Oh, Jack, do you think I could do that?"

"You are a strong lady, Aunt Adelina. I think you can do anything."

Not an hour after the dowager left, Jack heard the sound of hoofbeats, and went outside to meet Kitty coming up his drive.

"I have the most amazing news!" She dismounted deftly and clasped her hands together.

"Tell me!" He looped her mare's reins over one arm, took Kitty's with the other, and they strolled toward the stables.

Kitty's eyes sparkled with excitement. "This morning I went to the cottage to practice and as I came near, I heard voices. Jack, I believe your uncle and the dowager spent the night there."

"Aha! I thought as much."

"But there are no mattresses. I had the old ones disposed of a long time ago."

"I took care of that matter before Uncle Joshua arrived."

"You rogue! You mean you had a mattress put on that bed—and without telling me—because you thought that—"

"Yes, that is what I did and what I thought."

"Rascal!"

"Do you disapprove?"

"My hope is that they marry and spend their lives together."

"So do I."

"And there is one other little situation with the elder generation, Jack."

"Oh, what is that? A romance for Lady Euphemia?"

Kitty giggled. "My mother was disappointed you did not invite the maestro to your dinner the other night."

Jack snorted with laughter. "You cannot mean it? I shall have another party then. Tomorrow evening for eight instead of seven."

SEVENTEEN

Kitty felt a strange sense of foreboding the next morning as she prepared for riding with Jack and Mary.

Nell reported the news from the servants' hall. "Major Whitaker received a dispatch from Portugal well after midnight. One of the grooms had to take the messenger to Nether Acker after he arrived here."

It could not be good news, Kitty thought.

Her fears were confirmed when she and Mary met Jack at the Charsley stables. He tried to use a lighthearted voice and amuse Mary, but Kitty could tell he was preoccupied.

When they had reached the farthest meadow overlooking the Acker River, they dismounted and sent Mary off to gather wildflowers.

Kitty sat on a rock and waited for Jack to speak.

"I heard from Wellesley. He has had to withdraw back to Lisbon and is fortifying the hills to defend the city. It sounds as though the Spanish let him down."

"So you are more anxious than ever to return?"

"He wants me here in England, but I do not know how I will make myself stay. I need to be there, in the midst of things."

Kitty felt a tightening around her heart "Then we will soon say good-bye."

"Only for a year or two, Kitty. You can be here with everyone you love, and I will soon return."

"No, Jack. No."

He reached for her hand and laced his fingers through hers. "But why, Kitty?"

She pulled away. "I am not staying at Charsley Hall. Once Bea's baby is born, I must find another life for myself, someplace where I am not dependent upon the duke."

"But you said you have no money. No income."

"That is correct. I shall have to find a position that will give me a wage, as well as a place to live."

"But that means you will be . . ."

"A teacher, perhaps, at a school. Or a governess."

"But, Kitty, that is ridiculous. You are needed here."

"Pooh. I have done nothing that would not have happened without me, sooner or later."

"Damn it, Kitty, you are not thinking clearly. But let me tell you, if you leave Charsley Hall, do not think you can escape me. When I come back, I will find you."

She shook her head. "No, Jack."

Mary danced up to them and waved a bouquet of bright gold blooms. There was not time for another word.

Kitty tried her best to be cheerful when she, along with Bea, the duke, and Jack went to the church for the wedding of the first of the Three to meet the parson's mousetrap.

The duchess had provided the bonnet for Sally, her sister, the dress. The major had a new coat tailored for Tommy, and the duke gave him a pair of boots straight from the cobblers of St. James.

Although the father of the bride looked as if he had already downed more spirits than he needed, and her mother's tears flowed freely, the couple smiled throughout the ceremony, and stopped halfway out of the church for a romantic kiss. The looks exchanged between Sal and Tommy made Kitty's heart ache a little.

The wedding breakfast was blessedly short, and Kitty managed to avoid talking at length with the vicar. Jack said almost nothing to her, and she was relieved not to have to try to explain her jumbled emotions to anyone.

Jack's second dinner party at Nether Acker was jollier than the first, to everyone but Kitty. The dowager and Uncle Joshua were comfortable with each another, and Lady Dunmark fairly glowed with happiness.

Maestro Salsini, with melodramatic sighs of Neapolitan ardor, kissed her mother's hand and gazed into her eyes. "*Carissima!*"

Kitty could not believe her mother's reaction. Lady Dunmark smiled and gazed back at him, her lips parted and eyes bright. She obviously enjoyed the fellow's exaggerated attentions.

When Win came into the drawing room to take away the tea tray, he lost his composure for a moment at the positions of three couples, entwined together in a most indiscreet fashion. Bea sat beside Char, her head on his shoulder, gently moving her hand over her well-rounded belly, an angelic look in her eyes. Char stared into the fire, no doubt composing an ode to love.

Lady Dunmark curled up beside Signor Salsini, and Uncle Joshua and the dowager cuddled on another sofa. Only Jack and Kitty sat apart.

In moments, Joshua and Adelina left arm in arm, no doubt headed for their dark cottage and a few hours alone. Their looks and little touches said more than any words could.

When they had gone, Char stirred and stretched. "I believe, my darling, it is long past time for you to be in bed." Bea took a long breath and nodded.

"Lady Dunmark, Maestro, are you ready to accompany us back to the Hall?" Char asked.

Salsini rose and made an elaborate leg. "*Subito*, Your Grace. I escort Lady Dunmark home." He drew her arm through his.

Jack sent a footman for the carriage. "I will bring Miss Stone along later."

Kitty waited for her mother to object, but Lady Dunmark had either not heard a word or did not care. Her eyes never left the maestro's as he arranged her shawl around her shoulders.

Neither Bea nor Char said a word either, so wrapped up in each other were they.

At last, when Kitty and Jack were alone, he took her into his arms. "Kitty, we have to talk. Do you love me, Kitty?"

She whirled away from him. "I cannot, Jack. I cannot let myself love you if you are going back to the war. I know what kind of solider you are. Your men say you inspire everyone in the thick of the battle, take every risk. No, I would rather turn away from you now and seal my heart. I must go away and start a new life." Even as she spoke the words she knew how futile they were. She already adored him. No matter what she said, it was too late. Her heart was already gone.

"But are you not being selfish, thinking only of yourself? It is not only me that you wish to shun, but your sister. Your mother."

"Selfish?" She heard her voice rise almost to a shriek. "I do not have that luxury. And, the selfish one is you. Everyone, your precious general Wellesley, Lord Pearson, Uncle Joshua and the dowager, especially Char—all of them say you are needed here and in the House of Commons. In the field you are only one soldier who can take only one bullet. Here you can help the entire army by speaking in the House, encouraging the support of others. You can help all the people of this neighborhood on your estate, at Charsley, in the villages."

She stopped to catch her breath, but dared not look into Jack's face yet. "You have this romantic dream, Jack. I suspect you think that you can lead the final charge, brandish your sword and slash the entire French army. And you say I am selfish? How dare you?"

Jack's eyes glittered cold and hard. She suddenly knew what an enemy might feel seeing that degree of rage. Where a few moments ago, he had been gentle with her, pleading for her understanding, softly caressing her arm, now he was like granite, solid and unmoving. What had she done? Her words had made him like this.

In an instant, everything had changed. Everything between them was over. Finished.

He said nothing, just stared at her.

A log in the fireplace snapped.

She picked up her reticule and shawl and left the room, treading the familiar route to the main door. It was not far by the road through the village to Charsley Hall. She had followed it many times before on foot, on horseback and in an assortment of vehicles. Though she did not relish walking alone at night, she knew there was really nothing to be afraid of. She let herself out of the house and strode past the newly sheared topiary.

"Where do you think you are going, Miss Stone?" Jack's voice rang out before she reached the turn.

She looked back at him framed in the doorway. Against the light behind him, he was as black as the moonless sky, an ominous figure.

"I said, where do you think you are going?"

She pulled her shawl close around her. "Why do you ask such a foolish question, Jack? I am going to Charsley Hall." She began to walk again.

He was beside her in an instant, as if he had leapt over the space between them.

He stopped her by taking hold of her arm.

She tried to pull away, but he drew her against him and buried his face in her hair. "You cannot go away from me, not yet, Kitty."

She shivered and Jack led her back inside. He stopped

just beyond the door and kissed her. "Kitty, Kitty, I adore you. Do not turn away from me, my darling."

Kitty had never known such exquisite agony. Deep within, her body throbbed for him, for his touch, his kisses. But in her head, she knew it would never be. The tears streamed down her cheeks and he kissed them away.

"Oh, Jack, I cannot. I cannot let myself love you."

"My dear Kitty, you are breaking my heart. It is too late. You cannot deny we love each other already."

"Do not say that, Jack. It is not true." Through gritted teeth, she lied. "You think you love me, but you love something else more. Whatever that dream is, you want it more than you want me."

"No." His response was almost a sob. "How can you say that?"

"Because it is true."

He buried his face in her hair again. "Kitty, do not believe that, my dearest."

She pushed at him, but he held her more tightly. Each spot where his fingers touched her seemed to burn with a desire she had never before experienced. It would be so easy to give herself to him tonight, let all those strange feelings soar and forget all the careful strictures of her twenty-two years. Why not let herself know the ultimate in love, just this once? No one would ever have to know.

The fire built within her, and she pressed against him, letting his every exquisite caress fill her soul. She felt the pounding of her heart match the rapidity of her breathing. He kissed her cheeks, her lips, her throat, and she wanted more of him.

But suddenly he moved away, almost shoved her from him. "Kitty, forgive me. I forget myself."

Like a bubble bursting, her whole being felt suddenly collapsed upon itself, each tingle in her limbs now an ache, emptiness replacing the fullness of before.

He stood and walked to the fireplace, breathing deeply,

yanking his coat back into place, and running a hand through his hair. "I shall find Win to call for the curricle. It is long past time for me to take you back."

When he left the room, she put her face in her hands and let the tears flow again. He did not return immediately and she instinctively felt he wanted her to put herself to rights. She smoothed her hair and rearranged her skirts. Other than a few wrinkles and drooping curls, it took no time. But inside, it was a completely different matter. Every nerve in her body sent messages of frustration and pain. And dishonor. She had been about to offer herself shamelessly, go beyond everything she knew was right. Somehow Jack had felt that, and rejected it. Whether from kind consideration or refusal of her love, it did not matter. Her cheeks burned with embarrassment. Though she had said nothing outright, he had known what she was thinking. And he had stopped her.

When he opened the door and beckoned to her, she walked quickly out to the carriage, keeping her eyes down. They drove in silence down the dark lane and through the village where not a candle flickered in the windows of the sleeping houses.

As they came up the drive to the Hall, a footman leaning against a pillar tossed away a cheroot, then snapped to attention.

Jack took her arm and walked with her to her door. She shook her head as he was about to speak and he only gave her a bow.

"Good night, Major."

Running up the staircase, she fought back tears. She wondered if she would ever see him again. She had the sudden vision of him leaving this very hour and going to London, then off to Portugal without saying good-bye.

Nell waited in Kitty's room. "Miss, where have you been? I have been so worried. And you are crying."

Kitty ignored her. "Is my mother here?"

Nell nodded. "She came in a quarter hour ago. What is

happening, miss? You are late, and so was she. And she had taken her hair down already, and just shunned my help and closed the door of her bedchamber before I could even—"

"Oh, it is far too complicated for me to explain tonight. You must be tired too, Nell. Just go along to bed and you can brush my hair in the morning. I can hardly keep my eyes open."

"Yes, ma'am." Nell left the room, shaking her head and muttering to herself.

Kitty hoped her mother was all right, that she and Maestro Salsini had not done anything indiscreet. Oh, but what did it matter if they had? Why should her mother not have a little fling? It certainly seemed to be in the air around Nether Acker and Charsley Hall. Indiscretion.

That had been exactly what she had wanted. Jack had stopped her. And she would never know why.

She blew out her candle and crawled beneath the covers. A tear trickled onto her pillow.

Oh, Jack, I never knew what torture love can be.

She listened to the throb of her heart. What did it mean?

Was Jack correct and she could never turn her back on this love? Unlike her mild feelings for Char, which she had so easily ignored, there was something much deeper here. Or was that only a trick of those physical stirrings, nothing that truly had depth, but was only a passing whim caused by too many kisses, too many touches and too much sentimental yearning. And too many lovesick companions.

Kitty yanked the covers more tightly around her. It was all as silly as the duke's poems.

Lots of people survived quite nicely without indulging in the excesses of love. And that was precisely what she was going to do. Put it all behind her, the warm tingles, the melting kisses, the fluttering of her heart. They were nothing compared with the pain of separation and the embarrassment of rejection.

The next time she saw Jack—if there was a next time— she would thank him for the dinner party. How very improper it had been for her to forget to offer her appreciation for his efforts. Nothing more need be said.

Jack wandered among the trees behind his house. He felt helpless and confused. Clearly he could not have everything he wanted. It had stung when she said he was more needed here, that Wellesley had many other capable soldiers. Was it true he could be replaced on the battlefield but not here?

What really mattered was his love for Kitty. He knew she was not telling the truth when she said she did not love him, that her heart was not engaged, that she could go away and forget him.

Yet she was the only woman *he* had ever loved. None of his past flings had come close to approaching the way he felt about her. She had become a part of him. That feeling when he awakened of wanting to see her, share with her, listen to her music, hear her laughter, receive her wise counsel. How had this happened? How had his life become so entwined with thoughts of her?

And no thought even began to approach the way he longed for her, to hold her close, to make her his own. Those feelings he could not allow, or he would drive himself mad, bringing a kind of pain that transcended his wounds and filled him with frustration.

When Wellesley wrote he needed Jack more than ever, when Lord Pearson inquired how he was coming with his campaign to get Char involved, when the dowager asked him to support Char—those who depended upon him would consider it their own failure if he insisted on going back to Portugal.

As Kitty had so bluntly said, he was only one soldier of many there, while in England, he had a unique opportunity. In the field, was he not just another of those men whose combination of brains, strategic thinking, and just plain guts made them outstanding, but not too different from one another? If the army could do without General Moore, lost in the retreat from Corunna, it could do without Jack Whitaker. Even if Wellesley fell, God forbid, someone would rise to the occasion.

Without thinking further, he knew what he must do.

"Please ask Miss Stone to join me in the Ivory Salon."

Randall bowed. "Right away, Major."

Jack entered his favorite of the formal state rooms at the Hall, ideal for proposing marriage. If he had his choice, he would have chosen the rose cottage, but that was impossible with the dowager and Uncle Joshua there. He could hear someone—Kitty, he presumed—playing the pianoforte in a distant room, a sad sonatina in a minor key.

When the music stopped, he went to the mirror and touched his hair, his neckcloth, then turned to wait for her to come in. His heart began to pound like a blacksmith's hammer. Until this very moment he had put the awkwardness of their parting last night out of his mind. Now, he found his pulse racing with nervousness. Had she been so terribly offended by his passion that she wished never to see him again?

When she peeked around the corner and saw him, she stopped, keeping one hand on the edge of the doorjamb.

He tried to read her expression, but she looked quite neutral, neither smiling nor frowning.

For a moment, they simply stared at each another, then both spoke at once.

"You wanted to see me?" she asked.

"Good afternoon, Kitty," he said.

Another pause followed. Jack found his tongue frozen, his lips numb, his brain empty.

She took a small step forward and he strode to her, holding out his arms. With a little cry, she moved to him and no words were possible, for their lips were eagerly engaged.

He wound his arms around her and pressed her to his chest.

"My dearest Kitty, would you have me if I decide not to return to Portugal, to Wellesley's army?"

"Am I hearing you correctly? You are not going back to the war?"

"I am not. I want to stay here with you."

Her throat constricted, her eyes filled with tears. She slowly shook her head. "I cannot believe it."

He put his arm around her shoulders and hugged her to him. "I have given the matter a great deal of thought. You were right last night. My quest for battlefield glory has no real meaning. I can do far more here in England for the cause."

"Are you certain, Jack? Can you give up the war? It has been your dream for so very long, what you have worked for."

"I have thought about that, Kitty. When I consider what I have said to other men eager for war, when I think about the death and destruction, the tedium and the hardships, why do I dream only of the momentary triumph when there is victory?"

She shook her head but said nothing in reply.

"But more than anything, Kitty, I am staying here because I cannot deny the power of love."

"Jack, promise me you will not hesitate to tell me if you have misgivings. We must have no secrets from each other."

"And if you ever wish to go far away, alone—"

"You mean to be a companion to a fussy old lady? Or a governess to a passel of noisy darlings?"

"Or perhaps to escape a cranky husband or the cries of little ones of your own?"

"Oh, Jack, children, our children? They would be my greatest joy. I would never wish to escape your sons and daughters."

"Then let there be many of them, Kitty."

* * *

With a sense of warm hopes, Kitty watched the men load her harp on a wagon to carry them to Nether Acker. There she would take up residence after tomorrow's wedding ceremony when she would become Mrs. Whitaker.

Adelina, the dowager duchess of Charsley, had wed Uncle Joshua that morning in the chapel at Charsley Hall. They would spend the first night of their marriage in this little cottage. Both Kitty and Jack had promised not to tell why, but Kitty suspected that others beside the servants had figured out the situation.

The only person to whom the old affair made any real difference was Mary, and she was pleased to see her guardian so happy. Beatrice had already taken to the girl, and Miss Munstead would bring her to Nether Acker almost every day. Jack promised to ride with Mary several times a week.

Kitty found she was looking forward to his election to the House of Commons. She thought she might even enjoy becoming a minor political hostess, helping Jack in his work to further the army's needs. The cause was dear to his heart—but he made sure she knew that she was dearer still.

"Kitty?" Jack called to her from the lane.

She ran outside to his curricle. "Yes?"

"You will never believe it! Yates has found a taker for his tonic. Flossie Barker bought five bottles and after they drank all of them, she dragged him off to Mr. Drivel and next Sunday, they shall post the banns."

"At last, he has been caught in his own net!" Kitty laughed as Jack helped her up. "Now we have only to convince Bart he needs to say his piece to Nell."

"Your maid?"

"I told you there was something magical about that cottage."

He smiled down at her. "Whatever it is, Kitty, it inspires love. Enough to last a lifetime."

And then they kissed . . .

AUTHOR'S NOTE

The Battle of Vimeiro was an important victory for the British forces. If Wellesley had remained in command, instead of having to defer to other officers who arrived during or after the fighting, the British might have chased the French from the Peninsula in the next few months. Sadly, the war continued for five more years.

For an article on Vimeiro and pictures of the battlefield and the present-day memorial, go to *www.victoriahinshaw.com*, and click on Vimeiro on the left menu.

In my imagination, Jack Whitaker eventually left his wife and two children temporarily to join his general, later known as the Duke of Wellington, at the historic battle of Waterloo. Jack was rewarded for his heroism with the title of baron, becoming Lord Whitaker of Nether Acker.

More Regency Romance
From Zebra